Pen

PAPERBACK HERO

Antony J. Bowman was born in Sydney and works primarily in film, as a screen-writer and director. He graduated from the London Film School, wrote the feature films *Relatives* and *Cappuccino* to considerable acclaim, and has written and directed the new Australian film *Paperback Hero*. His adaptation of the script is his first novel.

PAPERBACK HERO

ANTONY J. BOWMAN

Penguin Books

Penguin Books Australia Ltd
487 Maroondah Highway, PO Box 257
Ringwood, Victoria 3134, Australia
Penguin Books Ltd
Harmondsworth, Middlesex, England
Penguin Putnam Inc.
375 Hudson Street, New York, New York 10014, USA
Penguin Books Canada Limited
10 Alcorn Avenue, Toronto, Ontario, Canada M4V 3B2
Penguin Books (NZ) Ltd
Cnr Rosedale and Airborne Roads, Albany, Auckland, New Zealand
Penguin Books (South Africa) (Pty) Ltd
4 Pallinghurst Road, Parktown 2193, South Africa

First published by Penguin Books Australia Ltd, 1999

10 9 8 7 6 5 4 3 2

Copyright © Antony J. Bowman, 1999

Design by Marina Messiha, Penguin Design Studio
Typeset in 9.5/13.5 pt Giovanni by Post Pre-press Group, Brisbane
Printed and bound in Australia by Australian Print Group
Maryborough, Victoria

National Library of Australia
Cataloguing-in-Publication data:

Bowman, Antony.
   Paperback hero.

   ISBN 0 14 026506 6.

A823.3

For Jeanie and Ella

ACKNOWLEDGEMENTS

I am most grateful to the following people for their encouragement and support in the writing of this novel: Robert Sessions; Sue Berger; Clare Forster; Julie Marlow; Thea Walsh and Rachel Scully.

The stars are with the voyager
  Wherever he may sail;
The moon is constant to her time;
  The sun will never fail;
But follow, follow round the world,
  The green earth and the sea;
So love is with the lover's heart,
  Wherever he may be.

Wherever he may be, the stars
  Must daily lose their light;
The moon will veil her in the shade;
  The sun will set at night.
The sun may set, but constant love
  Will shine when he's away;
So that dull night is never night,
  And day is brighter day.

Thomas Hood

1

Five forty-five a.m. In the outback, dawn always starts with great anticipation. Jack Willis knew that because he had it all to himself – a private showing. Each morning, brilliant colours were hoisted on a huge canvas that rose slowly from the surface of the earth. Never the same one twice.

'What do you think of that?'

Jack got no answer from Lance, his blue heeler cattle dog, who was curled up on the passenger's seat in the cabin of the rig as it rolled along the highway pulling the massive road train behind it.

'You're missing a good one, boy.'

Lance was thirteen. He had seen far too many sunrises. These days he preferred to sleep. 'Most people are still in bed. Yep, they're just letting it all slide by.' Jack smiled as the first warm ray of sunlight struck his weary, rugged face.

In all the years he'd been driving his huge road train across Australia he had never been disappointed by a morning sky. Every season had its own palette. Now it had the clarity of winter colours with the pink and grey nimbus clouds that spelt rain and, right up high, the cream-coloured stratus that turned pure white once caught by the sun. But in the desert the heat soon makes its harsh impact upon the landscape. The scattered mulga bushes, glittering with overnight dew, were already beginning to burn off to their usual daytime colour of parchment. Jack knew that in a few minutes the private dawn spectacle would be gone, as if it had never existed, and the red land would stretch out before him, arid and hostile, in the glare of the sun. He always marvelled that anything at all could live here; scorched in one season, sodden in the next. Rivers would burst their banks then evaporate during seven months of withering drought. In the dry season, rainless electrical storms set the bush ablaze. Finally, when the rains did bring relief, they added incredible life to the ochre-red soil, and thousands of little wildflowers and grasses would spring up.

But now miles of fine bulldust followed Jack's rig. Almost as far as the eye could see, the dust just hung there like a blazing red vapour trail. Jack peered out the window and rubbed his unshaven face. 'Not long now, mate.'

Lance lifted an ear slightly in polite acknowledgement of this information. The infamous Mundi Mundi Plains stretched about them. This land was so flat Jack could actually see the curvature of the earth. Broken Hill and its famous mines were not far away. Up ahead, a dot on the horizon soon became a faded, lime-green '64 Holden ute. It was loaded to the gunnels with an old orange couch, a laminex kitchen setting, a few personal effects, old broken suitcases tied with twine and three beautiful, black children, each with their eyes closed and their heads held high. The crisp morning breeze felt wonderful against their skin. The old rusted ute was flat out at fifty and running on bald tyres.

Jack hit his air horn as he passed. The children laughed and waved frantically. Jack wondered where they were headed. He was conscious as always of the contrast between the old beat-up vehicles the Aborigines drove and his own great, powerful white man's rig with its road train stretching out behind it like part of some invading army. Jack had quite a few Aboriginal mates. There was Johnnie Ngallametta, a stockman who literally *ran* old Mr Reece's Darling Station. Johnnie was one of many from families out of Cape York Peninsula. There was Sam Yunupingu and his wife, Neddy. Sam was a right little entrepreneur. He was a tour bus driver until the day he dug a rare black opal from the tread of his tyre on a trip back from White Cliffs. Sam bought the bus company. As the lime-green Holden turned again into a dot behind him, Jack wished the family all the luck in the world. He knew they would need it.

As Jack drove, from time to time voices would blare over his CB radio receiver. Like all the other truckers he had a CB set and anything else that would make the interior of his rig comfortable during his long journeys. Truckers will spend hours in the pubs of the outback debating what constitutes comfort. Everyone had sheepskin seat covers and they talked nonstop about their sound systems, although their taste in music varied enormously, ranging from country and western through current cult bands to classical. Last Christmas Mad Pete, a trucker from Menindee, had tried singing along to *The Best of Pavarotti*. His wife, Gladys, gave him the tape to help calm his nerves. His favourite was Puccini's 'Nessun Dorma'. Thank Christ he had been alone out there, Jack thought. He had sung along for months until he got a painful tongue cramp on a frozen-meat haul just outside Darwin. Pete thought he was going to die. He ejected the tape and hurled it out the window into the dry, red desert.

Jack's rig was a freightliner – the daddy of all trucks, he called it. Twenty-two wheels as a standard rig; another forty if he towed two extra trailers. The most trailers Jack had ever towed was three. That made his vehicle well over one hundred and twenty feet in length. These road trains replaced the work of the cattle drovers who used to drive huge herds of cattle to market across thousands of miles of dry, arid land. Nowhere else in the world do these road trains exist and Jack, like the other men who drive them, was proud of his gigantic machine, with air-conditioned comfort and a sleeping compartment second to none! The old-time drovers would have thought they were in heaven.

Lance yawned as Jack searched wearily through the selection of early-morning country radio. He pushed all the buttons. Nothing he liked. He gave a grunt of dissatisfaction causing Lance to open both his eyes and look up at him. Jack started going through his tapes and came upon Roy Orbison.

'The Big O, Lance,' he said.

Lance stretched, and rearranged his position to get more comfortable. He had a lot of hours of rest to pack into his busy day and wanted to get on with it. Jack grinned at him as he was inserting the tape. In his more energetic younger days Lance, as befitted a pure-bred blue heeler, was an obsessive wrangler. If Jack left him for longer than ten minutes he would find something to herd. Sheep, hens, cows – anything with legs.

The rig cab filled with the sound of Roy Orbison singing 'Crying' and Jack singing along. Jack's rendition of the song was quite admirable, although the acoustics within the cabin were not a patch on most motel bathrooms.

Jack sang his bloody heart out. God, he loved being out here. In his imagination he was on a stage behind a microphone singing a song about a man in love with a woman who had taken his hand, wished him well and vanished, before he realised he was in love with her.

After the song had finished, Jack picked up a biro secured to the dash by a length of string, and resumed writing on a notepad attached to a simple retractable steel bracket. Jack wrote silently for some time with his experienced eye darting between the clipboard and the empty road ahead.

'Wild – and – irrev-er-ent . . .' He looked up, pained. 'Hey, Lance, picture this: 1944, this bloke's twenty-one, an Aussie pilot in Bomber Command implementing operational flights over Nazi Germany during the Second World War.'

5

Lance yawned.

'An operation means bombing the shit out of them. You with me?'

Lance started to pant. Jack continued. 'Now, this bloke's on a lucky streak. It's his first tour of duty, and with every operation – apart from a few tracer scraps, courtesy of the infamous night-fighters of the Luftwaffe –' he makes it back to base. Every time his Lancaster flies out with another crew it never comes home. This bloke gets a new plane every time he goes out. Imagine that? Now, the plot thickens. While on leave, our gung-ho Aussie meets this beautiful English girl at an Officers' Mess dance organised by the air base . . .'

Jack looked down at his dog. Lance was asleep again. 'Christ, you're not listening to me at all, are you?'

High above Jack's rig in the cloudless, morning sky, a red biplane blocked the sun for a beat before it banked hard, levelled out and drifted lower to the horizon. That familiar spluttering of an old single-engine plane grabbed Jack's attention. He peered up, squinting his eyes against the direct desert sunlight. The biplane swooped into another aerobatics twist in the sky, stalled, and dropped down dangerously close to the ground. One more manoeuvre and it was heading straight for Jack's rig.

'Oh, shit, no!'

Jack hit the brakes. Hard. A punishing shudder engulfed them and Lance was jerked forward, off his seat and onto the floor. The sight of his startled dog flying for an instant through the air might have amused Jack if he had not been so aware of the numerous wheels of the great rig biting deeply into the roadway as tons of steel momentum ground to a halt. Out front, the biplane held its course, sitting just ten metres above the roadway. Closer and closer, until its red fuselage filled the windscreen. At the very last moment, full flaps and a deafening roar sent it up overhead. Jack's yell couldn't be heard over the sound of cascading dust and pebbles. Like heavy hail on a tin roof, the rig was completely engulfed in superphosphate.

Then, silence. Jack slowly looked out. Everything around him had turned white, as if dusted with snow.

'Bloody hell!' he yelled again. Lance struggled back onto the seat. Jack switched on the wipers to clear the dust from the windscreen, then climbed out to survey the damage. The superphosphate was a direct hit right down the length of his rig. No damage – just hours of cleaning up.

Jack sighed and urinated where he stood. The biplane however, although well behind him, was not finished. It banked steeply and set another course for attack. Jack heard the approaching roar.

'Oh, Christ!' He tried to urinate quickly. Impossible. The biplane was at full throttle, two hundred metres away. Too late. Jack scrambled for the cabin door. This time there was no phosphate; just a rude index finger held up in front of the pilot's goggled face. Within seconds the biplane pulled high into the sky and disappeared into the heat haze.

Luck—. The road sign for Lucktown began, then stopped abruptly. The other half of the sign had broken off years before when a passing trucker, falling asleep at the wheel, had run his rig off the road, clipped the signpost and careered into a paddock of lambing ewes. The trucker and all the sheep had survived unscathed, which was all that anyone was concerned about. At the time, and afterwards, it had never seemed important to replace the sign. The locals, after all, could hardly miss the town.

No one knew how the town had got its name. But it had started off as a mining camp and, one night over a game of cards, some of the miners must have decided that their scrappy bunch of tents and huts deserved a name. 'Lucktown' was probably ironical. Often humour was all that the miners had left as they trudged west from the cities to the inland deserts searching for that gold or silver strike that would put them on easy street. Mostly they were disappointed, but there were some who made their fortune. In 1883 a boundary rider had pegged a claim on a hill known as 'The Broken Hill'. The orebody under that claim was nearly eight kilometres long. A hundred years later, old Bill Peason had discovered a raw vein of pure silver while bulldozing his truck out of a gully during the rains of '82. But old Bill, who never had a penny to his name, promptly died of shock. His wife, Mabel, had the words *Too much, too late*, carved into his headstone.

While the silver mines were long gone, Lucktown was still the centre of the region. For many of the locals, this was the only connection to civilisation. A 'trip to town' was still quite an event for most people.

The beer was cold, and there was always reliable food at Ruby's Boomerang Cafe.

There was one remaining pub, of course; a milk bar; and a rundown Chinese cafe, whose reputation was severely damaged as a result of a rumour that its sweet 'n' sour dishes had changed considerably since the mice plague of '84. There was a grocery shop; an old mining claims office, converted into a clothing outlet for the Salvation Army; a cinema, converted into a seed and hardware store, and numerous other buildings 'converted' by progress. At the height of summer the main street had little to offer. Each shopfront had a small awning or verandah that gave shelter from the searing heat. The first satellite dish went up on the pub the previous June with very little fanfare. Most people thought it was an elaborate rain gauge until Artie Barnwell, the publican, switched on CNN.

The Boomerang Cafe was in fact the only substantial new building in Lucktown in the last three decades, and as Jack drove his superphosphate-covered great rig through the town's dusty, familiar main street, he thought that was probably only because there weren't any old buildings in the town that could be converted into a giant boomerang. Why George Vale, Ruby's father, had wanted his cafe to be built in the shape of a boomerang no one knew, but the place had thrived because, apart from the local people, all the truckers loved it.

Jack's rig roared off the main street, swung wide around the Boomerang Cafe and parked at the rear.

This confident manoeuvre assured everyone that this was 'his spot.' He and Lance slid down swiftly from the cab and made towards the cafe. As they passed another idling rig, a brown, wrinkle-faced woman peered down at them. She had her hair tied back in a long, grey ponytail. Her voice was raspy from too many cigarettes.

'When are we gonna go out and 'ave some real fun then, Jack?'

'When women quit drivin' trucks, Tammy,' he quipped, without even looking up.

'Wouldn't hold yer breath, love.'

Jack ignored her remark and kept walking. He had superphosphate in his hair and was still angry about what had happened out on the Mundi Mundi Plains. This morning business at the Boomerang was quiet. Suzie Barnwell, who helped out in the cafe most days, had plenty of time to look around while waiting for the usual orders of mixed grills and eggs to cook. At the counter, a small group of truckers ate breakfast completely oblivious to the decor about them, which resembled the service bay of an old aircraft hanger. Props, engine parts, tail pieces, helmets, wheels and a cockpit dial, all carefully dusted and polished by Ruby, adorned every inch of wall space.

Ruby's dad, George, had been a pilot. He'd built the Boomerang just after he returned from the Vietnam War, where he'd been a transport pilot for the RAAF flying supplies from Queensland to Penang then later, onto Da Nang, South Vietnam. Like his father before him, all he wanted to be was a fighter pilot. Unfortunately, his age – old at twenty-nine – kept him out of the prestigious 'single-seaters.' Flying had bonded this father and daughter. Sadly, the same couldn't be said for Ruby's mother, who eventually separated from George after he refused to give up aerial acrobatics above the town in his red Stearman biplane, which had resulted in one near-death experience over the Lucktown airstrip. It wasn't just the flying that Ruby's mother hated; she was even more jealous of the relationship Ruby had with George.

The half-dozen or so truckers in this morning were regulars. But even if Suzie hadn't known them all, she would have been able to predict that among them there would be one who was smitten with Ruby. Today it was the large red-haired bloke from Griffith. He was gazing adoringly at Ruby as she was listening to her walkman while playing a solitary game of pool on a table of torn felt. Suzie grinned to herself. Even in her greasy flying suit with her dark hair pulled back, Ruby looked terrific. As usual, she hadn't noticed that the red-haired bloke from Griffith was in love with her; she never noticed the succession of truckers who sat at the counter worshipping her with their eyes, while putting away their enormous breakfasts. Somehow being in love never seemed to put them off their food.

'Love,' she thought to herself, 'love, love, love.' She could still remember how charming Artie had been when they married. Now, twenty years later, she was forty-something or other and Artie was the publican of the Lucktown pub and the truth was, she worked in the cafe to keep away from his vicious temper.

Well, to keep away from Artie and because she and Ruby were, despite the age difference, good friends. That reminded her.

'I reckon you're always askin' for trouble,' she yelled, over the sizzling of sausages and bacon. Ruby turned to her with an inquisitive look. She removed her headset.

'What?'

'I said, you're always askin' for trouble.'

Ruby just grinned, and resumed her game. 'Ah, but you shoulda seen his face, Suz,' she said. 'He was so pissed-off.'

She put her headset back on and had a little bop to her private music as she lined up her next shot. Suzie flicked the bacon over expertly in the pan, shaking her head. Like everyone in the district, she knew that Ruby and Jack were constantly at war and had been ever since they were kids, when Ruby had decided that there wasn't a thing in the world that anybody was going to stop her from doing just because she was a girl, and a bit undersized for her age. Ruby had been fearless and feisty, and the small gang of Lucktown kids soon let her do exactly as she wanted, except for Jack. He was five years older, and one day he'd told her 'No'. No, she couldn't climb up on the steep roof of the old church with the bigger kids. Of course she'd scrambled up like a little monkey the minute he was out of sight and the war was on. The whole town was amused by it.

A moment later, Ruby turned to discover Jack standing there not five metres away. 'Speak of the devil,' she said.

Jack lunged at her. There was a shriek and Ruby was off around the pool table with Jack in hot pursuit.

'You've ruined my paint job,' he yelled.

'It'll wash!'

Not the answer Jack wanted. Ruby laughed. She did not really believe the fury in his stare. Suzie flipped a burning egg. 'Come on, you two.'

Ruby held up her hands to halt the moment. 'Okay, a truce.'

Jack was not convinced that this was what he wanted from Ruby – she'd played far too many pranks on him to be trusted. This had been going on for years.

'I promise – no more fertiliser,' she said.

Jack pointed his finger. 'One more of those,' he said, trying to quell his anger, 'an' I'll put sugar in your bloody fuel tank.'

Ruby stared at him, indignant. 'What? I'd crash!'

Jack nodded. He was now satisfied he had made his point, and headed for the counter. 'Flyin' out there like some mad bugger. You're just like your father.'

At this parting shot, Suzie sighed and shook her head. 'Shouldn't have said that, Jack,' she thought, 'Not a good move at all.' Watching them, Suzie just couldn't believe how two otherwise sensible people could get each other so wrong. You'd think after all these years Ruby would understand how proud Jack was of his rig – she'd be outraged if someone had dumped fertiliser all over her biplane. Ruby became indignant. Horrified, in fact. And Suzie could see it from her side. Everyone knew that Ruby had been brought up to be meticulous about maintaining her plane. Her father had always said he was a reckless flyer, but not a careless one. He wouldn't mind if he got killed trying some new bit of aerial acrobatics, but he was not going to get killed by avoidable mechanical failure. Sabotage was not a matter to joke about with pilots.

And then Jack had criticised Ruby's father to her face when he knew, like everyone else, that it wasn't a plane that killed George Vale, but a big rig like his own that had gotten out of control one night and jackknifed across the road in the face of George's oncoming car. It was as if, thought Suzie, they both had maps in their heads that showed them how to aggravate each other. She stood and waited for the explosion. It wasn't long in coming.

Ruby followed Jack across the room and yelled, 'Dad would've used wet birdshit!'

Before she could utter another word, Jack spun around, picked her up and hoisted her onto his shoulders.

'Jack, what're you doin'?'

Jack struggled with Ruby towards the door.

'We have a truce!'

'Yeah, sure we do, Rube,' he said, as he kicked open the flyscreen door and carried her out into the dusty main street of Lucktown.

Ruby's protest could've woken the dead. 'Don't you dare . . . Jack, put me down – now!'

Ruby was aware that all the truckers in the cafe and

some people from the street and the gas station opposite were following Jack as he carried her along. All the men were grinning broadly. None of them would have ever dreamed of taking on Ruby. Occasionally in the cafe a trucker would get aggro, start yelling and threatening to tear the place apart. Ruby would never say anything. She'd just walk over to the guy and stand there regarding him in a thoughtful sort of way as if he was some minor inconvenience, like a dripping tap. This absence of emotion usually did the trick. The trucker would find it hard to keep on yelling and threatening when she was looking so – preoccupied. He'd start to lose his thread, begin to glance around at other people. Everyone would avoid his eyes. Ruby would just stand there for a minute or so then she'd return to what she'd been doing and the crisis would be over.

Ruby kicked and banged her fists uselessly on Jack's back. She knew where they were going.

'Jack – you bastard. Put me down – now!'

Jack grinned as he got closer to the water tank. He really was pissed-off with Ruby. Ever since she'd been big enough to run after the older children she'd been at his heels, and then when he'd finally realised that wild little Ruby Vale was a part of his life and he might as well just accept it, she discovered pranks. Previously she'd just carried out dares. But at around eight years of age or so she'd begun to think up her own trouble, and it had usually been Jack who had been the butt of her fun.

He would always remember one very hot summer

afternoon – he was fifteen and she was ten. School was just out and Ruby was racing after Jack, as she often did, on her bicycle towards the river. Every afternoon, local kids would charge off to the waterhole to see who could swing off the rope first. Off the rope into pure heaven. No more heat, no more flies – just exhilaration and laughter. On this occasion, young Jack was first. He dived in and surfaced just in time to catch Ruby shedding all her clothes and jumping into the cool water. Ruby wasn't the strongest of swimmers, so he waited for her to surface.

Nothing – the water was still. Jack turned and called her name. Still no sign of her. All country kids have been told stories of waterholes. Those notorious places that harbour unseen dangers, from old tree roots to thick suffocating mud. Young Jack had seen local cattle get bogged and die at the edge of the river.

'Ruby,' he called out. Then again. He was frozen with fear as he dived under the muddy water searching for her. Gasping for breath, he tried time and time again, searching the bottom of the waterhole, feeling old car wheels, tin cans, rocks and bottles. Ruby, of course, was well hidden behind a low tree branch all this time watching his frantic search. Then, when she thought he'd had enough, she paddled out giggling, 'Ha, haa – fooled you.'

That incident, for which he says he never forgave her, was the first of many pranks. These days he considered the concrete water tank at the rear of the Boomerang Cafe a most effective form of retribution. One last lift and Jack had Ruby tumbling into the cold water. Her angry protest turned into furious gurgles. 'You bloody child, Jack.'

'*Now* we have a truce, kiddo,' said Jack, with a satisfied grin.

Ruby hated it when he called her 'kiddo', and he knew it. He was looking so pleased with himself she couldn't think of anything to say. In a confrontation with one of the truckers she could keep her cool, but Jack could always make her feel like she was a little kid trying to keep up with the older ones. Her immediate impulse was to splash out at him as she was getting to her feet, but he had thought of that and moved back out of range, still grinning at her furious face. Then she saw her soaked walkman and hurled it at him. To make matters worse, he caught it with the dexterity of an experienced fielding cricketer.

'Jesus!' Ruby screamed. 'And *don't* call me kiddo.'

Jack smiled, and turned away. By this time, truckers had gathered outside the Boomerang and were applauding Jack's show of masculinity. Out here, they believed, men were still in charge.

'You wait till Hamish hears about this,' Ruby added, with another scream. 'An' don't bloody think you're invited to our wedding.'

Jack reached the door of his rig, opened it and climbed on board.

'You hear me?' she screamed.

Jack paused, 'I'm the best man, Rube.'

2

The Lucktown pub. From the outside, still a rather elegant, Victorian two-storey building with wrought-iron laced verandah and peeling paint. Inside, a social watering hole for farmers, truckers, shearers and cotton-pickers. The local doctor and a farmhand drank side-by-side, discussing politics and the price of rabbit skins. The owner, obnoxious Artie, never had a dry night. He made good money from the pub. Most of it he kept well hidden from his wife, Suzie. Even though she worked nights at the pub, he only allowed her to pocket the money she made working for Ruby at the Boomerang. No one really liked Artie but unless you want to be a hermit, you can't have a war with the only publican in a small country town. Where else was there to go for a drink and a yarn?

Saturday night was the 'big one' in the bush. Ruby and her fiancé, Hamish, were on their way to the charity barbecue for the local Flying Doctor Service and had called in to the pub for a drink first. They were all dressed up for the occasion. At least Ruby, in a simple but pretty print dress, looked terrific in the eyes of the locals, who were used to seeing her in her old flying suit, or jeans and a shirt. Hamish, who was the local vet, looked like he usually did. He always wore moleskin trousers, a brown tweed jacket and a light-coloured shirt.

After two years of seeing him in exactly this outfit, Ruby had suggested a slight change. Perhaps a brighter-coloured shirt? Maybe a sweater? She thought he was a good-looking man – a tall Scotsman, ruddy-faced but firm-jawed, slim-hipped and fit. Hamish had grinned and said it would upset all the local sheep, who were used to seeing him dressed like this and hated change. He couldn't go around getting offside with his patients, could he? Then he started to laugh, and kept on laughing for quite a bit, as if he'd said something really funny. She had noticed before that he had a tendency to laugh at his own jokes. Nevertheless, Hamish was a very good vet, who would go and attend animals regardless of whether the farmers could pay him or not. He wasn't a local man. He'd moved to Lucktown a few years before, from the Queensland border town of Goondiwindi, to replace the previous vet who'd been accused several times of requesting sexual favours from the more mature women of Lucktown. Rumour had it that the old bugger did quite a few house calls.

Suzie had Hamish's beer poured the moment he and Ruby reached the counter. She knew what her regulars drank and where they liked to sit at the bar. The district engineer, for example, already had his schooner of VB and always sat on the fourth stool from the end beside Harry Grimes, the school teacher. Harry was a determined stout drinker who sat beside the mayor. And on it went, all of them total creatures of habit. Every evening at five-thirty those stools would be filled and enough beer was consumed to sink a Japanese ore freighter.

'G'day, Hamish.' Suzie dumped a beer in front of him without spilling a drop. Hamish took that first gulp that left froth on his upper lip. He sighed with immense satisfaction.

'Suz, you're a work-a-holic.'

Suzie was much more subdued in the pub. In the cafe she enjoyed the truckers' company when she fed them hamburgers and coffee, but some of these men were very different when they were full of beer. Artie was forever breaking up fights between drinkers. Some of the younger Aboriginal stockmen were often thought fair game by the tough, transient shearers who became totally obnoxious after too many schooners. But no one ever picked a fight this early in the evening.

'And how's the man of my dreams?' Suzie replied, with a weary smile.

'Much too old for you.' Hamish laughed at his own joke.

'He's right!' quipped Ruby.

Suzie leant forward, as if about to announce something of the utmost importance. 'I'm all packed, Rube. Just say the word and we're outta here like *Thelma & Louise*.'

Hamish leant closer still. 'Who?'

Ruby turned to Hamish with a deadpan expression. 'Suzie wants to know whether she can come with us when we move to Queensland.'

Hamish straightened his body, thought a moment, then gave a wry smile. 'Yeah, I reckon old Artie'd be into that.'

Suzie threw a cautionary glance to her overweight husband drinking with his mates at the other end of the bar. Her face drained of any emotion. 'Fucker wouldn't know what hit him.' Hamish looked startled. He had never heard Suzie speak like that.

Ruby said quickly with a grin at her friend, 'We could be a *ménage à trois.*' This brought a smile back to Suzie's face.

Hamish picked up his beer, the reference had shot right over his head. 'Well, I'll leave you girls to chat about whatever it is you like to chat about.'

Suzie watched Hamish wander off across the room eager to yarn with his mates. 'What is it they think we talk about?' asked Ruby.

'Buggered if I know. Recipes?'

'Penis size . . .'

Suzie screeched with laughter. Conversation in the bar died for a moment as all the men, including Artie, glanced across at her.

'What are you girls laughin' at?' asked one of the drinkers.

'Never you mind,' called Suzie.

'We could start a rumour,' whispered Ruby.

Suzie's gaze drifted back to the next schooner glass she was slowly filling in her hand. 'No need for rumours, love. Christ, I tossed up my lucky coin and ended up with numb-nuts over there.'

Ruby smiled compassionately.

'Tell me something, love,' Suzie continued.

'What?' Ruby took a sip of lemon bitters as a smirk drifted across Suzie's face.

'Does a vet have a good bedside manner?'

'None of your damn business.'

Suzie chuckled.

'Hey, Suzie,' yelled Artie. 'Stop bloody yappin', and fill some glasses.' Artie had a voice like fingernails on a chalkboard. A broad, nasal monotone that grated even when he was trying to be friendly. Which was rare. Suzie's mouth tightened. Then she saw the look on Ruby's face and said quickly with a defeated smile.

'Don't worry, love, he only yells at me in public.'

'I'd leave the bastard!' It wasn't the first time that Ruby had said this, and Suzie knew that it was true. Ruby would have got in her biplane and been miles away the first time Artie'd yelled at her. Suzie thought wearily of spending years thinking you'd made some mistake and it would all be fixable once you found out what had gone wrong. There was no one reason why Artie and Suzie's marriage was on the rocks. A child might've helped, Suzie once thought. But who needed a father like that? Those circumstances would've only made Suzie's life more unbearable. Artie was charming when they first met. Stayed that way for the first two years, and then he turned – completely resented being married. Suzie looked at Ruby and hoped that she would never know about all that.

In the meantime, she said dryly, 'Yeah, the world's just cryin' out for single middle-aged women.'

Suzie caught a glimpse of Jack entering the bar. Jack never dressed up for any occasion but when he had showered and donned a clean shirt, there was something definitely appealing about this tall, quiet man. Jack noticed Ruby and came over to the bar carrying her walkman.

'Does it still work?' Ruby asked.

'Tough to tell with your music, kiddo,' he replied, offering the machine back. Ruby had no intention of resuming their argument – or not here, anyway. Jack picked up a freshly poured beer from the counter, smiled at Suzie, and walked off towards Hamish and a group of drinkers.

'I reckon I could go for him if I wasn't past my use-by date,' said Suzie, quietly.

'Huh!' was Ruby's only reply.

Suzie watched Jack retreating. 'I like 'em a bit shy.'

'Shy? He was dropped at birth.'

'Yeah.' Suzie was enjoying this. 'So he chucked you in the water tank again.'

'He's such a bloody child.'

A grin spread across Suzie's face.

3

As she drove her little hire car down the main street of Lucktown, Ziggy Keane reflected that she'd seen places like this in films, and read about them in books, and that as far as she was concerned, that was where these places should stay. On the page and on the screen. 'Forget about the magic of the outback,' she said to herself, 'the lure of the inland. In real life—' Ziggy didn't get to finish her sentence. She had come to the far end of Lucktown's main street and saw before her a collection of massive road-train rigs all gathered around some large, oddly shaped structure.

'Invasion of the Road Trains,' she said to herself. Ziggy was very proud of her ability to come up with titles quickly. She was just congratulating herself on this one when she caught a clearer glimpse of the odd-shaped building inside the ring of road freighters. This was the Boomerang Cafe.

'Good God,' she said aloud. She'd been expecting the Boomerang Cafe to be like one of those quaint little cafes that she'd seen in touristy country towns within easy driving distance of Sydney. She had imagined a wooden boomerang sign and a variety of small tables with flowers and non-matching chairs inside – perhaps even a sideboard displaying a selection of homemade jams.

She now saw that this place actually was a boomerang. A giant boomerang. As she turned off the road to look for a parking space among the enormous road rigs, she remembered having heard of other big structures like this in other country towns and made a mental note to herself to add visiting these to her long list of things *not* to do: do not see the giant banana at Coffs Harbour and avoid the oversized merino at Goulburn. One big boomerang is enough in any lifetime.

Up close, the giant road trains were even more intimidating. Ziggy found a vacant space between two of them, and then changed her mind. Each of the huge vehicles had its engines running and the combination of engine noise and general vibration gave Ziggy the impression they were communicating with each other. Not a good parking space.

She quickly backed her hire car out of the spot she'd chosen and drove round to the rear of the cafe, where there was a much larger vacant space. Once she'd parked, Ziggy immediately forgot her nervousness about the road rigs. She was, as she always said, very focused – and she had a job to do. A simple mission. Catch a flight to Broken Hill. Hire a car. Drive to Lucktown. Find Ruby Vale.

Ziggy ran through her routine of what she always did before any meeting: she combed her hair, touched up her make-up, reapplied her bright, red lipstick and checked her perfectly tailored suit for threads and other specks visible solely to her and an experienced forensic scientist. She'd made only one compromise on this, her first and (she hoped) last trip to the Australian outback. After her session at the gym the previous Saturday morning she'd bought a brand-new pair of Nike cross-trainers which she now put on. She'd gotten the impression somewhere that the ground inland was rough, and with the price of designer footwear these days, she wasn't going to expose her favourite Italian shoes to scratches from mulga – it occurred to her at this point that she didn't actually know what mulga was. It was just one of those things that was always mentioned in books about the outback. She peered around as she was swinging her long shapely legs out of the little car but there didn't seem to be much of anything on the red earth. In the distance she could see some low scrubby parchment-coloured bushes, but where she now stood there was nothing but red-baked earth, which undoubtedly accounted for all the red-coloured dust that was settled on everything, including her small hire car, and would soon – she suspected – settle on her. Forget it, she told herself firmly, forget the mulga, forget the dust, forget the outback. Focus on Ruby Vale.

When the Boomerang was busy, it was extremely hard not to be affected by the energy of the place. The din of dozens of men talking over the music, food orders being yelled out across a smoky room, and that lingering smell of fresh coffee. No sooner had Suzie wiped down a table than four more truckers slid into the booth to yarn and joke with their mates. These huge men had huge appetites. The Boomerang was famous for its breakfasts: eggs, bacon, sausages, tomatoes and toast.

Suzie handed out over-sized mugs of tea and coffee to quell the men's desire to flush it all down as quickly as possible. A jukebox played most of the time: Motown, Dusty Springfield and The Bee Gees featured heavily. This morning, as Ziggy entered, no particular music could be deciphered over the hub-bub of conversations and cheerful greetings.

Ruby was working the grill, completely absorbed by the music on her walkman – REM, her absolute favourite. Ruby had a lot of favourites. Midnight Oil, the old Aussie group, was terrific; My Friend the Chocolate Cake, silly name, great group. There were other faves: Annie Lennox; The Cranberries; Alanis Morissette; and The Pretenders. Her father used to like Chrissie Hynde – he thought she was very sexy. 'I'll Stand by You', one of her more recent songs, made Ruby cry. George would've loved it.

Suzie was the first to notice Ziggy coming towards the counter. She had become aware of a sudden silence as she was putting some cups away and turned to see a tall, elegant woman with short-cropped blond hair in a light-coloured suit walking through the busy cafe. Conversations seemed to collapse about her as she passed. Each man stopped eating to leer at her, their incredulous eyes moving up and down her body. Hair, bust, hips, legs – several sets of startled male eyes came to a halt at the sight of Ziggy's Nike trainers. A couple of truckers wondered to themselves if this unbelievably gorgeous woman had something really terrible wrong with her feet.

'Can I help you, miss?'

Suzie thought that this fashionable city woman was handling the attention well. She said quite calmly, 'Yes, I'm looking for . . .'

A wolf-whistle cut her off. Ziggy sighed, then smiled. At least her tactic of acting like the men weren't there had worked; no one had grabbed her – yet.

'They're harmless, love. What'll you have?'

'Iced tea, please.'

Suzie reached back into the fridge for cold water. 'Milk 'n' sugar's on the counter.'

As she was saying this, a smallish thin man in a western shirt moved up beside Ziggy. Not an unfriendly face, just a person of little significance encumbered with a slow, annoying drawl. Ziggy eased further down the counter as he came out with one low, slow question.

'S'cuse me, girlie, did you park yer car out the back?'

Suzie came to the rescue.

'Now, Joe, let her have her tea.'

The thin man thought a moment, shrugged and drifted away.

Suzie returned with cold water and a tea bag. Ziggy smiled, with very mild appreciation, reminded herself never to ask for iced tea in the outback again, and attempted once more to ask her question.

'Could you tell me where . . . ?'

'Hey, Rube. Where're my eggs?' screamed a voice that penetrated even Ruby's headset. Mad Pete was in town. No one pissed-off this huge, smelly trucker, although Ruby knew he really had a heart of pure gold under all that bluster.

She looked up from the grill and yelled back at him. 'I'm not your wife, Pete.'

Mad Pete chuckled and squeezed up to the counter beside Ziggy. Ruby's voice was music to his ears. He loved the way she yelled back at him. He was feeling happy with the world. He lit a cigarette and turned to exhale thick smoke into Ziggy's face.

'Want one, miss?'

Ziggy instantly held her breath and prayed that Mad Pete and his foul smoke would go away.

'Eh?' Mad Pete was persistent.

'No – thank you,' replied Ziggy, adding a little gratitude to her tone just in case he should turn nasty. Ziggy then turned to Suzie and pointed at Ruby.

'Is that Ruby Vale?'

Once again, the thin man interrupted in his slow annoying drawl. Weeks must pass before he finished his sentences.

'Girlie, I gotta tell you . . .'

All this was too much for the city girl. 'Can't you see I'm busy?' she flared at him, showing her irritation.

The thin man backed off, a little shaken.

'Okay, suit yourself.'

While she had everyone's attention, Ziggy again turned to Suzie.

29

'I'm here to see Ruby Vale.'

Suzie smiled. 'Rube, there's someone to see you, love.'

Ruby was used to doing several things at once: cooking different orders of food, keeping an eye on the customers and making sure there was never any trouble because she stopped it before it started. She looked relaxed and seemed to be preoccupied with the grill, but a careful observer would have noticed that she had not put her headset back on. The combination of this strange woman, Mad Pete and Joe looking really anxious about something concerned her. But she stopped cooking, wiped her hands on her apron and came to join Suzie at the counter with a casual air.

'What can I do for you?' she asked.

Lucktown got the occasional unexpected female visitor, and all visitors – whether male or female – came to the Boomerang for information about the district. People would often say to strangers, 'Go and see Ruby. If she doesn't know, she'll know how to find out.'

Mostly the female visitors were public servants, academics or journalists researching isolated communities – sometimes there'd been so many visitors in Lucktown doing studies of its isolation that Ruby and Suzie agreed the place was in danger of not being isolated any more.

Ruby figured that this woman looked too smartly dressed to be a public servant or an academic, so she must be a journalist. Or maybe an eccentric millionaire who wanted to buy a roadside cafe. She was going to have to sell the Boomerang when she and Hamish got married. He wanted to move back to Queensland and said they needed every penny they could get. Though who was going to buy the Boomerang was quite another matter. The For-Sale sign had gone up months ago but there hadn't been any offers.

Ruby had enough time to do this quick mental review of her business affairs because the woman was just standing there gazing at her in silence as if she couldn't quite believe what she was seeing. Finally Ruby thought she should say something.

'Hi!' she said with a smile.

Ziggy was bewildered. This attractive young country girl with her large dark eyes was nothing like what she'd been expecting. She'd pictured a serious-faced woman in her fifties with glasses – yes, definitely glasses.

Just then the ear-piercing screech of air horns ripped through the cafe. Ziggy jumped with fright but the truckers ignored the announcement of Jack's arrival. Without slowing down, Jack confidently swung his huge rig around the side of the cafe heading for his usual parking spot. He didn't notice Ziggy's little Nissan rental car. How could he? – it would have appeared smaller than a Coke machine from the front seat of Jack's rig, and he was travelling fast.

It was too late when Jack hit the air brakes. Once again, poor old Lance slid off the seat and onto the floor. Ziggy's car was history; nothing could stop the thirty tons of steel and rubber.

Inside the cafe, the explosive sound of glass and tortured metal brought all conversation to a complete standstill. Ziggy hesitated, but asked the first question.

'What on earth was that?'

The extremely long silence from everyone didn't help her sense of anxiety. She glanced from face to face. Why did it look as if everyone knew the answer except her?

'Stuffed if I know,' said Ruby, trying to make it sound as if loud explosions happened on a regular basis around the Boomerang. Of course she'd guessed as soon as she heard the screech of Jack's brakes and seconds later, the impact. But she didn't know what to say to this unknown woman whom she was sure was not going to take the news well.

'Ooh –' began Ziggy, suddenly realising. The truckers were all leaving their tables and heading towards the door to investigate the situation. Ziggy hurried after them with Suzie and Ruby, grinning wryly at each other, at the rear.

Jack backed his rig off what remained of Ziggy's obliterated rental car. As all the truckers noted, there wasn't any damage to his vehicle except for a few minor scratches to the heavy bull bar that protected the front of the grill and the cabin. But the little Nissan hadn't stood a chance. The truckers all shook their heads, very impressed, and thought that if Jack had deliberately set out to pulverise the little car he could hardly have done a better job. It didn't resemble a car any more. It looked like a Foster's can some kid had been bashing at enthusiastically with a brick.

Indeed, this was Ziggy's first thought when she saw it, having pushed her way to the front of the locals. A week or so before she'd been to an art gallery in Sydney where there was an exhibition of sculpture made of bashed and welded drink cans, and for half a minute she thought she was gazing at it again until a blue-grey dog appeared, gave the wreck a perfunctory sniff and then raised a leg and urinated upon what Ziggy now realised was the tyre from her destroyed car.

To the locals, Ziggy's bewildered stare seemed to last an eternity. Jack, who had parked his rig and joined the group, finally saw that he was going to have to say something. This tall, blond-haired, really striking woman was staring at what remained of her car as if she were mesmerised. He asked the obvious, 'Yours?'

She came out of her spell, swung right round and snapped at him, 'What if I had been in it?'

Jack thought this was unreasonable. He could understand her being shocked and upset but couldn't see why she was getting angry about something that clearly hadn't happened. He walked over and inspected the remains of the Nissan, taking his time, like a bushman might when contemplating a change in the weather. Then answered without a hint of emotion, 'You'd be dead.'

Ruby hid a smile behind her hand. Men chuckled and drifted closer to the wreck in the hope of salvaging something of use.

Nothing was ever wasted in the bush. The remains

of that door panel. That'd beat nicely into a weather cover for the river pump. Those wheels? They could be knocked out – put 'em straight on a box trailer made from the remains of the chassis.

Joe, the thin man, approached Ziggy shaking his head. 'You just wouldn't listen . . .' But before he could elaborate Ziggy cut him off.

'Are you a cop?' she inquired, sarcastically.

'Yep! Sergeant Buckingham at your service.' Joe offered his thin, bony hand and a genuine country smile. 'Buckingham, like the palace. Pleased to meet you, ma'am.'

Ziggy's tolerance began to plummet. 'Where's your uniform?' she demanded.

'I'm off duty.'

Ziggy took a moment. Could this man be lying? Was she being teased with that dry, rural humour? One cautionary glance around the faces of the locals instantly gave her the answer. The man was definitely not lying.

'Well, thank God you're here, officer. You can deal with this mess.'

Sergeant Buckingham shook his head. 'Insurance job if you ask me, girlie.'

'Insurance?' Ziggy exploded with anger. 'You should be charging this idiot with negligent driving!'

The truckers started to laugh. They were beginning to enjoy this city girl's sense of humour. She was a real hoot!

Jack stepped forward hesitantly. 'I'm sorry about your . . .'

He was about to say 'car' when Ziggy turned on him again. 'What am I going to say to the rental company?'

In tense situations Jack had a habit of pausing before he spoke. From being around arguments and brawls in dozens of country pubs he knew that the most dangerous thing you can do in a fight is to say the first thing that comes into your head. His impulse now was to say, 'For godsakes, lady, the local police sergeant is telling you it's an insurance matter; you've got twenty witnesses.' But instead he said, 'You could tell them that you parked behind the Boomerang Cafe in Lucktown.'

'Oh, I suppose,' inquired Ziggy sarcastically, 'this is your very own spot?'

With almost perfect timing, a trucker stepped forward and wiped the thick dust off a hand-painted sign nailed to a nearby post. It read: *Jack's Spot.*

Ziggy was too furious to reply. She wiped her brow, brushed away an annoying fly, then told herself, Forget about this. It's just history now. You've done the important thing, you've found Ruby Vale. Now get the job finished and get out of town, somehow.

She turned towards Ruby and to Ruby's surprise, she smiled warmly and said, 'Ruby, I'm Ziggy Keane from Zane Publishing based in Sydney.'

Ruby smiled back at her and nodded casually. Then she became aware that Jack had drawn closer to her and seemed to be looking concerned.

'When you've got a moment,' Ziggy was continuing, 'I'd like a word – inside.' Without waiting for an answer, Ziggy strode off back into the cafe.

Ruby looked at Jack, her eyebrows raised.

'What does she want me for?' Then suddenly a possibility hit her. 'Jesus, you don't think she's one of those lottery people?'

'Ahh . . .' was all Jack was able to utter before Ruby jumped to a conclusion.

'You know, they drive all over Australia handing out cheques the size of ouija boards? Hey, wouldn't that be great!'

'Rube . . .' Jack said, trying to make her listen.

'You'd think she'd be more friendly if she was handin' out money.'

'Rube!'

Ruby stared up at him. His firmness was uncharacteristic unless they were headlong into an argument.

Jack continued, hesitantly. 'I've, ahh . . .'

'Jesus, what Jack?'

Jack grabbed her by the arm and escorted her a safe distance from other ears. 'I've gotta talk to you. Look, I've kinda . . .' He then chuckled as if excitement was about to overpower his worried face. 'I've written this – this book.'

'A what?' asked Ruby. A smile of disbelief came across her face.

'A book. You know, a book!'

'What kinda book?'

'It has your name on it,' he added.

'You've written a book with me in it?' asked Ruby.

'No, it's got your name on it – not in it!'

Ruby glanced around wondering who else might be listening to this absurd conversation. 'You mean, like I wrote it?' she asked.

Jack nodded, then shrugged, as if it was no big deal.

'Jack, why on earth did you do that?'

''Cause it's a – well, you know, a romance novel.'

She laughed incredulously. 'How could *you* write anything *romantic*?' But as she said it, Ruby realised that nothing was ever simple with Jack. It never had been. 'So that's why she's here.' Before Jack could answer, Ruby felt a huge favour looming. She exclaimed in exasperation, 'Why in hell didn't you use Suzie's name or Tina from the hairdresser's? Why didn't you just make one up? Why did you use mine?'

Jack knew the answer to this question but was finding he couldn't say it in a way that would make sense to her. 'It made it all feel real. If I put a real person's name on the book instead of a fictional one, it made me feel that I really had written a book.' He hadn't thought anyone would publish it. Whenever he read articles about would-be novelists in the newspapers, there were always accounts of how many rejection slips the novelists received before their books were finally accepted for publication. This was his first book. Zane Publishing was the first publishing company he'd sent it to. The only reason he'd sent it there was because it was the last publishing company in the alphabetical listing in the phone book. He'd been going to send it to the first publisher listed and then work his way forwards but, at the last moment, he'd changed his mind and decided to work backwards . . .

The return address had been a problem because he wanted to use his mailbox at the post office but he knew a parcel going there in Ruby's name would create all sorts of talk, until he realised a way out. Ruby and Hamish's wedding. He would tell Brenda at the post office it was a wedding present for Rube and Hamish.

Three months later he'd gone into the post office and Brenda, on sighting him, had immediately said, 'Well, that parcel you've been expecting hasn't come, Jack, but there's this letter addressed to Ruby in your box – reckon that could be about your present?'

'Yeah, I guess, Brenda,' he'd said, casually. As she passed the letter over to him, he'd noticed it was very thick. Outside in the cab of his rig with Lance at his side, he'd discovered why. He had kept reading the important parts of the letter out aloud to Lance '. . . enjoyed your manuscript very much . . . we are prepared to make an offer for Australian rights . . . paperback format . . . please see copy of contract enclosed.'

Jack became aware that Ruby was gazing at him with an exasperated expression.

'I was going to tell you, honest.'

'You should have asked, damn it!'

Ruby's exasperation was partly directed at herself. Jack's face had taken on a solemn look that she'd always found touching and she was sure he knew it.

'You're right,' he admitted.

'You bet I am. And don't give me that bloody look.'

'What does this Ziggy Keane want anyway?'

This was exactly what Jack was wondering. There'd been nothing in the three letters he'd received from Ziggy Keane to suggest that she would one day appear unexpectedly in Lucktown. In fact the letters, which were about revising and proofreading his manuscript, were so bland and dull and businesslike that Jack had begun to imagine Ziggy Keane as a glum-faced, dour person who by some fluke had missed out on a career in accountancy.

'Which just shows you,' he said to himself, remembering Ziggy's long legs and elegant, curvy body, 'how wrong you can be.'

Ruby was glaring at him, waiting for an answer. He decided it wouldn't be a good idea for her to know how astonished he'd been by Ziggy's arrival.

'Just a chat, I reckon.'

Despite his nervousness, Jack found he was becoming excited. It must mean something, Ziggy Keane suddenly appearing like this.

'Please, Rube, just see what she wants, then I can deal with it.'

Ruby pointed her finger. 'You'd better.'

Suzie stepped out from the rear door of the Boomerang and yelled out at the top of her voice, 'Rube, this lady's waitin' for you!'

Ruby sighed. 'Righto.' She then looked back to Jack. 'So she thinks I wrote it?'

'Ahh . . .'

'Yes or no?'

'Yep!' said Jack, with a smile. And after one more moment to consider all this, Ruby turned on her heel and walked purposefully back towards the cafe. She passed Suzie at the door.

'What's going on?' inquired Suzie.

'Ask *him*,' said Ruby, gesturing towards Jack, who was following behind.

Before anything further could be said, Ziggy was at Suzie's side at the door. She seized Ruby's arm and steered her into a booth.

'Sweetie,' she said, 'your book is about to go through the roof. All we want to do is get you to Sydney for publicity. Oh, and – um – sign a revised contract so we can publish it overseas.'

'Sydney?' Ruby interrupted.

'Yes,' said Ziggy who wanted to deal quickly with the other more important matter: getting that revised contract for overseas rights signed. She took the new contract from her briefcase as she started describing to Ruby all the glamour of a high-profile book launch.

'We're getting television appearances lined up,' she said. The new contract was spread out before Ruby now but Ruby hadn't even glanced at it. Instead, she was staring at Ziggy fearfully, 'I can't go on TV.'

'Why ever not?' asked Ziggy, surprised. 'Look we're only talking a few days here, at the most.'

While speaking soothingly to Ruby, Ziggy was throwing cold looks at Jack, who had now come over to the booth and was listening to their conversation. He ignored her gaze, his eyes were fixed on the contract on the table before Ruby. She hadn't glanced at the contract. She was going pale at the thought of appearing on television. Imagining herself as a novelist is one thing – pretending to be one is another. She had a sudden inspiration, and looked up to Ziggy. 'I can't, I'm gettin' married,' she said, the relief in her eyes hoping that statement would just fix everything.

'When?' insisted Ziggy.

'Three weeks. Then we go to Queensland.' Ruby was so pleased to have that off her chest. No one could interrupt a wedding.

Jack came to Ziggy's rescue. 'This publicity stuff sounds pretty important, Rube.'

Ruby stared at him. Her eyes narrowed to slits.

Ziggy turned to Jack in appreciation. 'There you go, even your fiancé here . . .'

'Jack's *not* my fiancé.' Ruby corrected her quickly. 'My fiancé's a vet, and his name is Hamish.' She now stared straight at Ziggy. 'Sorry, Ziggy, this isn't gonna work.'

'You can get married anytime, sweetie. Look, we have a serious window of opportunity here.'

Ruby remained silent. A who? A window of opportunity? What in the hell did that mean? Ziggy was conscious that Suzie was now within earshot and plainly listening. Meanwhile, Jack leant in closer and mustered concern for Ruby's wedding predicament. 'Rube, why don't you and Hamish get hitched in Sydney?'

'Brilliant!' Ziggy's exclamation made Ruby jump.

'No!'

'Okay then,' Ziggy knew what to do. 'Why don't you let us arrange and pay for everything here with a professional?'

'A professional what?' Ruby asked with suspicion.

By this time, Suzie believed it was well and truly time she became involved. She pushed in to make up a threesome. 'They do everything. Flowers, food . . .'

She turned to Ziggy, 'Could we have one of those big tents?'

'A marquee?'

Suzie turned back to Ruby with a teary smile. 'Rube, this could be the weddin' you always dreamed of.' And then with a look to Ziggy. 'You see, during the drought Hamish often didn't get paid and they could never really afford . . .'

'Suz!' said Ruby, bringing everyone to silence.

An indignant look passed across Suzie's face. 'I *am* the matron of honour,' she said quietly, as she untied her apron. 'But as I'm not needed, I'll get back to the pub an' do deliveries.' She turned on the spot and left. Ruby sighed. She hated upsetting Suzie.

Ziggy waited for Suzie to exit before she homed back in on Ruby. 'Well?'

Ruby remained silent.

'Big wedding sounds good, Rube. Everything paid for,' said Jack, who was trying to read the revised book contract upside down.

Her delight of the very thought of it was inching across Ruby's face. She had resigned herself to a small wedding after Hamish said it was stupid to go into debt just to get married. Even their planned honeymoon in the Blue Mountains was on hold until they were relocated to Queensland and could afford a week off.

'You won't be sorry. Believe me, this is what we do for our people,' beamed Ziggy. She tried her mobile but it was out of range, so she leapt up confidently and headed towards the payphone on the wall. Ziggy couldn't believe how well things were going. There hadn't been a single inquiry from Ruby Vale about the new contract. All she was interested in was getting married. Getting a signature on the new deal would be a cinch.

Our people? Ruby was thinking. Where the hell is she from, Mars? She looked up at Jack, hoping to be let off the hook but he just smiled at her.

'You gotta admit, it sounds good,' said Jack.

'Sweetie,' said Ruby, mimicking Ziggy's city voice, 'this is what we do for *our* people!' Ruby sighed, and glanced away. 'What if someone finds out? Jesus, we can't lie to people, Jack.'

'I'll split with you sixty–forty.'

Ruby pondered this.

'Okay,' he conceded, 'fifty–fifty on the next book.'

Ruby looked horror-struck. 'Next book? What next book? Jack, I'm meant to be gettin' married and movin' to Queensland. And next week I'm supposed to be puttin' eight tons of super on Jim Drinan's place.'

Jack knew not to interfere with Ruby's flying. Do that at your peril. He trod cautiously. 'You know rain's predicted all next week.' Jack added a look of concern. Again, Ruby sighed and looked away.

'Bugger you, Jack,' she said below her breath.

'Rube, how often do I ask you to do anything?'

Ruby quickly turned back to him. 'All the bloody time!'

Jack stopped dead in his tracks. Just long enough for Ruby to concede.

'Okay, I'll do this one thing. But not by myself, yer

43

hear? You've gotta come down to Sydney with me.'
Jack was so relieved he didn't make any objections as
Ruby continued, 'Once only – now say it to me. Go
on! Ruby will do this once only!'

'Once only!' Jack repeated.

'And Hamish agrees.'

Jack lost his grin. 'You can't tell Hamish I wrote this!'

He looked so embarrassed by the idea of Hamish
knowing that she agreed, 'Okay, but only if Hamish
doesn't mind me changing the date. And – it's a one-
time favour. Fly to Sydney for a coupla days, do the
book thing and get outta there.'

Jack smiled at her, relieved and grateful.

'Will they really pay for everything?' she added, just
to make sure.

'Cross my heart, hope to die,' said Jack, crossing
himself on the wrong side of his chest.

'Other side, Jack. Your heart's just here,' she said,
tapping herself above her left breast. 'Least mine is!'

As Jack sheepishly crossed himself correctly he
asked, 'Rube, is it okay if we drive?'

'Drive?' Ruby rolled her eyes and turned to leave.
Jack grabbed her.

'You know how I am with flyin'.'

'Okay, we'll bloody drive!' Ruby made her way back
in behind the counter. 'Christ, you're a pain in the
bum.'

Meanwhile, at the payphone, Ziggy continued her
chore, watched closely by an amused trucker who
commented to his mates that she ordered people
around like a bloke. The truckers agreed that she

certainly didn't look like one – but they could never trust a woman who came on so strong. Ziggy huddled closer to the phone for more privacy. 'Anything will impress them, Errol. Small marquee in a garden – basically they're beer 'n' finger-food people – okay.' With that, she hung up. The trucker was taken aback. 'Don't ya say goodbye to each other in the city?'

Ziggy ignored his observation and turned to address everyone in the cafe. Clearing her throat first, she announced, 'Excuse me all, I need a lift back to Broken Hill. I have a flight to Sydney at four.'

There was no response. Everyone in the room simply stared at her in silence. Ziggy cleared her throat once more. 'I can pay half your petrol if that's the deal.' Still no response. It was quite unnerving now as everyone just stared. 'Okay, I'll pay for it all!' Ziggy knew that this would do the trick. When in doubt, throw money at it. But nothing happened. Ziggy thought she could have heard a pin drop. She realised she had read the situation wrong. Perhaps she ought to be lighter, more friendly – make a joke?

'What's wrong? Is it the way I'm dressed?'

'Yes, take it off!' was the instant reply yelled from some distant corner of the room. The cafe erupted into laughter. Ziggy flushed and silently cursed Lucktown. What made it worse was that it was Jack who finally came to her rescue.

'I'm carting a load east,' he said.

'In your truck? Don't you think you've done enough?'

Jack shrugged, but Ziggy knew only too well that he

45

was her one chance to get out of Lucktown and said briskly, 'Okay, Mr who-ever-you-are, but before we hit the road we just have to finish up the formalities and get Ruby's signature on the dotted line. Otherwise –' she made her voice light and bright but she fixed her gaze firmly on Ruby, 'there won't be any catered-and-paid-for-wedding, will there?'

She paused. She'd rehearsed this speech and saved it for the last moment, determined that Ruby would not get a chance to object. She had no guilt about doing this – it was, after all, a fair and reasonable contract. 'Here we are,' smiling her biggest smile, Ziggy expertly flicked the contract open at the last page and a half-second later was sliding a pen towards Ruby.

But as Ruby was reaching for the pen Jack said suddenly, 'Hamish'll want to see that contract, Rube.'

'Hamish?' Ruby looked at him in astonishment. Ziggy had turned and was staring at him too. Jack felt awkward, but knew he had to go on talking. He hadn't even tried to imitate Ruby's signature on the first Zane Publishing contract he'd signed, figuring that there was no reason why anyone at the company would want to check it. However, now he knew that if Ruby signed this contract, anyone who took the most casual glance at the two contracts would notice the difference in their signatures immediately.

'Yeah,' he said firmly, 'as you're going to be married to him, Hamish is going to want to see any contracts you sign before you sign it.'

'Really,' Ziggy exclaimed, 'this is positively feudal.

There's no reason why Ruby can't sign this contract without her future husband's say so!'

Ruby glared at Jack but she had registered what Jack meant and said, 'Yeah – you're right. Hamish will want to see this before I sign it.'

The way she repeated the last four words let Jack know she understood, and he would have let out a sigh of relief except that Ziggy had turned on him in a fury, 'I can't believe in this day and age – do you mean –' she demanded of Jack, becoming incoherent in her exasperation, 'that we can't leave this godforsaken place until Ruby's fiancé has deigned to allow her to sign a contract that's absolutely nothing to do with him? Where is he anyway?'

'I couldn't leave until tomorrow morning, anyway,' replied Jack, calmly, 'I won't have a load till then.'

'Am I expected to stay here?' Ziggy gave the cafe a disbelieving look, but Ruby only smiled. She stood up, folded the contract neatly and put it in her jeans pocket.

'Lucktown has a beaut pub,' she said with a smile.

******

Lucktown did indeed have a beaut pub. It rarely accommodated anybody, as tourists were scarce in the isolated little town. The last one, some years ago now, had been a leather-coated, exhausted Japanese motorcyclist who had been determined to speed right across the continent of Australia without stopping. Over-nighters got nothing more than a bed and a towel, but the pub had an atmosphere that stirred the imagination. Built during the days of the silver rush, it boasted a history of infamous and colourful clientele. Over the years, stories of the Lucktown pub's former guests naturally became greatly exaggerated but nonetheless important as a reminder of the town's colonial history.

'Suz, I gotta guest for you,' announced Ruby, as she escorted a reluctant Ziggy into the public bar of the hotel. It was rare for Suzie to be in the pub during the day. 'Days' were for the cafe – a time for Suzie to be with her friend Ruby, joke with the truckers and listen to music on the jukebox. Her nights were very different. No music and no friends – just obnoxious drunks raving on about how good they once were in bed or how rich they could have become. It was common knowledge why Suzie worked such long hours. Artie saw to that.

As Ziggy surveyed the unused blackened fireplace and the huge carved bar with brass accessories she saw that the place must have been elegant – once. Now an ancient mirror, bordered by ornate dirty crystal lamps, reflected the tired figure of Suzie as she wiped down the counter-top with slow, deliberate strokes.

Suzie only glanced at the two women briefly, and didn't meet their eyes. 'Twenty-eight bucks,' she said, in a flat tone. 'You get fresh sheets an' a towel, an' I do breakfast.'

Ruby caught her breath. She'd noted her friend's odd manner and the way she was holding her head. In the mirror she saw that one side of Suzie's face was red and swollen. Ruby moved closer, manoeuvring to see more. Suzie could not hide any longer, so she turned and covered the side of her face with a wet dish towel. 'Don't say anythin', Rube. Promise!' A single tear rolled down her cheek. Her face was so sore she couldn't even feel the tear's delicate trail.

A slow but tremendous anger mounted within Ruby as Ziggy inched forward, horror-struck by the sight of Suzie's face. 'Do your rooms have a bath?' Ziggy asked inanely, unable to think of what to say.

'Yeah, down the hall.' Suzie's voice was strained.

By now, Ruby's anger was so intense she had started to pace back and forth with short little steps that showed her anxiety. 'The bastard!' she spat out, with enough venom, Ziggy thought, to kill a horse. Ruby could see that Artie had used his clenched fist against Suzie. She would have fallen hard under the impact of such a blow. This was not an angry slap, but a vicious, deliberate punch to the face. What was wrong, Ruby wondered, with Artie, who'd once held Suzie by the hand and looked into her loving eyes and betrothed himself? What happens to married people?

At that moment, Artie entered the rear of the bar carrying a dozen bottles of Johnnie Walker scotch.

'Here – how long is it gonna take you to load this on the shelf?' he demanded of Suzie, in his thin, whining voice.

Ruby couldn't hold back; she exploded and lunged at Artie like a wild animal. His red, fat face turned a sickly purple with alarm. The slug to the side of his face came as the next surprise and caused him to drop his precious bottles. There was a loud crash as the box hit the floor. Artie looked at Ruby in horror.

'You bloody bitch!' he yelled, lunging towards her. Suzie tucked herself safely in behind the bar.

'Christ, Rube, what are you doin'?' she screamed.

Ziggy had retreated back towards the entrance door as Ruby seemed more than ready to take Artie on.

'Come on, Artie, you fat bastard. You love beltin' women, don't ya? Try me!'

'Ruby, no!' screamed Suzie again.

'Come on, take a shot, you mongrel,' yelled Ruby.

Ziggy didn't know where to look. Her agonised smile fell upon Suzie in the hope of some sort of intervention. Nothing. Suzie was frozen to the spot.

Ziggy then took a half step forward. 'Ahh, could I see my room now?' No one seemed to hear her.

Ruby tensed up even more. She shuffled her weight lightly between her feet and further beckoned Artie with her clenched fists. Ruby knew she was only good for one more shot. The bastard was unfit, but big. If he slugged her she'd certainly go down.

A bush radio station announcer droned on with wool market reports. His monotonous tone seemed incongruous with the tense stand-off in the Lucktown public bar.

'Rube, this is silly,' said Suzie from behind the bar, hoping to end the confrontation.

'Oh, yeah? So is your bruised face, Suz. Real silly!'

Finally it was clear that Artie had thought twice about lashing out at Ruby. He broke the tension with a forced grin and walked from the bar murmuring obscenities under his breath. The atmosphere around the three women was electric. Ruby, with an immense sense of triumph, faced Suzie with a proud smile. Suzie's look was full of gratitude, but she knew that her husband was not going to change.

'You okay?' asked Ruby.

'Nothin' a piece o' steak won't fix,' smiled Suzie, as she placed the wet cloth to her face again. 'What about you?'

'I'm fine. Don't you worry about me.' Suzie turned to Ziggy with a painful grin.

'Welcome to Lucktown. You can see how it got its name.'

'Yes!' Ziggy found she was laughing with relief. 'Lucky you live here.'

Suzie laughed until the hurt in her face pulled her short.

Ruby took the wet cloth from her, rinsed it under a cold tap and filled it with ice cubes from the freezer. Then, with four smashing blows on the bar top, she pulverised the ice and handed the compress back to Suzie.

'Ice does the trick.' Ruby then turned to Ziggy. 'Right, come on, let's find you a room.'

When Ruby returned to the bar after taking Ziggy to her room, she told Suzie her news.

'You'd better go and tell Hamish right away—'

'I can't—' Ruby began, but Suzie interrupted.

'I'll go down to the Boomerang.'

'You oughta be lying down,' said Ruby gently. She did want to go and tell Hamish the news and it wasn't the sort of thing you talk about over the phone.

'It'll take my mind off things here,' said Suzie, removing the icepack and carefully touching her cheek. 'Coupla pills and a good coat of make-up – I'll be right. I'd rather be out of here anyway. That reminds me,' she added, 'how did our city girl like her room?'

There are times when it's better to turn things into a joke. Ruby knew that Suzie would have loved to do up some of the rooms at the hotel, make them modern and comfortable, but Artie refused to spend the money, figuring that no one would stay overnight in Lucktown by choice and there was nowhere else to stay. So the rooms were clean, but grim.

'Well,' she said thoughtfully, 'I think she liked it more than the sight of her car after—'

'—but not much more,' said Suzie dryly. Both of the women burst out laughing. 'Well, no one asked her to come here,' said Ruby, and added, 'You go and fix yourself up; I'd better get back to the cafe.'

During the quieter parts of the day the Boomerang could, and occasionally did, run itself. Anyone who hadn't paid for their meal would just leave the cash and collect the change on their next visit. Newcomers would either wait for Ruby or Suzie to return or, if they were in a hurry, one of the regulars would set off to the grocer's or the butcher's and find them – somebody would always know where they were.

On her way to the door, Ruby came to a halt. 'Oh Christ!' She had just remembered where Hamish was. 'He's at Darling Station, the old Reece place – Mr Reece is having his sale today.'

'Hell,' said Suzie. The two women stood looking at each other.

'With all the drama we've been having today I'd forgotten.'

'Poor old Mr Reece,' said Suzie, as she raised her fingers to her cheek. 'That place has been in his family for generations, hasn't it?

Ruby nodded. 'Hamish said he'd probably stay and help as long as he could – I can't turn up there in the middle of the sale just to talk to him.'

'Course you can,' said Suzie firmly, 'Mr Reece will be pleased to see you. Anyway, it's important to talk to Hamish as soon as possible. It's no little thing you're doin' – how many weddings have you postponed?'

'None,' said Ruby, grinning at her.

'Neither have I,' said Suzie. 'More's the pity.'

4

The disbursement sale. It's the most dreaded moment for anyone on the land. Inevitably it's when there is no one to take over, or when farmers are too old to adapt to new farming technologies, that they have to sell out. Sell everything they own, usually for a rock-bottom price. More than likely it is forced upon them by a bank that has carried the farming business far too deep into debt; or by bad seasonal markets, or by the folly of Mother Nature who's delivered too many drought years in a row. Whatever the reason this was not a good day for old Mr Reece, who was leaning on a rail with Ruby as they watched his prize merinos go under the hammer.

'You know, Ruby,' he chuckled, 'during the wool boom we used to get a pound a pound. They used to call me Reece the Fleece.' His voice, as usual, was far too loud because he never remembered to change the batteries in his hearing aid.

An Aboriginal man with a greying beard and a sweat-stained hat rode up swiftly to the edge of the yards on a proud chestnut horse. For some time he just stared solemnly at the sheep.

'Anything left in the bush paddock, Johnnie?' Mr Reece asked.

'That's the lot, boss.' Johnnie Ngallametta was visibly upset. He avoided eye-contact with Ruby and Mr Reece, pulled sharply to the left on the reins and immediately kicked his chestnut into a canter back towards the homestead. Mr Reece shook his head – he knew exactly what was on Johnnie's mind.

'He's a good bloke, eh?' smiled Ruby.

'The best. Darling Station's all he's ever known.' Mr Reece paused a moment at the thought of the drastic consequences that the sale of the homestead was going to have.

'A long time ago,' he said sadly to Ruby, 'I promised Johnnie he could stay here forever!'

'Oh.' Ruby's gaze followed the black stockman's back.

'I thought we'd all be here forever. Life's a bastard, eh?'

'What will he do now? Where will he go?'

'He got a job with the local council, driving a grader.'

Ruby nodded. They both knew how long that would last.

Mr Reece sighed. 'I give Johnnie a month then I reckon he'll go walkabout.'

Ruby was about to say 'Yeah, he'll hate it,' then stopped herself. It would only make Mr Reece more miserable. She wondered if Jack could think of any other places where Johnnie might find a job. She knew that he and Johnnie Ngallametta were friends, but she guessed that Johnnie was too proud to tell Jack how desperate things were for him. 'Jack travels all over,' Ruby said to herself, 'he's in a position to hear of a place on another property. Line it up for Johnnie – Mr Reece'll give him a good reference – and make it sound like Johnnie will be doing the new owner a favour.'

At the thought of this plan, a smile spread across Ruby's face. Hamish, who was standing on a makeshift platform above the pens of sheep with the auctioneer, looking down at her, reflected on how vivid and alive Ruby's face was. The auctioneer was taking a quick slug from his whisky flask as one lot of sheep were run out and another lot brought in. Due to the time of the year, the auctioneer was having a hard time lifting the price of the animals. When he started his call again Ruby was mesmerised listening to him shouting the price bids. Hamish, catching her eye, smiled. Ruby responded with a wave that inadvertently secured the next bid.

Hamish rolled his eyes in despair and mouthed a firm instruction for her to keep still. Ruby mouthed her reply with a grin. 'Sorry.'

There was no real need for Hamish to stay at the auction after he'd given Mr Reece's livestock a clean bill of health. But, as all inspections had been completed by mid-morning and there were no other animal emergencies in the district, Hamish had decided to stick around and help the old man with the sale. It was always difficult to watch strangers poking around on the trestle tables covered with boxes of rusted century-old tools, horseshoes, rabbit traps and other nameless odds and ends. The agricultural equipment was first to go: the Massey Ferguson tractor; the dual-wheeled Dodge truck; a broad-acre plough; a small Caterpillar dozer; four trailers in various stages of re-building; a Willys army jeep that had never given a day's trouble until the new owner tried to drive it away; and fencing equipment. It went on and on – everything this man, and his father before him, had collected. An agricultural museum was going under the hammer.

For the auctioneer, trying to get an enthusiastic bid was like squeezing blood from a stone. His voice droned on saying just about anything to interest buyers. Old Mr Reece was just about to lose hope when Ruby brushed an annoying fly from her face. Up went the bid again. Hamish leant over to the auctioneer and whispered something in his ear. The man was furious that he had to break his stride and bring the proceedings to a halt. Hamish climbed off the platform and walked over to Ruby. 'What are you doing?' he asked in a loud whisper.

'Gettin' me a good price,' barked Mr Reece. 'A price I deserve.'

Ruby smiled, loving the spirit of this old man.

'That may well be so, Mr Reece,' explained Hamish. 'But you can't bugger up the auction.'

'I was swatting a fly,' admitted Ruby.

'Ruby, it's illegal – that's all I know.'

Ruby took him completely by surprise by suddenly embracing him. Her huge affectionate hug embarrassed Hamish.

'I gotta talk to you,' she said, then stretched up to kiss him.

Hamish glanced around hoping there weren't too many witnesses to their private moment.

'Rube – after my buck's party, eh?'

'Hamish, something really amazing has happened.' She gave him a big smile. 'Guess what? We can have a big weddin' and we won't have to pay a cent!'

Hamish was torn between her excitement and his need to return to work.

'Everything!' Ruby added. 'They'll pay for food, drinks and a big marquee . . .'

'Yer comin', Hamish?' yelled the auctioneer.

Hamish waved his acknowledgment and turned back to Ruby. 'Rube, I said I'd help out here.' He was conscious that all around people were watching him.

Everyone stared, waiting for him to make a decision.

'All we gotta do is put it off a week,' Ruby added casually.

'Who's paying?' asked Hamish.

'Well . . .' She proceeded carefully. 'I've got this . . .'

The auctioneer cut her off. 'Come on, mate, leave your bride for the big night an' get back to work.'

Farmers chuckled. Hamish smiled back at them pretending to enjoy the attention. He turned to face Ruby. 'Rube, we don't need hand-outs.'

'It's not a hand-out.'

'Why don't we talk about it later, eh?'

Disappointment crossed Ruby's face as Hamish disappeared back into the huge flock of sheep.

******

Ruby kicked around Darling Station for some time waiting for Hamish to finish helping out with the sale of the sheep. She knew Suzie could cope with the Boomerang. Timing was everything with Hamish. She'd weighed up Jack's charade in her mind and knew that if she decided to help him she would certainly get the wedding she deserved. She also knew that it was difficult to rush a country man like Hamish into a decision, especially if it had anything to do with a wedding. Usually, the women decided everything.

That's it! thought Ruby. I'll just tell him that's what's happening and not to worry himself. Yeah, that'll work.

The Reeces' homestead was a grand but sprawling affair built during the late eighteen-hundreds and built-on in the nineteen-thirties. It had deep verandahs on all four sides with a silver-painted bull-nose iron roof. Ruby remembered how she used to play in the once lavish garden and climb the proud, aging trees. It used to be one of the showpiece places of the district. When Mrs Reece was alive, everyone knew that when she wasn't working her fingers to the bone helping Mr Reece with sheep and cattle she'd be in that garden, fighting the elements, trying to build her Shangri-la. It was sad to see it overgrown and neglected.

Right there, by the verandah post, was where Jack had teased her when she couldn't hit tin cans off a fence with Mr Reece's .22 rifle. Ruby became a great shot the moment she realised Jack was giving her false instructions about the sight alignment.

'Sorry, Rube. Got a bit caught up.' Hamish's voice

broke Ruby's concentration. Ruby looked over to see him entering through the garden gate. 'Anyway,' he continued, 'I've been beeped by the surgery.'

'You're a good man, Hamish Wilson.'

Hamish chuckled, placed his arm around Ruby's waist and escorted her out of the garden and away from the homestead.

'Why can't we buy this place?' sighed Ruby.

Hamish threw back his head with laughter. 'That's a good one, Rube. We've gotta be tight-belt people. We can't even afford a new car yet.'

Ruby wondered how long it would take before they had a real honeymoon.

'Now what's all this about someone payin' for the weddin'?' asked Hamish.

'Don't worry – it's all sorted out.'

Hamish was relieved. 'Great!'

Ruby took a deep breath. 'We just shuffle the dates: I go to Sydney for a coupla days, do the business, fly home, and we have a wonderful big wedding that won't cost us a cent!'

'You still haven't told me who's payin'.'

'Book publishers. It seems my name's on somethin' they've bought.' Jesus, was that a lie, Ruby thought? If it wasn't, it was bloody close.

'You're kidding?' Hamish's pager went off again. 'Bloody hell,' he said, while awkwardly fiddling with the pager. He quickened his pace. 'Come on, Rube. Never rains but it pours!'

* * * * * *

'What on earth!'

Ziggy Keane was jerked awake. It took her a moment to realise where she was. Lucktown. She was still in Lucktown. The room was dark. She stretched out a hand to turn on the bedside lamp but her hand groped uselessly in the empty darkness. There was no bedside table, no bedside lamp. 'Lucktown,' she said to herself, and got out of the bed, went to the door and felt around for the ancient rope pull which served to turn on the room's one light – a bare bulb suspended from the ceiling in the centre of the room.

Ziggy sighed deeply. By six o'clock that evening she felt she'd exhausted all the simple amusements – rental car demolitions, wife bashings and the like – that Lucktown provided for visitors, and decided to go to bed. She'd taken a couple of sleeping pills that were conveniently in her bag on the assumption that these would be sufficient to knock her out until morning. It was a long time since she'd had twelve hours sleep but it seemed to be the only useful thing she could do. Unfortunately the sleeping tablets which always worked in Sydney when she took them to wind down, didn't seem to be as effective in the country. It was now only ten o'clock on a Friday night in Lucktown.

The room was suddenly full of noise as if downstairs in the bar there was a football crowd cheering a goal. Ziggy became aware that it was this same noise that had wakened her earlier. She stood and stared around the bare depressing little room – the narrow bed; unshaded light; battered wardrobe containing several wire coat hangers so deformed you couldn't use them; the chest of drawers that Ziggy hadn't even tried to open for fear of what she'd find; and a threadbare towel that had probably once been white but was now dyed an unpleasant shade of red by years of Lucktown dust. As she gazed about her, Ziggy noted an odd rust-coloured stain on the worn linoleum floor, and was wondering glumly if some previous guest had shot him- or herself at the prospect of a night in Lucktown, when she had an inspiration. In the wardrobe with the deformed coathangers was her briefcase, which contained her dictaphone. She could actually make some use of her extended stay in Lucktown. She could go to the Boomerang and interview Ruby Vale about her novel – and she could also use the visit as an opportunity to see if Ruby had signed the contract.

As usual, the thought of that contract made Ziggy's heart beat more rapidly. She was very ambitious and knew that one of the surefire ways to get ahead in publishing was by discovering a bestseller. Even a big international company like Zane Publishing – which produced a whole range of books and had a dozen bestselling authors both in Australia and overseas – was eager to find that one, rare, elusive manuscript that could become a runaway popular success. It wasn't only the money that a blockbuster brought a publishing company – it was also the prestige. Other authors were always eager to sign with a publisher that had had a hit book, and good staff from other publishers were always keen to work for a successful company. Blockbusters meant money, glamour and power. 'All my favourites,' said Ziggy Keane to herself, as she combed her hair. And she'd very nearly missed out on Ruby Vale's book, *Bird in the Hand*.

Of course she'd realised that Ruby's manuscript was competent and worth publishing even though it was a first novel by an unknown writer. But she hadn't really paid it much attention. The decision to publish the manuscript had been based on reading the first twenty pages, the last twenty pages and an editor's favourable report. 'OK – Australian market only,' she'd scrawled on her report. She wasn't much interested in romantic novels. It was Ella, her secretary, who really made Ziggy aware of the potential of *Bird in the Hand*.

One morning the previous week she'd come into Ella's office and found her secretary sitting having a cup of coffee and reading Ruby's book. Ziggy had been astonished. She wasn't surprised that Ella was reading the novel – all the staff were encouraged to read company publications – it was the sight of her reading it in the office. Ziggy had never before seen Ella doing anything at work that wasn't immediately related to her duties as a secretary. She was very conscientious about her work and was never known to have private phone calls, file her nails or flick through fashion magazines while at her desk. The only way that Ziggy could get her to take a break was by insisting on talking to her over a cup of coffee. Most people in the company thought her too serious, and weren't surprised that – at nearly forty – she was still unmarried. But Ziggy knew she had attended the Aboriginal school of hard knocks and also that her grave, beautiful, dark face hid a wonderful laconic sense of humour.

Ella's eyes met Ziggy's and she said shamefacedly, 'I took this home last night but I couldn't finish it – I really had to find out what happens at the end.'

Bells started ringing in Ziggy's head. Ella was a fast and voracious reader. In the time that Ziggy had worked with her, she'd known her to read hundreds of books, but she had never seen Ella have a reaction like this.

Ziggy cancelled all her calls and meetings and locked herself in her office with a copy of *Bird in the Hand*.

The following day there was the monthly publishing meeting, which was always chaired by Errol Ruben, Zane Publishing's flamboyant managing director. After going through the agenda items, Errol had looked around at his senior staff.

'Anything new?' he inquired.

'Yes, Errol,' said Ziggy, trying to keep her voice clear and calm, 'I have re-thought our entire strategy about that first-time novel *Bird in the Hand* and am proposing an immediate new print run. We're contacting all the major talkshows . . .'

Everyone around the table knew what this meant. Ziggy Keane was confident she had a winner. She was conscious as she went on outlining the new publishing and publicity strategy that Ralph Seaton, across the table, was watching her closely. Ralph was roughly forty. Ziggy was certain that he lied about his age, but he cut a fine figure in an Armani suit and he was

Ziggy's chief rival for promotion at Zane Publishing. When she finished speaking she waited to hear what he would say. He couldn't rain on her parade without appearing jealous and ungenerous in front of all their colleagues, but she was sure he'd find some way to undermine her.

'That's wonderful, Zig,' he said, pulling his lips back in a bright smile. 'What about overseas?'

Ziggy felt herself go chill. She knew that for a book like this Zane would want to have overseas rights. But all she had was Ruby's name on the Australian contract.

'That's in the bag,' she said, trying to sound relaxed. 'We sent her out a contract last week and she's signed it. I'm going to pick it up when I go out to Lucktown next Friday to discuss publicity.'

She was sure Ralph suspected she was lying, but Errol was saying, 'Have fun in the dustbowl, Ziggy, and congratulations. Next?'

Back in her office, Ziggy had instructed Ella, 'Get me to Lucktown, wherever it is, next Friday, by whatever means it takes – and remember that for *the past week* you have known I am going to Lucktown next Friday.'

Ella had grinned.

******

Ziggy decided to leave the Lucktown pub by the side entrance, not wishing to encounter either its unpleasant owner or the crowd of drink-crazed locals who were making all the racket in the front bar. But as she was hurrying down the side hall she had a sudden glimpse through an open door of the front bar. The long, narrow room was crowded with men. They all had their backs to her and were roaring at something out of her sight. She thought it was the screen showing the game she had supposed they were watching, until a figure came into view. It was a tall, fair-haired man. He was bare-chested, wearing a kilt and – Ziggy stopped, appalled – a blindfold. As she stared, she realised he was attempting to walk along a row of bar tables. At the end of the row, leaning against the wall, was a bored-looking woman in a Carmen Miranda outfit. The man in the kilt was plainly trying to make his way towards her. He was also drunk as well as blindfolded and relying on the other men for directions.

'Left,' the men were yelling, 'Left, left.' After hesitating, swaying back and forth above them for a moment, he stepped left – and landed on the floor with an almighty crash. There was a roar of cheers and laughter. Ziggy raised her eyebrows and kept walking.

Across the road from the pub, Ruby was closing the Boomerang Cafe for the night. The last lonely trucker, filled with hamburger and strong coffee, had left with enough sustenance to get him over the border to Alice Springs – if he was lucky. Kangaroos were the biggest danger for the truckers at night. It was difficult to stop a thirty-ton truck when an animal suddenly hopped out, dazed, into your headlights. Mad Pete said he hit a camel once not far from Broken Hill. 'Felt like running into a fuckin' brick wall,' he had said.

Ruby sighed, and took one more look around the cafe before dousing the lights. Suddenly, she was startled by the entrance of Ziggy.

'What's going on over there? I can't sleep for the noise,' she said, as she flopped down in a booth.

'Men being boys,' smiled Ruby.

'How do you cope? You got coffee?' she asked, although it was obvious that Ruby was finishing up. More cheering came from across the street. 'Sounds like some primal thing.'

Ruby switched on the hot water urn. 'It's Hamish's buck's party.'

'Ugh,' groaned Ziggy. 'I'm really getting to see all of Lucktown's major tourist attractions. I expect that awful trucker person's there, too.'

Ruby was just about to say that Jack would be keeping an eye on Hamish, but Ziggy was going on, 'Do you know what they're doing over there?'

Ziggy was too insensitive to notice how Ruby had stiffened at her contemptuous tones and it didn't occur to her to look at the other young woman's face as she blithely described what was happening to Hamish. To make things worse, at the end of her description there was another very loud crash. Ruby glanced over towards the pub, her mouth tightening. As Ziggy was speaking she'd gone to turn the urn on to make the coffee. It occurred to her that the water might take some time to reheat, but she decided this didn't matter. In her present mood she would be happy to serve Ziggy's coffee with a dash of rat poison.

None of this showed in her voice, however, as she placed the cup of tepid coffee on the table before Ziggy. Instead she said, in tones almost as bored and superior-sounding as Ziggy's own, 'Really – is that all? It sounds as if Hamish is getting off real lightly. I've known of blokes who've woken up the next morning in the middle of the bush, miles from anywhere, to find they've got no clothes on and they're covered with sticky molasses and shackled by a chain to a tree stump. Of course,' she added casually, 'not all of them survive.'

Ziggy, who was setting her dictaphone upon the table, gave Ruby a startled look.

'What's that for?' inquired Ruby.

Ziggy smiled at her naiveté and switched the machine on. 'Thought, seeing I'm stuck here, we might as well chat!'

A sudden anxiety gripped Ruby. She couldn't do this. What if she said all the wrong things? 'Are you really gonna pay for my wedding?' she asked quietly.

'Sweetie, this is the tip of the iceberg for you. Now, you've got to be honest and tell me everything about yourself. When do you write? I mean, seeing what responsibilities you have here . . .'

'I fly a crop-duster plane as well,' Ruby added, without thinking.

Ziggy shook her head in amazement. 'See what I mean?'

Ruby smiled modestly, and slid somewhat reluctantly into the booth opposite Ziggy.

'Tell me about your characters,' Ziggy asked. 'God forbid they're drawn from people around here!'

Ruby thought for a moment before answering. 'Does it seem that way to you?'

Ziggy laughed. 'Okay, let's start with your next book.'

Ruby took a deep breath. 'Next book?' Ruby abruptly stood up and started to reorganise the cruets and sauce bottles on each table. 'Ahh . . . it's about . . . love . . . honour, and the war!' Ruby smiled. Thank Christ she'd managed to pull that off.

'Which war?' Ziggy said, switching on the dictaphone.

Ruby moved towards a selection of photographs hanging on the wall. Many of them featured Ruby with her father, including one of them standing by a huge pig at the Broken Hill Agricultural Show.

'Boer! . . . yeah, the Boer War,' she replied confidently.

This immediately appealed to Ziggy. 'Good setting!'

'You think so?' asked Ruby.

Ziggy didn't let up. 'What's it going to be called?'

Ruby felt she was on a roll. 'Umm, *Love in . . . Africa*.'

Ziggy thought about this. A long, uncomfortable pause.

'You don't like it?' asked Ruby.

'No – I think it's great!'

Ruby's face showed instant relief. She returned to the booth and slid in again. 'I don't want to give too much away.'

'No, Ruby, we can't be doing that.' Ziggy looked at Ruby with genuine affection. She switched off the dictaphone. 'Tell me this. Were you scared when you hit that creep in the pub?'

Ruby smiled pensively at the thought, then looked straight up at Ziggy. 'I was absolutely shitless!'

'You were great,' Ziggy said with a smile. She stood up. 'Oh,' she added casually, 'about the contract—'

'Yeah – it's signed,' said Ruby, interrupting her. 'It's around somewhere—' She got to her feet and went over to a shelf behind the counter where she kept various bits of paperwork: bills and order slips and deposit books. This shelf was not far from the grill and Ziggy noticed that the contract had acquired a few spots of oil. But Ziggy didn't care. It could have been returned to her covered with egg yolk and tomato sauce so long as it bore Ruby Vale's signature.

'So it was all right with Hamish, was it?' she added.

Ruby looked at her inquiringly.

'The contract – Hamish read it and he approves?' asked Ziggy, who was feeling fond of Ruby now and sincerely didn't want to be the cause of any conflict between Ruby and her fiancé. Ruby, however, merely nodded and said, 'Yeah it was okay with Hamish,' in a rather vague manner as she went again to turn out the lights.

Hamish, over the road, was feeling pretty vague himself, but he was determined to make his way along the zigzag trail of bar tables to where the girl from Broken Hill awaited him. In Hamish's drunken memory that girl in her Carmen Miranda outfit had looked very attractive – curvy, nice tits. He was going to get to her if it killed him.

He took another step and found he was walking on air. His huge, drunken body fell like a stone. The men cheered with excitement. Carmen Miranda sighed, and checked her face in a mirror. Hamish struggled to his feet.

'I'm okay, I'm okay!' he said, turning abruptly and bumping his head into a pillar.

'Will someone help out this poor fucker?' screamed Carmen Miranda in a broad, squeaky voice. Men grinning broadly surged forward in reply to her request. This was not what she meant. 'Not me, you bastards!' she yelled, and kicked out viciously as they came into range.

Jack was observing all this behaviour from the rear of the bar. He shook his head and sipped the cool foam off the top of his beer.

By this time, Hamish had scrambled back up onto the row of tables.

'Go right, Hamish,' Jack yelled. 'Go right!'

Hamish stopped when he heard Jack's voice. Now there's someone he could trust. 'Is that you, Jack?' he asked, already dreaming of cavorting with Carmen Miranda.

'Yeah, mate. Go right!'

A deafening uproar from the other men tried to persuade Hamish that Jack was wrong – he must go the other way! Hamish ignored them, knowing that Jack would never betray him.

'Now, left – two steps and left again!' yelled Jack. Hamish moved on excitedly. But unfortunately, too much alcohol had clouded his brain – Hamish turned right.

'I said *left*, you silly bastard!' screamed Jack.

This time, Hamish's fall rendered him motionless on the floor of the public bar.

******

Half an hour later, tired, drunk men stumbled out of the Lucktown pub laughing and joking, still grasping cans of beer. No one cared what time it was – no one cared that tomorrow would bring terrible hangovers. No one cared that Hamish was near death. It had been a good night.

Hamish had one arm draped about Jack as he was helped into the street. In his other hand, he was still holding a half bottle of Johnnie Walker. 'Geez, Jack – did I get laid?' he asked, slurring every word.

'You were up there for our enjoyment, not yours,' replied Jack, trying to keep the man upright. Jack manoeuvred Hamish to a bench in the street outside the pub.

Hamish flopped down, amused. 'I'm gonna be a bloody married man.'

'That's a terrifying thought, mate. But someone's gotta do it.'

Hamish chuckled and took another swig. 'Ruby says she's written this story an' some mug's gonna pay for a big wedding if we change the date. What do you reckon, Jack?'

Jack just gazed out into the darkness of the street.

'Eh?' insisted Hamish.

'Written a story?'

Hamish cut his next swig short. 'Tell you what,' he slurred, 'I don't mind someone else payin'.'

'That'd be good.'

Hamish tried to sit upright on the bench. He looked at Jack, suddenly wondering why he hadn't thought to ask the question earlier. 'When did Ruby write a book?'

'Beats me,' said Jack, holding his gaze into the street.

Hamish took another swig. 'Well, I'll be buggered!' he said, with complete bewilderment. 'These fillies sure take some breakin' in.' He then laughed at his own joke. Jack sipped his beer hoping that Hamish was drunk enough to forget soon what he was talking about.

Hamish placed his scotch bottle on the ground beside the bench. 'Ruby'll have to slow down a bit if she wants to be a vet's wife,' he mumbled.

'Yeah,' said Jack, keeping his voice neutral. As Hamish was talking he'd been thinking about Ruby's father and wondering what he would have thought of this tall, blond, solid Scotsman his daughter was intending to marry. Though he himself liked Hamish, and could see what a hard-working responsible bloke he was, he had a feeling that these were not the sort of qualities that would have appealed to George Vale, and he knew that George would have been outraged at the idea of anyone trying to tame his adventurous daughter. Still, he thought to himself, George Vale hadn't made much of a success of marriage and he'd brought up his daughter to be almost as wild as he was. Hamish would bring some stability into her life. Jack grinned to himself. He had realised that George

Vale would never have approved of Hamish because Hamish disliked flying almost as much as Jack himself did.

Hamish, who was trying to sober up, had noticed Jack's grin but had thought of a completely different reason for it.

'You seein' that Flying Doctor nurse?'

Jack shook his head, 'Nympho?'

Hamish looked at him astonished. 'I took her out once to a Picnic Race Ball. She wasn't like that with me.'

Jack laughed, 'Just kiddin'.'

Hamish felt very relieved, 'Jesus, for a minute I thought I'd really missed out on something.' Both men laughed, and Jack took a swig of whisky.

'Good women are thin on the ground, mate.'

An old utility truck rumbled by with its exhaust pipe dragging along the ground. Sparks off the roadway lit the underneath of the vehicle. Hamish gave the driver a casual wave as it disappeared into the night with no tail-lights.

Both men stared after it into the darkness for a while, then Hamish said with a burp, 'Don't tell Ruby, but I quite fancied that bit of crumpet in there. She had great tits.'

'Not a word, mate.'

'How does—' It took Hamish a while to start the question, and he had to repeat himself while he tried to find the right words, 'How does a bloke really know if he's really—' despite his efforts, he could not think how to say what he wanted to ask.

'—if he's a good lover?' Jack asked.

Hamish smiled, 'Yeah.'

'Chemistry.'

Hamish was delighted, 'That was always my best subject!'

Jack laughed, stood up and pulled Hamish to his feet. 'Come on, let's get you home.'

'Where do yer think Ruby is?' moaned Hamish, as the blood quickly escaped from his head now that he was upright.

'Believe me, mate. She's the last person you need to see right now.'

A surge of nausea overcame Hamish; he fought it back. 'I'm okay, I'm okay.' His knees were weak but his spirit was strong. Hamish turned to Jack with a kind of sincerity. 'You're a good mate, Jack. I just want to thank you.'

'Yeah, yeah,' Jack retorted, dismissing his friend's drunken words. 'Look, Hamish. Why don't you stay here at the pub?'

'Great bloody idea,' said Hamish. He immediately spun around on the spot and smashed his head against an iron verandah post, then fell like the proverbial ton of bricks.

Finding a room for Hamish was easy – Suzie saw to that – but carrying the six-foot, drunken Scot up the narrow staircase proved to be more difficult than carrying a mattress. Suzie, dressed in her dressing-gown and slippers, held Hamish's feet, while trying desperately not to wake Artie in their bedroom across the hall. Jack, at the other end, was trying to drag Hamish upstairs one step at a time. It was a big challenge. They tried twisting, turning, and at one time, folding him. Suzie dropped one of Hamish's legs and burst into giggles.

'What the bloody hell's goin' on out there?' A scream from Artie.

'It's okay, Artie,' yelled Jack. 'I got it under control.'

As he spoke his eyes met Suzie's and they both began to shake with laughter. Hamish lay between them, halfway up the stairs. Somehow, in their attempts to lever him upwards, he'd gotten wedged crossways between the banister and the wall, and he now lay there like a massive living barricade.

'Might have to take the wall out to get him free,' whispered Suzie to Jack. Her bruised jaw was aching from laughter, but she didn't mind. She looked down at Hamish and added, 'He's covered in bruises. There won't be enough ice in the country to make packs for all the damage he's done to himself.'

'Just as well he's a vet,' said Jack, cheerfully. 'He can give himself a shot.'

Suzie giggled again.

5

The next morning, Jack thought that he wouldn't have minded one of the injections Hamish used for the cattle himself. The day started clear and crisp – a perfect morning – but Jack only *just* managed to get himself out of bed and over to the Boomerang Cafe desperate for his first mug of Ruby's black coffee. The atmosphere was alive. Ruby and Suzie were working like Trojans to get breakfast in front of twenty truckers. Orders were yelled across the room above the sound of Diana Ross singing 'Baby Love'. Business was good.

Jack grabbed the only remaining stool at the counter as Ruby scuttled past holding three breakfast orders.

'Morning,' Jack said, not knowing whether she had heard him. Ruby placed down the orders, skimmed back past the coffee machine, filled a mug for Jack and then promptly dumped it in front of him as she headed the other way.

'Where's Ziggy?' Again Ruby had not heard him. Or maybe she wasn't listening? Eventually, she stopped and looked at him for the first time. Even at this hour of the morning her faultless skin was glistening from perspiration. She was trying to keep her hair from falling over her face with a blue bandanna.

'This is a good look,' said Jack.

'I'm not sayin' one more word to you.' With that, she turned to face Suzie, who was already overwrought. 'Suz, can you look after him?' 'Him' meaning Jack. Suzie rolled her eyes and nodded reluctantly.

'What have I done?' queried Jack, smelling his clothes to lighten the moment.

Ruby threw down a dishcloth and approached him with dark, angry eyes. 'Have you seen Hamish this morning?' Ruby punctuated this by pointing to a booth in the far corner of the cafe. Jack turned to see the groom-to-be lying face-down on the table.

'You bastards. You shoulda stopped it.' Ruby knew, only too well, that Jack didn't have an excuse.

'Why?' he said.

Ruby cursed and spun away back towards the grill. Jack picked up his coffee and slowly made his way over to Hamish. A few truckers and other suspects from the night in question commented rudely on the vet's inability to hold his drink. Jack slid into the booth opposite Hamish. He knocked on the surface of the table. Hamish didn't stir.

'Guess what, mate. Ruby's changed her mind.'

Hamish said nothing as he lifted his aching head.

'Want another scotch?' Jack added.

Hamish slowly surveyed the cafe. The noise seemed to rip through his brain like a buzz-saw.

'Did you bring a gun?' he moaned, with whatever strength he had left.

'You need another drink, mate.'

Hamish slowly lowered his face back down onto the table. 'You wait till it's your turn,' he muffled. 'We'll have gaps between those tables like the Grand bloody Canyon.'

Jack chuckled and pulled himself up and out of the booth. 'No one wants to marry me, mate.' He returned to the counter with his coffee. Ruby flashed past him with another order of bacon and egg sandwiches. 'He'll live!' he said.

Ruby turned on him. 'I don't know why I'm doin' you any favours. Consider our deal off! Finished! Kaput!'

'Look, kiddo . . .'

Ruby swelled with fury and threw a wet dishcloth at him. This was the last straw. 'Don't call me *kiddo*!'

Jack ducked and the cloth flew across the room hitting Ziggy square on the face just as she entered the cafe.

'Oh, shit!' sighed Ruby.

Ziggy peeled the disgusting cloth off her face and looked around the cafe like an irate school teacher.

'I'm sorry, Ziggy,' Ruby said, hiding a smile.

Jack turned on his stool towards Ziggy. 'Breakfast?'

It took a moment for Ziggy to contain herself in front of these morons. 'I don't eat breakfast,' she replied, with pure ice in her voice at the very notion of there being any relationship between herself and food in the morning.

Jack shrugged. Christ, and the day had hardly started. He helped himself to pastries from the counter. 'Put 'em on the tab, Rube.'

'We don't have a tab, Jack,' she answered, mimicking his tone.

Jack ignored her and exited the Boomerang with Ziggy in tow while Ruby looked after him with an exasperated expression. Suzie noted the look on her friend's face and for a moment thought of asking Ruby why she and Jack couldn't just let each other be. But as she moved rapidly about the cafe taking orders and pouring coffees, she changed her mind. They'd always been like this. Why should they change now?

Ruby, however, seemed to have been aware that Suz had been watching her because she said suddenly to Suzie in a quick whisper, 'I got something to tell you – about Jack.'

Suzie grinned, 'I'm real keen to hear it. Let's get this lot fed first, eh?' said Ruby.

It took an hour of grilling, toasting, brewing and backchatting to get all the truckers out of the Boomerang and on the road again. Afterwards, Suzie sat on the back step smoking a cigarette while Ruby told her about Jack's book and the charade they were playing.

Suzie was astounded. 'Jack Willis has written a romance book! And you're pretending to this publisher woman that you wrote it?'

'I said yeah yesterday, but this morning I was so wild at the bastard that I told him the deal's off.'

'And give up a big weddin'?' Ruby shrugged. 'What did Hamish say?'

'Not much.'

Suzie smiled. 'You mean he doesn't know the truth?'

'How can I tell Hamish that the best man at our wedding has just written a romance novel?'

A good question. Suzie smoked in silence, trying to imagine what the reaction would be in Lucktown if the news about Jack's book got out. Most of the local men had to get drunk before they even kissed a woman. The idea of a bloke they knew, a local bloke, writing a romantic novel was, well, unimaginable.

But at the same time Suzie found herself thinking about the book. She wasn't a great reader but she did enjoy a good story and she'd occasionally wondered what it'd be like to write a book. To go into a book-shop and see a book with your name on it. For a moment she felt envious of Ruby. Fancy going into a bookshop and seeing Suzie Barnwell in gold letters all across a book. She knew she would have said 'Yeah', too, if Jack had asked her.

But Ruby's situation was different. Suzie didn't think it was a good idea going into a marriage and keeping secrets from your husband. Especially with a man like Hamish. Rube's fiancé didn't show his feel-ings in public, but Suzie had seen his face when he looked at Ruby the very first time he saw her.

'Well,' she said, grinding out her cigarette with the heel of her shoe, 'it's a shame for Jack but I think it's good you're out of it. Hamish wouldn't say much but you know what they say – still waters run deep.'

'I wouldn't know about that,' said Ruby, jumping

up with a grin, 'none of the creeks around here ever have more than a foot of water in them unless there's a flood.'

Suzie laughed.

******

'This road to Broken Hill's so straight,' Jack said to Ziggy, 'that even the crow flies right above it.'

Jack liked this analogy, but the humour of it seemed to go right over Ziggy's head. She was sitting across from him in the rig with her nose held up and a pursed look around her mouth. This was because of Lance, who was occupying the stretch of seat between them. Within minutes it had become apparent that Lance and Ziggy weren't cut out to be travelling companions. In those rare moments when he was awake, Lance had an inquiring mind. There were always things he wanted to know about: Was that really a flea under his ear? Had he caught a burr up the top of his back leg? Had that flea now moved to his ribs? Every time one of these important questions occurred to him, he had to bestir himself, sit up and investigate. And every time he bestirred himself, dust and loose hairs would rise as if someone was shaking a carpet in a high wind.

'Don't you ever wash him?' Ziggy demanded.

'No need. He jumps in the dam every other week.'

Ziggy mumbled something hostile and edged farther away from Lance in the hope that his hairs wouldn't invade her precious clothing. But Lance just

82

yawned and settled down to sleep so she felt safe, at least for a while.

Jack tried another conversational overture.

'Years ago, when they were building this highway, the engineers reckoned they ought to put some bends and curves in it, just to make sure the drivers stayed awake.'

There was no response from Ziggy.

The highway climbed over a rise which overlooked a flat, dry river basin. Jack thought the view was breathtaking and slowed the rig so that Ziggy could appreciate it. But she exclaimed, 'God, it's so empty!'

Jack smiled. This was clearly no time for him to give a lecture on the beauty of the Australian outback.

High up on the inside of the cabin Ziggy had noticed an old black-and-white photograph of the Sydney Harbour Bridge. That wondrous monument to fine old Scottish engineering, pictured with a brilliant shaft of sunlight illuminating the crest of the arch.

'Where'd you get that?' she asked.

'You like Sydney?' responded Jack, without answering her question.

'I love it. I should think you'd hate it!'

Jack was about to explain his dad had taken the photo when Ziggy cut him off with a crisp. 'It's changed. A great deal,' as she returned the photo to its place.

Lance woke up and reorganised himself before settling down to sleep again. Ziggy gave a little start as several long hairs landed on her skirt. Jack suppressed a grin as he watched her reach into her handbag, extract a tissue, and use it to carefully remove the hairs from her skirt. Then the tissue was folded and placed neatly in the bag he kept for rubbish. He reminded himself that he must remember this scene in case he needed it in another book and said quietly under his breath, 'She removed the dog hairs from her skirt with all the precision of a brain surgeon conducting an operation.'

'Did you say something?' inquired Ziggy.

'Just reminding myself of something,' answered Jack.

She gave a half nod and fixed her gaze on the landscape with an expression on her face that suggested she was looking at one of the most awful places on earth. Jack tried to concentrate on thinking about his next book, but nothing seemed to be happening in his head.

World War Two, Bomber Command, the twenty-one-year-old fighter pilot and his English lady friend – they'd all disappeared. Jack told himself that he needed to be able to write to really focus on thinking about his book and he'd taken his clipboard off its bracket before Ziggy had gotten into the rig, but he knew this wasn't true. What he really wanted to do was talk to Ziggy about writing and, though he'd tried several times to think of a way of introducing the topic, he'd felt too shy and awkward to start. But it was frustrating having this real live publishing person sitting there next to him in the truck, and being unable to say a word to her about the one thing he spent most of his life thinking about.

Finally he had an inspiration.

'Is Ruby a good writer?' he asked.

'Is that any of your business?' inquired Ziggy in her curt way.

The funny side of the situation was beginning to strike Jack. She's got a point, he said to himself with amusement, you should've thought about all this before you decided to get the book published under Ruby's name.

'No,' he said aloud.

Ziggy smiled. 'I suppose out here everybody knows everything.'

'Just about.' Jack grinned.

Ziggy's eyes caught a row of paperbacks arranged on shelves high along the side of the cabin. She read off the authors 'Wolfe; Carey; Keneally . . .' For a moment, as she looked about, Jack was thinking that he could finally have a talk with another person who was interested in writing. 'What? No *Guns 'n' Ammo* magazines?' Ziggy asked.

The situation was too funny for Jack to do anything but burst out laughing. However, at the same time he decided that Ruby Vale's writing career was going to come to a halt. His next book was going to be published under another name and by *another* publisher. Ms Ziggy Keane was bright and attractive – and he was sure she was good at her job – but he had the feeling that their relationship had gotten off to a bad start, and it wasn't going to get any better. She always seemed to be on the lookout for a chance to put him down and it was getting on his nerves. 'This time,' he said to himself, 'I'll start at the front end of the alphabet.'

'I suppose you already know about Ruby's new book?' asked Ziggy.

Jack was stunned, and Ziggy knew it. 'Ah, it seems you don't. It's called *Love in Africa*.'

'What kinda title is that?' Jack asked firmly.

Ziggy turned to him with a condescending look. 'Jack, we don't sell romantic novels to truckers.' Ziggy enjoyed that remark. The way she said 'trucker' made him sound repulsive. Jack glanced out his side window – bloody hell, he thought, how did he get lumbered with this female?

Ziggy didn't let up. 'I think *Love in Africa* sounds fiercely romantic. Don't you?'

Jack just peered silently out the side window. *Love in Africa*? Christ, what had Ruby been saying? He wondered if she'd been taking some revenge on him for not keeping Hamish out of trouble at his buck's party, when suddenly there was a loud thump on the rig and Ziggy gave a shriek, 'What was that?'

Within seconds Jack realised what had happened. He'd been too preoccupied with thinking about his book and Ruby to notice that there had been a small flock of emus running parallel with his rig on the passenger's side. Any other passenger would almost certainly have commented but Ziggy had clearly thought these long-necked wingless creatures as uninteresting and unimportant as everything else in outback Australia and now, looking back, he could see that he'd really hurt one of the young ones. It had fallen by the side of the highway.

Jack hit the brakes hard. Ziggy screamed and Lance,

once more, slid off the seat. These plunges to the floor seemed to be happening with such regularity that the dog was nonplussed.

'What are you doing?' Ziggy was agitated. 'You're not stopping?'

'You stay in the cabin.'

A squeamish look came over Ziggy's face as Jack scrambled out. When Lance attempted to climb back on the seat, she pushed him back down with her foot. 'You stay there, you beast!'

Jack walked down the side of his rig and discovered the wounded young bird hopping about on one leg. Some distance away the anxious parent squawked, ran forward in a brave attempt to retrieve the young one, then retreated as Jack waved his arms in the air. Jack bent down to inspect the creature. Most of its underbelly was covered with blood. One leg seemed broken and there was a severe gash on its breast.

'Come here, you poor bugger.' He scooped up the bird and held it firmly to his chest. Even though the young emu must have felt terrified there was little resistance from its wounded body. 'Open the door,' yelled Jack.

Ziggy popped her head through the window and peered down at them. 'You're not bringing that thing in here?'

'You bet I am. Now, open up the door – slowly.'

Ziggy did as she was told. Jack lifted the young emu up into the cabin.

'Oh, my God!'

'Spread out Lance's rug on the seat.'

Ziggy scrabbled frantically to lay out the rug, and Jack lowered the emu onto the seat between them.

'Now, hold the bird firmly with your hand.'

Ziggy grew pale and stared at him. 'What?' she said, weakly.

Lance immediately reached up to the emu and started to lick its wound.

'He's eating him!' shrieked Ziggy. 'Oh, God, *do something*!'

Jack shook his head despairingly. 'He's just helping out.'

Lance looked up at Ziggy with blood all over his mouth, like a wolf after a kill.

Unwillingly, she stretched out an arm to draw the emu's body towards her and hold it firmly down on the seat. Jack thought that he'd never forget the sight of her elegant white manicured hand with its perfect red fingernails reluctantly gripping the bird.

'Now, with your other hand,' he continued, 'pinch the gash to stop it bleeding.'

Ziggy looked at him with open-mouthed horror.

'Come on,' Jack insisted, 'before the poor bugger bleeds to death.'

Without saying another word, Ziggy reached under the emu, grasped the wound with her fingers and clamped it firmly shut. The bleeding stopped immediately and, much to her amazement, the young bird lifted its head and looked at her with big, dewy eyes. Ziggy forced a smile and glanced over to Jack.

'See – you're savin' a life,' he said with a smile.

'I am?'

'New experience?'

Jack hit the accelerator. The rig roared into life once more and headed towards Broken Hill with Ziggy sitting half sideways in her seat, one hand securing the young bird and the other holding the wound closed. As she did so, Ziggy remembered the first time she'd ever heard the word 'emu'. It was on a chilly morning while on a school excursion to the London Natural History Museum on Cromwell Road.

There were hundreds of things there for a little girl to be frightened of or entranced by: skeletons of big strange animals, stuffed bodies of familiar ones, exhibitions and photographs and demonstrations. Somewhere she'd found an egg. It was so big – a good eight inches in length – and had such an odd, greyish, mottled surface that she thought it was prehistoric – they had learned about dinosaurs at school and knew about extinct animals. But later that evening, huddled in their tiny South Kensington flat, her father had said no, 'It's not from a prehistoric animal,' he explained. 'It must've been an emu egg. From Australia.'

She knew about Australia. Her father, who was a civil engineer, had always dreamt of emigrating there.

'Have you heard the noise they make?' Jack's voice cut in on her memories. 'It's sort of like a rattle – sounds like the noise an old wooden bridge makes when a truck goes over it.'

'What are you going to do with it?' she asked.

'Know a bloke with a chicken farm just outside Broken Hill,' Jack answered. 'He knows what to do with them.'

If Jack had realised what ideas this last comment set off in Ziggy's head he would have chosen his words more carefully. His chicken-farmer mate had no sense of humour but was very kind. He was particularly fond of emus, and Jack knew he'd care for the young bird until it was strong again – and then he'd conscientiously prepare it to return to life in the bush. While he noticed that Ziggy seemed as reluctant to hand over the injured bird as she'd been to take it on in the first place, it didn't occur to Jack that Ziggy was thinking sadly that her new young friend was going to end up in grilled sandwiches prepared for busloads of international tourists visiting Broken Hill and eager to sample local bush tucker.

6

Zane Publishing occupied an entire floor of a tower building in the heart of downtown Sydney. From her office on the fortieth floor, Ziggy was able to gaze out over the beautiful Botanical Gardens on one side and the Opera House and Harbour on the other. She called it her little piece of heaven, and her brief experience of the heat and dust of Lucktown made her appreciate it even more.

'That's it,' she said to Ella, who was waiting for her in her office when she arrived back at work. 'In the future I'm never going anywhere unless I can see the Harbour Bridge.'

Ella smiled, and handed her a takeaway cappuccino from the Italian café at the foot of the building. No one could make coffee like Felix. He got Ziggy started on egg-white froth by insisting that, years ago, it was the way northern Italians used to make it. 'Protein coffee,' she'd said doubtfully the first time he'd made it for her. Now she was addicted.

Ziggy was about to thank her, when a voice said from the doorway, 'From what I hear, that's a good policy. Did you remember to initial the "full liability" box on your car-rental contract, Zig?'

Ziggy hated being called Zig, but she made sure that there wasn't the slightest indication of her feelings in her voice or expression as she turned to face Ralph Seaton. 'I wasn't anywhere near the car at the time,' she said smoothly. 'Fortunately, the local police sergeant almost saw it happening and took over the case immediately.'

Ziggy thought with amusement that nobody in Lucktown would have recognised this description of the accident but all the facts were accurate. However, it was the first time in the history of Zane Publishing that any employee had managed to get a rental car demolished, and Ralph thought he ought to keep on pushing the issue.

'Word is that you parked irresponsibly,' he said.

Ziggy smiled, and ignored his remark. 'Ruby Vale is quite a woman,' she went on before Ralph could say anything further. 'She writes a hit novel in between running a trucker's cafe and flying a crop-dusting plane.'

'She's also only about twenty-five years old, and totally gorgeous,' she added. 'Or at least she will be,' Ziggy said to herself, 'once we've got her out of overalls, fixed her hair and put her in a George Gross frock.'

'We're planning to have big blow-up photographs in the foyer,' she added aloud to Ralph.

'Yes, well, time's money, Zig,' said Ralph, managing to imply, as usual, that she'd been keeping him away from more important matters.

'Yes,' said Ziggy with a smile, 'success is money too. Have you had a chance to read the book?'

Ralph didn't answer. Instead, he just gave a wave and turned away quickly.

'I think you won that round,' Ella said dryly.

'Yes, but I need to win every single round and then some,' said Ziggy, grimly. 'This place is a real boys' club.'

As if to prove her point, a moment later Ziggy's boss, Errol Ruben, appeared at the door.

'Ah, my demolition derby queen has returned,' he announced. 'Give me the *good* news.'

'Ruby Vale is coming to Sydney,' Ziggy said, after greeting Errol.

'She's really quite impressive for someone...' Ziggy said, before being cut off by Errol's flamboyant hand gesture.

'Just hand me contracts, darling. Contracts!'

'It's a done deal,' said Ziggy. Errol smiled broadly and gave her a rather vague look as he disappeared. It was a look that Ziggy was familiar with. 'One day,' she said to herself, 'I will have my own publishing company.' Keane Publishing had a nice ring to it.

******

Ruby loved the sound of rain on a corrugated iron roof. Her father, George, had loved it too. They used to spend hours in the cafe playing pool while waiting for the saucepans and buckets to fill with rainwater. In those days there were about five leaks in the roof, and every time it poured Ruby would pray that her father would never fix them.

On this night, Ruby counted twelve leaks in all. One day, she thought, somebody will have to do something about the roof.

After she'd put out sufficient pots, pans and buckets, Ruby placed her headset back on and switched on her walkman. REM played 'Losing My Religion'. She closed her eyes, lifted her arms and started to dance in small, tight circles around the pool table.

She didn't realise that Jack had come in and was watching her as she danced. It was a sensual moment as she spun around with her hands outstretched completely oblivious to her private audience. Jack leant on the doorjamb and grinned as she sang through to the end of the song. Eventually, she pulled off the headset and set up a configuration of balls on the pool table. Ruby's trick was to attempt to sink as many balls as possible without having to cross the torn section of the table. That bottom right-hand pocket always eluded her.

'G'day.' Jack had to yell above the sound of the rain.

Ruby jumped so high the pool cue actually shot forward like an arrow. 'Jesus!' she screamed, and turned to see Jack standing there in a rain-soaked oilskin coat. 'What are you doin' bloody creepin' in here?'

Jack removed a large manuscript of handwritten pages from the recesses within his oilskin. 'I brought my book,' he said, shaking rain from his arms.

'What for?' she snapped. 'I'm not goin' anywhere for you.'

'Because you haven't read it.'

Ruby moved behind the counter and started to make coffee from the urn. 'I suppose you want one?' she asked, pouring hot water over instant coffee.

Jack walked forward. 'Got any real coffee?'

Ruby looked up – a plain stare.

'Okay, that'll do. Yes please.' Jack placed the manuscript on the counter near her. Ruby glanced at it briefly.

'That's a book?'

'Yep!'

Ruby gave a wry laugh.

'Has Ziggy phoned yet?' Jack asked.

Ruby scanned some of the handwritten pages lying before her. She bent down for a closer inspection. Much of Jack's scrawl was difficult to decipher. Ruby lifted up one page and pointed to a word. 'How am I expected to read this?'

Jack leaned over to inspect. He had had to write most of it while driving his rig, so some of the words were barely legible.

'Looks like chicken scrawl,' Ruby added.

'That says *"balabushka"*. It's a . . .'

Ruby was quick to interrupt. 'I know, famous pool cue. Paul Newman had one in the *Color of Money*.'

Jack smiled, and nodded his head.

'Dad used to say if I had a *balabushka* I would've had the edge on him around the pool table,' said Ruby, with melancholy in her voice. Jack poked at the torn bit of felt on the pool table to hide the fact that he had a lump in his throat. He knew how much

Rube missed her Dad. He also knew that just before George Vale had died, he and Ruby had been planning a big holiday – flying around the country together in the biplane. Unlike Jack, Ruby had never travelled – hadn't ever seen the sea. And she'd never got the chance to do so. Jack had been miles away – way out in Western Australia on a job – when he got the news. Heard it over the truckers' CB radio system. Everyone on the road knew George Vale or knew about him. Jack hadn't been able to get back for the funeral, but he'd sent flowers – a bunch of wild flowers that he knew Ruby would like. Fortunately, it was just a few weeks after George's death that Lucktown's new vet arrived, and the rest, as they say, was history.

Ruby, glancing at Jack as she tidied the pages of the manuscript, guessed he was thinking about her father, and for the first time it occurred to her that though she still grieved for her dad and always would, she'd been lucky to have had such a father. By the time his father left, Jack couldn't have mourned much for Tom Willis, though he might have grieved for the father he'd lost long before.

Ruby remembered her own father saying that years ago, when he'd first met him, Tom Willis had been a great bloke. Bright, full of ideas, enthusiastic. He hadn't been popular – too independent-minded for that. He had criticised the local landowners for overstocking their properties and he had stood up for the Aborigines. Sadly he never had any discipline. He wouldn't persevere at any job, once he became bored or decided he wasn't going to make money immediately. There was always another get-rich scheme over the horizon. Jack's father was a drunk and a gambler who dragged his wife and son all over the state to prospect for anything of value. Everything but knowledge it seemed. Jack's father believed only in what he could hold in his hand. Sadly, that was never much more than a bottle. But, fortunately for his family, Tom Willis was never abusive. He had his good times. An opal strike near Cootawundi proved extremely lucrative until he lost it all through neglect over a claims deal with a local sheep station owner.

In another scheme, Jack's father planned to round up brumby horses and sell them off for pet food to the local abattoir. This he was going to do after fattening them on land leased from the council. But it all fell through when the abattoir closed without warning, making it far too expensive to ship wild horses to the next major town. Needless to say, Jack wasn't very close to his father and good grades at school meant nothing to his dad. Tom gave his son no praise when a short story of Jack's appeared in a local newspaper when Jack was just fourteen. Here was a father who wanted his son to be a chip off the old block. Sometimes he did make money and he'd sweep his wife and son off to Sydney where he'd set up a company to exploit vast mineral deposits he thought he'd found, or to sell unusual stones and fossils from the outback to tourists. Sooner or later they would all be back to the plain little Lucktown cottage that Mrs Willis had inherited from her father, and that she sensibly refused to sell to support her husband's dreams. Jack's parents eventually divorced when he was fourteen, Mrs Willis staying on in the little Lucktown cottage for a couple of years until her health failed and she went east to live with her sister. From the time he was seventeen, Jack was more or less on his own.

Jack mistook the reason for the serious look on Ruby's face.

'Look, I'm really sorry about what happened to Hamish at the buck's night,' said Jack.

'That's okay,' replied Ruby, with a quick shrug. 'He'll live.'

'Where is he?'

'Out helpin' Robbo bury dead sheep.'

'In this weather?'

Ruby nodded.

'Mr Nice-guy, eh?' added Jack.

'Yeah, every mother's dream.'

An awkward silence dropped between them as the rain outside intensified. Jack glanced around the cafe to check the water level of Ruby's pots and pans. Ruby watched his face. Jack was a handsome man underneath that unshaven face. He'd always been different, or indifferent, as Suzie liked to point out.

She glanced down at his manuscript. 'Okay, what do I do with this?'

A broad grin erupted across Jack's face. 'Read it. In case they ask questions.'

Ruby flicked through the manuscript, daunted by the prospect of getting through it. 'Jesus, isn't there a proper printed book with a cover and everythin'?'

'Nope – not yet.' Jack rubbed his unshaven face. 'I gotta get cleaned up.'

'No, it kinda suits you,' she said. Jack looked at her in bewilderment. 'Maybe,' she added with a shrug. 'Sometimes!'

Jack could not resist the moment. 'I should have a word to Hamish . . .'

'Don't you dare! He hates beards,' Ruby said, and punched him on the shoulder.

They both paused, aware of the moment. More and more these days, no matter how often they argued or how hard they pushed each other away, they knew they'd miss each other. Who else, Jack thought, would have the nerve to dump superphosphate on his rig? Who else could he throw into the water tank behind the cafe? Who else? . . . Jack sighed, and turned to retrieve his oilskin coat.

'Anybody home?' Suzie burst into the Boomerang with a plastic garbage bag over her floral dress. 'Bloody hell, what a night, eh? Mind if I have a cuppa tea?'

'You don't have to ask, Suz, you know that,' Ruby said. Suzie removed her garbage-bag raincoat and carefully hung it on a hook to dry.

Jack noticed her bruise – now quite red as the soreness had spread across her face. 'What happened to you, Suz?' he asked.

'It's that swing door from the bar kitchen. Wouldn't you think I'd learn, Jack?' she smiled. 'Anyhow, I can't stand Artie and his drongo mates yappin' on about tits. So I came over to talk to you.' Suzie lit a cigarette, took an enormously satisfying draw deep into her lungs and smiled again as if to dismiss the whole incident.

Jack grabbed his coat. 'Well, I must be off. You keep away from swing doors, Suz.'

'Righto,' she said brightly. Jack shook his head gently and looked to Ruby with a thankful smile. 'Night, Rube.'

'Night, Jack.'

Suzie and Ruby watched Jack as he went through the procedure of climbing back into his large, cumbersome, oilskin coat.

'You look like the man from Snowy River,' said Ruby, admiring his wet-weather look. Jack secured his hat with a tilt, smiled and walked back out into the rain.

Suzie took another draw on her cigarette. 'I still can't believe a bloke as quiet as that could ever write a romance novel.' Ruby answered her by holding up the manuscript of handwritten pages.

'Is that it?'

Ruby nodded.

'Mind you,' Suzie went on to say, 'I reckon that city girl got a whiff of him. What's her name, Ziggo?'

'He can't stand her – couldn't you tell?' questioned Ruby.

'Hard to know what he likes,' Suzie took another draw. 'He's never in one place long enough for anyone to know.' She looked at the manuscript. 'Does this mean your little charade is on again?' There was even more disapproval in her tones as she added, 'And you still haven't told Hamish?'

Ruby said quickly, 'Suz, blokes like Jack don't

normally go around writing romance novels. Anyhow, I promised I wouldn't say anything.'

Suzie smiled. 'What changed your mind?'

Ruby sighed. 'I'm just doin' him a favour.'

'No you're not. You're doin' it 'cause you want a nice big wedding.'

'Yeah,' agreed Ruby.

'You just be careful, love. You can't go around risking upsetting a good man like Hamish just to help out . . . somebody you've been fighting with all your life.'

'Yeah,' said Ruby thoughtfully. 'We've always fought, but you know when we made deals we always stuck by them. I'd feel bad about backing out on our deal just now when I'm going away. In any case it's just for a coupla days. I go to Sydney, come back again and I'm getting a great wedding and honeymoon and share of the profits and stuff.'

'Well, be careful,' Suzie repeated.

'Suz, are you goin' to be this bossy at my wedding?' asked Ruby.

'Only if I can get this bruisin' to go down,' replied Suzie. There were times when Ruby just wanted to hug Suzie and never let go. It frustrated her that her friend could, on one hand, have such a handle on Ruby's life but be so horribly resigned about her own miserable existence. Ruby hated the sacrifice.

7

The morning was so clear and crisp that Hamish could hear Ruby's Stearman engine for miles, while all he could see was a red dot in the sky, looping and twisting. Mack, the service mechanic at the Lucktown Airport, joined Hamish at the window of his Land Rover. He too looked up as he heard Ruby push her biplane into a stall.

'What the hell's she doin', Mack?' Hamish asked, anxiously.

Mack watched as Ruby did one more barrel roll. 'Buggered if I know. Havin' fun I reckon.' Mack thought that Ruby was the gutsiest flyer in the region.

George Vale had taught Ruby to fly when she was fifteen years old. She had taken to it like a young eagle from a treetop nest. A little hesitation, a stretching of the wings and she was gone. Ruby was a natural. The many hours she spent as a child rugged up against the altitude as her father dusted crops – not a moment was lost on her. For Ruby's twentieth birthday, George had prepared his red biplane to hand over to her. He wrapped it in yellow and white ribbon and fixed a card to the prop that said: *Dearest Ruby, It's your turn to fly. Happy birthday. My love always, Dad*. It was that following evening, two days before her birthday, that George was killed. He never got to see his daughter fly solo.

'I just heard her engine stop,' said Hamish, frantically.

Mack peered up casually into the shy. 'Nah, she's just stallin'.'

All this was too much for Hamish. He climbed out of his Land Rover and walked onto the airstrip. The Lucktown Airport was not so much an airport as an overgrown cow paddock with a number of tin shed hangers. Flying Doctor pilots had often had to buzz the strip before landing because cattle had broken through the barbwire fence. No one really knew who was responsible for the airstrip's upkeep. Most of the local flyers just chipped in when work was required. Usually the strip was so dry that it never needed mowing.

Ruby started her long descent from the western end of the strip. With the throttle back the biplane glided silently down to earth. Hamish felt much happier when Ruby was only a few feet off the ground. Finally, the biplane bounced on its elastic undercarriage; Ruby hit the throttle again and the engine roared, pulling the aircraft to a halt. A sudden dust storm erupted around Hamish as he was approaching the biplane.

Ruby cut the motor, pulled off her helmet and shook out her hair. Her skin was bright from the cold morning air.

'Want a ride?' she asked with a big grin.

'What were you doing up there, Rube?'

'Flyin'!' Pure pleasure was written all over her face as she grinned at him again.

'You worry the hell out of me.'

'Safer than drivin', Hamish.'

Jack sounded his air horns as he drove his rig into the airport. He parked beside the hangers creating a cloud of red dust that promptly settled on Hamish's Land Rover.

'Wouldn't you know – I've just washed the bloody thing,' groaned Hamish.

Ruby glanced at her watch. 'Damn, I'm running late.'

'Jack can wait. I'm not gonna see you for a few days.'

Ruby switched off her electrics, folded her helmet and scarf and scrambled out of the cockpit. Hamish noticed that her flying suit was in desperate need of a wash. 'Hope you're not going to Sydney like that!'

'Course not!' Ruby unbuttoned her suit in one sweeping action.

'Tad-ahhh,' she announced. Underneath she had on clean denim overalls over a red T-shirt. Ruby threw her arm around Hamish and escorted him across the airstrip towards Jack. 'I'll phone you the moment I get to Sydney. Even sooner!'

Hamish grinned, and hugged her back. 'Rube . . .' Hamish was hesitant. 'Look, I know I haven't had the chance to say just how, you know, great it all is.'

'What?' asked Ruby, stopping and looking at him.

'The book!'

'Oh, yeah, it's great!'

'I'm really proud and everything. I mean, it's certainly something to do when you're married, eh?' Hamish smiled, to soften the edge of his remark. He was good at beating around the bush. Ruby said nothing. It was all too difficult.

Jack poked his head out of the cabin of his rig. 'G'day, Hamish. Don't tell me you've been airborne?' he asked.

'No way. I hate the bloody things.'

'Yeah, know what you mean.'

Hamish looked up to Jack and shaded his eyes against the morning sun. 'Good of you to give Rube a lift, Jack.'

'No worries. It's on the way, mate,' Jack said casually. He opened the door and called to Lance to jump out, 'Go on, good dog . . . Go on. Go to Hamish.'

Old Lance hesitated for some time. Going to Hamish meant being treated like a 'dog' to which Lance was no longer accustomed. Especially these days when Jack always allowed him inside the house and always fed him breakfast. None of Hamish's dogs ever got breakfast and they all slept outside on smelly hessian sacks. Lance knew it wasn't going to be any holiday for him.

'Come on, boy,' said Hamish, showing a little impatience.

Eventually, Lance jumped down. 'I take Lance – you take Ruby. Good swap, eh?' Hamish said to Jack, in a weak attempt at being funny.

'No way, Lance eats like a horse!' Jack retorted.

Hamish threw his head back with laughter and turned to Ruby.

'I love you, Hamish,' she said, reaching up and kissing him and completely throwing him off guard.

'Yeah, yeah, me too,' he replied, always embarrassed at showing his feelings. Hamish and Ruby hugged once more. Then Jack suddenly blasted his air horns. Ruby jumped with fright.

'Jesus, Jack.'

'Sorry,' he said feebly. Ruby grabbed her overnight bag from the Land Rover and climbed up into the cabin of Jack's rig. She smiled down at Hamish as the rig roared into life and headed off away from the airstrip. Hamish returned to his Land Rover and opened the rear door.

'Come on, you mongrel, hop in.'

Lance leapt inside then turned to watch as Jack's rig disappeared up the road. All he could see now was a long trail of dust winding out towards the highway. Lance whimpered as Hamish started the Land Rover and drove away.

******

Frank Sinatra was singing 'New York, New York' incongruously as Jack's rig barrelled east through the desolate outback landscape. Deep red-brown rocks pushed up through scattered mulga bushes, which were dusted with a fine, red powder that would stay on the branches until the rainy season.

'This is Hamish's favourite song,' screamed Ruby, as

she turned the volume up high and sang along. Jack joined in although slightly mocking her. Afterwards he said that the surrounding wildlife would never be quite the same.

Ruby reached back into the storage section of the cabin and pulled out her overnight bag. After a moment of digging about inside, she looked up to Jack in astonishment.

'What?' he asked.

'My walkman.'

'What about it?'

'I didn't bring it! Jesus, I can't lie 'n' cheat without my music. We gotta go back.'

'I'll buy you another one in Sydney.'

Ruby was horrified. Her music was her solace. Closing her eyes in exasperation she sat and cursed quietly.

Jack leant forward and picked up the thermos from a holder between the seats. 'Tea?' he asked, light-heartedly. Ruby snatched the thermos from him, her face still set and angry. 'We should get a few things straight, Rube,' Jack began.

'Yeah,' she interrupted. 'No Roy Orbison on this trip.'

She softened the remark by handing him a black coffee. Jack said nothing, but he wasn't pleased. Music was one thing they never had in common. Even as kids, Ruby used to turn her nose up at any selection he made from the jukebox at the local milk bar. Reflecting on this, Jack decided quite correctly, that Ruby did this just to annoy him.

'When we get to Sydney, I don't want you winging it!' he ordered.

'What else can I do?' asked Ruby. She was right, of course. But Jack knew, only too well, what she was capable of.

'You don't trust me, do you?' she asked.

'It's not about trust.'

'What then?' Ruby insisted. Jack paused. It was a delicate situation. On one hand he needed Ruby to go through with this book charade. On the other, he was very aware at how quickly she could screw it up for him. Underneath, he trusted Ruby. But she had a very mischievous streak.

'*Love in Africa*. What kinda stupid title's that?' he demanded.

'Jesus, Ziggy loved it!'

'Is there some sort of story connected to this?'

'Yeah, 'course there is.'

'Well, you can forget about it,' commanded Jack.

Ruby smiled. 'Might be a good one for all you know.'

Jack chuckled at the irony of all this. Oh, if only Miss Ziggy 'Armani' really knew the truth. 'And another thing,' Jack continued, 'you're gonna have to watch your mouth; no more "damns" or "Jesus" . . .'

'Oh shit, Jack,' Ruby snapped back, 'if I can't say damn or Jesus, what can I say?' Jack stared at her.

'I'm just kiddin'.' Jack thought, not for the first time, that Ruby could look demure and dangerous all at once.

He shook his head. This trip was really going to try

his patience. He could see he might even live to regret the arrangement. Without another word, he set the cruise control and settled back to take in the changing landscape. Studying the countryside always calmed him.

Jack particularly liked dry riverbeds. He wasn't sure why, as they usually indicated the desperation of drought – of dying livestock and withering crops. Yet in each dry riverbed there was always the stand of ironbark and bluegum trees, which never seemed affected by the drastic seasons.

As usual, the landscape worked its magic and he got an idea. 'I think I'll be your manager,' he said to Ruby.

'What do you know about being a manager?' she asked.

'More than you know about writing books.'

'Whose name's up there, eh?' Ruby teased.

'It's just a name, Rube.'

'Yeah, but it's mine!'

She was right, of course. Jack decided that he had nothing to lose, so he selected a Roy Orbison cassette from the music rack and slid it into the player. 'California Blue' was one of his all-time favourites. As it started to play, the look on Ruby's face was excruciating.

'You shoulda been a Traveling Wilbury,' she said, with as much sarcasm as she could muster.

'How could you not like this?'

'Maybe in another life,' Ruby said, as she launched a mock Orbison duet, rolling her eyes and hitting the high notes with an exaggerated wail.

Jack punched the eject button so hard the cassette popped out onto the floor. Ruby picked it up and placed it carefully back in its plastic case. 'We don't want to get bulldust in there, Jack,' she said sweetly.

Jack remained indignant.

Ruby looked at him. 'What?'

'Have you read my book yet? I've . . .'

Ruby held up a finger to halt further questioning and dived back into her overnight bag. She pulled out the manuscript and proceeded to organise it into some sort of neat pile. 'I've just started it,' she explained, holding up the first half-dozen pages. Suddenly, a wind-draught snapped the pages from her hand and sucked them out the window. 'Oh, shit!' she dived for the window and peered back along the highway. Within seconds the pages were committed to nature. 'Bugger!'

'Well done, Rube.'

'Don't worry, Jack. I've read those ones,' she said, checking the remaining manuscript just to be sure. 'Yep! Anyway, they're biodegradable.'

With some reluctance she started reading *Bird in the Hand* again.

As the rig roared on through the outback, they passed a hand-painted signpost in the middle of nowhere that read absurd distances to far-off cities. Rome 21,567 kilometres in one direction, and New York 13,100 kilometres in the other. 'There isn't a sign for Sydney,' Ruby said the first time they passed one of these signposts.

'They like to keep up the suspense,' said Jack with a grin.

It was outback humour.

As Jack and Ruby approached the town of Mildura, they passed in-roads to small, neglected rural towns with boarded windows on their cafes and shops. These tiny communities were being bypassed as travellers now speeded through the outback on newly constructed highways. It was rare for anyone to want to break their trip by slowing down through a country town. Even home-cooked fare could not entice them. All that folks wanted these days, Ruby thought, looking up from her reading, were 'in and out' fast-food joints placed strategically along the highway. Eat, fill up their tank an' take a pee. She hoped that the old Boomerang Cafe wouldn't suffer a similar fate as more of the border regions of the outback were opened up through foreign investment. Already the huge Japanese irrigated cotton farms around Bourke had changed the region. Much of the change was positive, but it still made life extremely difficult for many families trying to scrape a living off the land.

Jack noticed that Ruby had stopped reading and was turned towards him.

'What?'

'Who's this Virginia girl? She's just like me.'

Jack laughed, which only antagonised her. 'This girl is just like me.' She repeated the words slowly.

'Rube, she's from an Adelaide shipping family.' Jack emphasised the words 'Adelaide shipping family' as if members of Adelaide shipping families were quite unique and there could be no possible comparisons between one of them and Ruby sitting beside him in her overalls with a smudge of bright red dust high up on her cheek. But Ruby merely said, 'Okay – it's me with money.

'Christ,' she added after reading on for a moment, 'It's like looking in a mirror.' Ruby returned to the page and moved over to the next. At one point she became so involved she started to read out loud and commented as she went.

'Read it to yourself, Rube.'

Ruby glanced up and smiled, 'I like this bloke "Brian".'

Much of what Ruby said about his book gave Jack cause to be pleased. Ruby wasn't overly romantic but much of his prose seemed to sit well with her. That is, when she wasn't complaining about his illegible handwriting.

It seemed to Jack that the safe thing to do would be to change the topic, so he explained to her that like most truckers, he was going to avoid the heavy traffic going into Sydney from the south-west.

'The trick,' he said, 'is to head a little north quite early in the run, take the Sturt Desert Highway north-east to Hay and West Wyalong, then go over to Bathurst for the motorway run into Sydney.'

'If we go on the Great Western Highway we get to see the Blue Mountains,' said Ruby, looking up from the manuscript. 'Have you seen them?'

'Yeah,' said Jack for whom the Blue Mountains meant narrow winding roads, heavy traffic and fog.

'Are they really blue?'

'Nope.'

Ruby slapped him. 'Yes they are – it's the blue gum trees. Why don't we stop there the night? They have bed and breakfast places overlookin' these huge gorges . . .'

'How do you know?'

'I read up when Dad and I were planning our trip. It sounds really beautiful.'

Jack changed gear in his rig to pass a slow car and caravan. Two icecream-covered faces appeared pressed against the rear window as the rig roared by and pulled in sharply ahead of them.

'No point stayin' in the Blue Mountains. It's only an hour and a half to Sydney.'

Ruby shrugged. 'Yeah, I suppose we don't have time, do we.' She turned to him and grinned. 'How 'bout on the way back?'

Jack smiled. 'Okay, you gotta deal!'

She returned contentedly to the manuscript and was absorbed in it when, ten kilometres from the Hay turnoff, just as darkness was falling, they had to stop to change a tyre. Unless a truck blew one of the front steering tyres it was difficult to tell if any tyres on the trailer had given out. Usually it was a retread that ripped off like an onion skin as a corner was taken at speed.

'Sometimes, it's just the sheer weight of the load that does it,' Jack explained. 'No real damage unless, of course, some unsuspecting motorist is unlucky enough to be passing at precisely the moment the tyre sheds its skin. But that's rare,' he added.

'Well, how come I see so many strips of rubber along the highway?' asked Ruby.

'Will you hold the torch still,' grunted Jack, as he struggled to load the heavy spare wheel onto the locking bolts and wished she'd chosen another time to demand a lecture on truck tyres.

'What if another one blows?'

'Ruby, please, let's just get this one on.'

'Okay,' she replied nonchalantly, holding the torch with one hand and using the other to support a section of manuscript which she kept reading while Jack grunted and strained and secured the wheel ready for bracing.

He was standing back looking at his handiwork and reviewing the dirt and grease he was now covered with when she asked, 'How do you write the sex scenes?'

'What?' Jack asked, caught completely off guard by her question.

'I'm curious,' she said, 'I mean, do you read *Playboy* and erotic books an' stuff?'

Jack smiled, and picked up the wheel brace. 'Ruby . . .'

'What?'

'Shine the light.'

'Okay, okay.' Ruby returned the beam to the wheel nuts as Jack engaged the huge brace and struggled to tighten each one.

'I read *Women in Love* when I was eight.'

Jack's wheel brace gave way under the pressure. He fell hard to his knees. 'That musta been an eye opener.'

'Well, only the five pages Annie Deleny ripped outta her brother's book 'n' passed round the school,' Ruby added.

Jack chuckled, and retrieved the wheel brace. 'I didn't lay eyes on that book until I was fifteen,' he admitted.

'Women mature earlier, Jack.'

Ruby directed the torch beam onto the pages of the manuscript. 'This "Virginia" girl says "damn" all the time. I do that.'

Jack was back on the wheel. 'Torch,' he yelled.

'Sorry.' Ruby shone it back to the wheel. 'Brian is kinda like you.'

Jack felt exasperated. 'What makes you think that?'

'He drives a truck,' she said with a shrug, 'lives in a small town.'

'Nah, he gets killed,' said Jack, casually.

'You get killed?' Ruby shined the beam back onto the page.

She only heard the thump as Jack attempted to stand in the darkness and hit his head on the under-side of the trailer.

******

Some two hours later, Jack and Ruby pulled over to the side of the road again. This time it was to sleep. They tossed up a coin just out of Narrandera to end an argument regarding the two shabby rooms at the infamous Wheat Silo Motel. Jack won.

'No,' insisted Ruby, ignoring the outcome of the toss, 'let's sleep under the stars.'

Her head was raised and she was watching as the clear bright stars of the inland appeared in the black night sky. She was so obviously imagining flying her biplane in that cloudless perfect sky that Jack soft-ened and agreed.

He built a fire within the cleared area off to the side of the road. Despite the heat of the day, the nights could turn quite chilly. As they were gathering more wood, a few metres from their camp fire, Jack pointed out the skeleton of a six-foot snake laying across a huge ant nest. The ferocious black ants had systemati-cally removed every piece of meat from the carcass. Apart from a crushed skull, the skeleton that remained was a perfect specimen.

'Look at the size of that bugger,' said Ruby. She moved closer and inspected the remains with Jack's torch. 'What happened to his head?'

'I reckon someone's whacked it and threw it on the ant nest.'

'That's a bit cruel.'

Jack grinned, 'That's not the way most people see it, Rube.'

'They're part of nature.'

'That's true – they do a lot of good. Mind you, she was still a king brown, six-feet long and angry!'

'How do you know it was a she?'

Jack pointed. 'Look, she was about to give birth.'

Ruby bent down for a closer inspection. She poked the skeleton with a stick and discovered fine eggshell remains within the skeleton.

'Jesus!' Ruby turned back to Jack. 'Poor thing. How do you know she was angry?'

'Wouldn't you be?'

Ruby set up forked sticks around the fire so that

they could toast the Big Macs they'd bought in Nar-randera for their dinner. They washed their hamburgers down with beer from the esky. A feeling that she was having an adventure made Ruby excited and giggly. As she was sipping her beer, Jack said firmly, 'Don't you get drunk – you've gotta finish my book.'

'I'll read myself to sleep,' promised Ruby. After a moment's thought she added, 'I reckon I could write stuff, you know.'

Jack looked at her. He'd had a difficult day. Although he'd expected that the experience of being in the rig beside Ruby while she read the manuscript would be a bit hard on the nerves, he hadn't expected it all to be quite as complicated as it had been. First he'd found himself being really pleased when it was clear she was enjoying the book, and this had surprised him. For obvious reasons it was convenient that she liked it, but he hadn't expected he would care so much about her opinion.

Then he'd been taken aback when she decided that his heroine, Virginia, was based on her. He knew that he had a bit of a guilty conscience about this because there were a few features of Rube's and a couple of characteristics that he'd borrowed – well, pinched – to flesh out his description of Virginia. For example, Virginia had Ruby's fine, strong legs and her cute feet, which he'd always liked even when they were kids. And he'd made Virginia's feet a little flat too – just like Ruby's were from not wearing shoes. (This had been a bit of a problem because he wasn't sure that young Adelaide shipping heiresses were allowed to run around without shoes.) Jack was sure that every time he'd borrowed from Ruby, he had done it subtly, and he'd tried to mix it up with other things. Virginia danced with her eyes closed but hated flying just as much as he did. And she didn't know one end of a pool cue from another – Brian had had to teach her how to play. Yet Ruby had been convinced Virginia was her, as she'd said, with money.

He hadn't taken quite as seriously her idea that the hero, Brian, was based on him. Readers can never believe authors make up characters – they're always convinced they are based on someone real. He had known there was no point in getting into an argument with her about it, even though he was irritated by the confidence with which she announced her opinions.

For Ruby to have opinions about his book was one thing; but for someone who'd never written anything longer than a letter in her life suddenly deciding she could write a novel too – that was something else.

'You can't even tell a good story,' he said.

'I can so,' she answered. 'Do you know what a bunyip is?'

'It's just a myth, Rube.'

'Not if you're Aboriginal.'

'True.'

Ruby looked at him across the camp fire.

'You know,' she said, 'the three peaks in the Blue Mountains,' she held up three fingers creating a sudden triple shadow across her face, 'called the Three Sisters?'

Jack nodded.

'There were these three sisters whose father was a witchdoctor. They all feared the bunyip, so while the witchdoctor bloke was searching for food he left his daughters safe on the side of the mountain. While their father was down in the valley, the sisters accidentally started a rock slide and woke the sleeping bunyip. Now, I don't know how big he was but this bunyip was really furious and started to search for the culprit . . .'

'This a long story?' Jack interrupted, with a smirk.

Ruby glared at him but continued unfazed, 'Fearing that the bunyip would discover his frightened daughters, the witchdoctor pointed his magic bone and turned them into stone – just until the bunyip had gone.'

'Let me guess – he ran out of batteries?'

Ruby started to get angry with Jack's glib remarks. 'The bunyip was so pissed-off he chased the witchdoctor. Now he was so scared he changed himself into a lyrebird and hid in a cave.'

'Who, the bunyip?'

'No – the witchdoctor. Everyone was safe. But unfortunately, the witchdoctor had lost his magic bone. To this day, he's still down there calling out to his daughters and trying to find it. Isn't that the saddest story you've ever heard?'

'One of the best, Rube.'

Ruby was irritated by his dry tone, 'Well, I think it is.'

During supper and more esky-cooled beer, Ruby

encouraged Jack to play her REM music on the rig's cassette player. Ruby opened the doors to allow the soulful, slow ballad 'Everybody Hurts' play out across the darkness of the desert. Jack lay back on his palliasse and watched as Ruby danced, barefooted. She was so beautiful, he thought, as she spun and gyrated against the extraordinary light of the fire. Ruby caught a glance of her long shadow that danced behind her like a puppet.

'Come on, Jack. You can do this.' Ruby had almost lost herself in the haze of alcohol and smoke.

Jack chuckled and drained his beer. No way was he going to dance around a bloody camp fire.

Ruby suddenly stopped. 'Damn, I gotta pee.'

Jack waved an arm generally at the huge, empty expanse of dark countryside surrounding them. As she left the camp site he rose to tidy up and douse the fire. He called out to her,

'I'm hittin' the hay, Rube.'

There was no answer from the darkness. Not even the sound of a foot cracking a twig. It was very quiet and still. He felt for a moment as if he was alone and called out, 'Rube—', then added, 'Watch out for tiger snakes.'

He half expected Ruby to come charging back into the lights of the rig with her jeans still around her knees. It was rare that a tiger snake would bite anybody at night while they were having a piss, but he knew that stranger things had happened. Like all the locals, Jack had great respect for all snakes, but particularly for tiger snakes. If disturbed near the nest, these reptiles could inflict three venomous strikes before the victim even realised they'd been bitten. Ruby would not be wise to piss on a tiger snake's lair.

Jack did his rudimentary check with a torch down the side of his rig. Ropes, flaps, tyres and anything that might resemble an oil spot on the ground. Oil always meant trouble.

Suddenly, from above, a heavy rope cascaded down on top of him. Like a huge serpent, it curled around his body – almost engulfed him. With snakes on his mind, Jack jumped aside and took the rope to the ground.

'Hello!' Ruby called out, from high up on the trailer. Jack sighed.

'Shit, Ruby,' was his only reply.

Ruby carefully peered over the top edge of the trailer. 'You okay?'

'What the hell are you doin' up there?' he asked, and added to himself, 'apart from giving me a heart attack.'

'You said you liked snakes,' she remarked sweetly.

'Not *on* me,' he said. 'Now, come on down, you can sleep in the cab.'

'You take the cab. I'm sleepin' up here!' she replied.

'Okay, but don't whinge to me tomorrow when you're covered in bloody mosquito bites.' Jack pulled a blanket and pillow from the cabin and threw them up to Ruby.

'Mozzies don't like me,' said Ruby. She was right. Jack, on the other hand, had to fight them off with sticks. Even in his cabin, tucked in under a blanket with the windows closed, Jack went on a killing spree with a rolled-up magazine. Eventually, there was silence.

Up on the trailer it took Ruby some time to organise her sleeping arrangements. Once she was settled she fixed the torch so she could go on reading and Jack was just beginning to drift off to sleep when he heard her voice intoning, 'I felt invigorated by her persuasive scent that lingered in every crevasse of my being, stirring my emotions into a whirlwind . . . something exquisite, an ecstasy beyond my experience . . .'

Sighing, Jack yelled out, 'Rube – what are you doin'?'

'You wrote all this on a Shell napkin.'

'It's not meant to be read out aloud. He's thinking it while he's riding his horse.'

'Oh!' Ruby read on.

'What?' Jack called out, hearing the pain in her voice.

'Brian's drowning in a swollen river?' gasped Ruby.

******

Breakfast next morning was in Bathurst, or at least it was for Jack. They were surrounded by travelling salesmen gorging themselves on hot meat pies, as dozens of families with obnoxious, over-tired children spilled Coke and chips across the plastic tables and polished floors. Ruby sipped her coffee, ignoring both the crowd around them in the busy BP roadhouse and the plate of scrambled eggs before her, while she finished the novel.

Jack devoured his bacon and eggs and found himself eyeing Ruby's plate.

'You gonna eat that, Rube?' he finally asked. Ruby was totally absorbed in his manuscript with only one page to go.

'What?' asked Ruby, looking up in a daze. Jack smiled and pointed to her meal.

'Have it, have it!' she said, without taking her eyes off the page. Jack ate the scrambled eggs as Ruby eagerly finished the last page. For some time after she just stared and said nothing at all. Jack glanced up to her as he ate.

'Rubbish, eh?' he quipped, with a mouthful of egg.

A solitary tear slid down Ruby's cheek. She quickly wiped it away with the back of her hand, picked up a napkin and blew her nose.

'Not that one, Rube.' He grabbed the napkin from her. 'I'd like to keep the original manuscript.' It was the Shell napkin he'd previously written on.

'Sorry,' pleaded Ruby, weakly. 'How about I learn this page by heart?'

Jack shook his head and stood up. He gathered his keys and wallet and headed for the cashier.

'Hey, I'm not a bad writer, am I?' called Ruby, just as he was passing a table of kids who stopped sucking loudly on their milkshakes to stare at him.

Jack turned back to her. 'Don't let it go to your head, kiddo.'

With that, he turned and strode off through the crowded cafe. Ruby quickly gathered up the pages of his manuscript and pocketed a slice of dry toast from the table. As usual, being called 'kiddo' irritated her, but then she suddenly grinned to herself and looked over towards Jack, who was now some ten metres away, paying the cashier.

'Jack?' she yelled out across the cafe, bringing everyone's eyes on her instantly. 'I still don't know why you had to go and kill Brian.'

Absolute silence filled the cafe. Necks strained to see who this girl was talking to. People paused with their spoons full of food frozen in mid-air, and stared at Jack. A couple who were leaving the restaurant at the same time hastily pulled themselves out of his way. Jack was conscious that the staff of the place who knew him slightly were gaping at him open-mouthed. He guessed that this was his last visit to this particular roadhouse. He walked what seemed a very long way to the door, his face going red with embarrassment.

8

The last stage of the trip to Sydney began in silence. Jack ignored Ruby as he sat with his gaze focused on the road. For the first time ever she felt slightly guilty about the prank she'd played, and sat quietly. Once they were in the mountains, though, she was so excited she kept exclaiming, and Jack found himself responding to her delight.

Soon the city of Sydney loomed in the distance under a slight industrial haze. Due to roadwork, Jack had been forced to detour from a section of the highway and take the more scenic Bell's line of road past Bilpin to Kurrajong Heights. Truckers generally loathed this spectacular route as the road down the mountain was a twisting and dangerous alternative for big rigs. Ruby loved it. It was like the start of a huge adventure. She'd never seen mountains like these before. A plateau, covered with a forest of blue gums, suddenly fell away to reveal orange-coloured cliff faces leading down into bottomless gorges. She had read about the famous, melodramatic-looking hotel called the Hydro Majestic, built in 1904 on the very edge of a precipice, and pointed it out to Jack enthusiastically, as if he might have missed it. Then she saw, shrouded in morning mist, the peaks of the Three Sisters.

'No bunyips,' said Jack with a grin, finally forgiving her.

'They come out at night,' said Ruby firmly.

Jack had decided that as this was Ruby's first visit to Sydney she was entitled to enter the city the proper way – by crossing the Harbour Bridge. Although it would have been easier for him to take the more direct route into the city from the west, he looped around to the north without telling Ruby what he was doing. His huge, long rig looked incongruous in the heavy morning traffic and several thousand business-suited motorists stared in astonishment as Jack deftly negotiated the rig's great bulk through lines of cars less than a quarter of its size.

Ruby hung out the window like an awestruck child. Her first glimpse of the Harbour made her gasp and he remembered that this was the first time she'd ever seen the sea. Because of the high, solid safety barrier, usually people in cars cannot see much from the bridge but Ruby's vantage point from the high cabin of Jack's rig gave her an unobstructed view. Hundreds of feet below, the morning sun glistened on the majestic white sails of the Opera House while the wake of busy harbour ferries and hovercrafts left patterns on the calm surface of the water. Ruby stared down at the ferries, unable to believe that people actually travelled on them to work. The idea of travelling across the water seemed so magical that it seemed impossible people could use the ferries for something so ordinary as going to the office.

'It's just like being on a bus to them,' said Jack.

Ruby shook her head in disbelief. Just then an enormous container ship blew its whistle as it was passing under them on its way to the industrial wharves of Balmain. The sound was deafening – the tone so deep it seemed to reverberate up their spines. Again and again the giant ship hooted as it attempted to cut a swathe through the smaller craft below. Ruby's face shone with sheer exuberance as she craned over towards Jack's window to see the container emerge from under the bridge.

Jack knew that everything he'd gone through so far to get the large rig into the city would not compare with the problems he was now going to face in the central business district. Parking his rig was his first concern. Most of the narrow streets were built in the early eighteen-hundreds, so the whole procedure would not be easy for a forty-foot rig. Parking restrictions made it even more difficult, but he had the good luck to turn into a sidestreet just as two tourist coaches were pulling away from the kerb leaving a once-in-a-lifetime's bonanza of parking spaces.

He and Ruby had just gotten out of the rig when a voice behind them suddenly announced, 'Yer can't park there, mate.' They turned to see a young cop as he stepped off his Kawasaki 1200cc motorbike in jodhpurs and shiny, knee-high boots. It was the cop's reflective sunglasses that annoyed Jack more than anything. He always liked to see people's eyes.

'Yeah, I know, but I don't reckon I should move it until the mechanic checks out my air-brake valve,' said Jack, with as much concern as he could muster.

'You got brake trouble?' asked the cop.

'Yeah, I've got a bloke comin'.' Jack shook his head in despair. 'Nearly ran over an old lady 'round the corner.'

The cop cursed under his breath and looked around to see if the rig would disrupt traffic, but it was parked beside four parking meters and the cop knew he didn't have a case.

Jack dived into his pockets searching for coins. 'Rube,' he called out. 'You got some money for these meters?'

'Sure have,' answered Ruby, wasting no time locating some loose change in her pockets. Ruby approached the first meter and read the instructions. 'Jesus, they want dollars!'

Ruby dived back into her pockets. The traffic cop shook his head, climbed back onto his motorbike and started it up. He was not totally satisfied – but what could he do?

Jack and Ruby entered a crowded elevator that would take them to the floors occupied by Zane Publishing. Both stood self-consciously in the crowd of suited businesspeople. No one uttered a word as the silent machine hoisted all ten of them rapidly up to the highest floors. Jack did detect some slight signs of life, a few nods and a smile. He half-expected Ruby to say something to break the silence – in the country it would be considered peculiar, all these people crammed in together but acting as if no one else was there. However, Ruby was feeling too intimidated to speak in this small space with all these over-dressed office workers. She also realised that the people in business suits were not impressed by her and Jack's neat but casual clothes. Indeed, all their fellow passengers were wondering why this pair of window cleaners was not using the service elevators.

When Jack and Ruby stepped into the foyer of Zane Publishing, they were spellbound. They didn't realise it, but this was exactly the response that Errol Ruben wanted them to have. The first day he'd arrived at Zane Publishing as the company's new boss, he'd glanced around at Zane's pleasant but functional foyer and said, 'I want this redecorated.'

'How do you want it redecorated?' his rather nervous second in command had inquired.

'So that people are impressed,' responded Errol, in the tones of one who is stating the obvious. 'That way,' he added, 'the minute they walk through the door they're more likely to do what we want.'

The second in command had nodded but it'd been obvious to Errol that instantly impressing people was not one of the things his second in command did well. Later that day, Errol had sent down instructions: parquet floor, a couple of tapestries, state-of-the-art lighting, mahogany reception desk, Balinese carved wooden tables and, off to the side of the reception area, a display stand to show off Zane Publishing's latest releases.

Jack and Ruby were gazing around when Ruby

suddenly saw her name – it was emblazoned, gold on green, on a huge exhibit in the display area. 'From Zane this month: *Bird in the Hand* by RUBY VALE.'

'Jack, look at the size of my name!'

Upon hearing her excited voice, a pretty receptionist glanced up to take charge of the situation. 'Can I help you?' she said, with a patronising air, and was just about to add, 'Have you inquired at the service manager's desk on the lower ground level?' when Jack came over to her, his boots noisy on the parquet floor. 'This young lady's very attractive,' he said to himself, 'but getting a smile out of her will be a real challenge.'

'I'm with Ruby Vale,' he supported this with a gesture back towards Ruby. 'That's her over there.' The receptionist's cool stare made these words sound like a lie. 'We're here to see Ziggy,' he concluded.

The receptionist was not convinced. 'And you are?' she asked, in a way that made Jack feel she was raising her eyebrows even though she wasn't actually doing so.

'Jack – Jack Willis.'

Ziggy's purposeful walk in high heels across the parquet was hard to ignore, as was the surprise in her voice when she saw Jack.

'Jack?'

Ruby turned to Ziggy with a smile. 'Hello, there.'

Ziggy was clearly flustered by their arrival. None of this had been entered in her daily schedule. 'Ruby, you should've called from the airport. I could've sent a car.'

'We drove,' said Ruby, casually.

'You drove?' Ziggy's face showed disbelief.

'Yeah, in Jack's rig. He can't fly. Gets real air-sick, don't you, Jack?'

'Yep,' Jack admitted, shaking his head. 'Can't even stick me on a carousel.'

Ziggy thought twice before asking her next question. 'You didn't park in the street, did you?'

'Yep, we had just enough room. Mind you,' he said, turning to the receptionist, 'your girl here might need to nip out and feed the meters a few times.'

'You won't mind, will you, Samantha?' asked Ziggy, knowing quite well that Samantha had never been asked to do such a thing before, and *would* mind.

'No!' she replied, icily. 'Not at all.'

Jack dumped his ignition keys down onto the mahogany reception desk. 'If you need to move it, make sure you build up air pressure before you take off.'

The receptionist glared. She then forced a smile and looked at Ziggy. Was this guy for real?

'Just kiddin',' Jack said, taking back the keys. 'Made you smile, though, eh?'

His wisecrack was not a hit with the sullen receptionist. Not his type anyway, Jack thought. None of these city girls really took his fancy. Ziggy was perhaps acceptable in doses. Well, small doses.

Ziggy ushered them into her office where she introduced them to Ella, and casually added, 'There's a meeting already set up this morning to finalise publicity for Ruby's book – could you tell Errol please that Ruby is here and will be attending this meeting?'

Ella nodded demurely but was not fooled for a

second. It was obvious to her that Ruby Vale and her whatever-he-was had just dropped out of the sky and taken Ziggy by surprise, but no one else at Zane Publishing was going to know that. As far as Ella was concerned, Zane Publishing was going to believe that Ziggy Keane was completely in charge.

In the brief interval before the meeting Ziggy gave Ruby and Jack a brief run down on Zane Publishing and its personnel, then she swept them off to the meeting.

'Right, sweetie, let's go.'

Ruby nodded and swallowed nervously for the hundredth time.

The Zane boardroom was dominated by a large, oval dark-granite table. The whole room was very smart with black leather armchairs and glass-fronted shelves showcasing the books published by the company. The meeting was informal by Zane's standards, but to Jack and Ruby, as they gazed at the opulent fittings, it was intimidating.

Errol ushered Ralph, Ziggy, Jack and Ruby into positions around the granite table as Ella organised coffee and biscuits for everyone. Ruby rose to help out. Picking up the coffee percolator before a startled Ziggy could stop her, she announced, 'Righto, who's having what?'

Errol smiled politely and pulled out a chair for Ruby to sit. 'Miss Vale, please. Ella will take care of the coffee.'

'Oh,' said Ruby, embarrassed. 'Thank you.' She sat down and glanced to Jack for reassurance but none was forthcoming. Jack had caught sight of the Sydney Harbour Bridge through the huge plate-glass window. Ella continued to pour coffee around the table.

'No sugar for Jack – thanks, Ella,' Ruby said, thinking she should probably quit while she was ahead. Errol moved to his seat at the head of the oval and sat down with his usual lordly confidence.

'Miss Vale.'

'Oh, call me Ruby,' she insisted.

'Ruby,' Errol continued, 'I'm sure you're going to approve of what we have prepared so far.'

Ruby's hand had immediately gone into her pocket. She withdrew a folded piece of paper. 'Invitation list,' she said, with a huge grin, waving it above her head like a flag. Errol glanced at Ziggy indicating to her to take charge of the situation.

Ziggy was caught off guard. 'Oh, the wedding. Yes, we're onto that!' Just what 'that' meant, no one was sure. Ziggy stalled for time by sipping her coffee. Ruby passed her invitation list over to Errol, who reluctantly received it as if it were an oily rag and held it with the very tips of his fingers.

'Quite a few guests, my dear.'

'One hundred and ninety-five,' boasted Ruby.

Ziggy suddenly choked on her coffee. 'Oh, I'm sorry, how dreadful!' she exclaimed. Hot liquid had spluttered across the table. Ella immediately presented half a dozen paper napkins to clean up. 'Thank you, Ella.' Ella soaked up spray from the granite table as Ziggy checked her French linen suit for spots.

Ralph always enjoyed anything, however trivial, at

Ziggy's expense. He smiled, grateful that he wasn't in the line of fire and turned to Ruby. 'You live in the outback and you know one hundred and ninety-five people?' Ralph asked. All heads turned to her for the answer.

'Not counting Hamish's brother's family,' she rattled off. 'There are six of them, but they live in Singapore.'

'Six?' asked Errol, appalled at how the numbers were growing.

'That'll make two hundred and one ... but I wouldn't count on them comin' 'cause his brother's got a bad kidney, I think.'

Jack smiled to himself as he tilted his chair back. So far, Ruby was doing fine.

Errol leant forward onto the granite and peered at Ruby with concern. 'Ruby, surely you were considering a more intimate affair?' he asked, in a firm but friendly tone.

Ruby glanced back to Jack hoping that he would support her on the numbers. She should've known better. He shrugged suggesting that she ought to be flexible. Ruby gave him a cold look.

'Maybe,' she said rather reluctantly.

'We'll come to something amicable.' With that, Errol dismissed the wedding and handed her a series of newspaper clippings instead. 'Here. I'm sure these early reviews will buck you up.'

Ruby took them, glancing back to Jack.

'Read them out loud,' said Errol. 'We've very proud of you.'

Ruby cleared her throat – twice – before glancing

down at the page. She read the first one to herself for a moment, then gave a short nervous laugh.

'Read them out loud, Rube,' directed Jack. Ruby looked quickly at him, knowing that he could be getting back at her for the incident in the cafe – among other things. There was a silence as she braced herself.

'A timeless, raw lust to her work that doesn't kowtow to vogue niceties . . .'

'Great!' interrupted Jack.

'No Rodeo Drive sexual caresses for this woman . . .'

By now Jack was grinning broadly with pride.

'Her primal sexual overtones are the stuff of epic romance. A female Wilbur Smith of the love jungle.' Ruby looked up, relieved she'd made it through. 'Wow!' was all she could say.

'Right, Ziggy, on to business,' said Errol, turning his attention back where it belonged.

Ziggy wasted no time. She was now ready to take charge. 'Tonight, we'd like to include you, Ruby, in our Christmas reception at the Art Gallery.'

'Christmas?' Ruby repeated, perplexed, knowing it was still months away.

'Yes,' replied Ziggy. 'We traditionally have it earlier than most firms; that way we don't clash with others. Now, this would mean an appointment for a complete make-over at say, three . . . ?'

'A what?' asked Ruby.

Errol noticed Jack was again preoccupied with the view of the Harbour Bridge. Jack had never seen it from this angle before, and it reminded him of his father and the photograph he had in the cabin of his rig. It was the only thing of his father's that he'd kept. His father had been in Sydney at the time seeing a lawyer about some case he was trying to mount over a disputed mining claim. Jack supposed he must have been in the office of some lawyer or mining company and, seeing the view, decided to take a photograph to send to Jack and his mother back in Lucktown. In the intervening years when Jack had visited Sydney he'd wondered where his father had taken the photograph from. Now he realised it must have been this building – no, he thought, this building is too new. But the one next door. That was older – and lower. His father had gone onto the roof, leant over and captured the precise and particular angle that emphasised both the grace and the strength of the great bridge.

'Jack, we must thank you for escorting Ruby safe and sound.'

Errol's words didn't break Jack's fixed gaze. Everyone leant back to see what he was looking at. Jack was jolted out of his trance, 'I'm sorry,' he said, 'it's the bridge.'

'Yes – and no doubt you're anxious to have a look around the big city,' suggested Errol, condescendingly.

'Jack's my manager,' said Ruby, rather swiftly.

'You betcha,' Jack added. Fortunately, there was no coffee in Ziggy's mouth or it would have spurted all over the conference table again.

Ralph enjoyed the moment as he quickly picked up on Ziggy's little oversight. 'Ah, I didn't know that.'

'Well, splendid!' declared Errol. 'This means we should include you, Jack.'

'Splendid!' repeated Jack with a nod.

******

After the meeting, Ziggy handed Jack and Ruby into the care of Eugene, an intense-looking but utterly charming Irishman who was going to be Ruby's driver during their stay. Eugene's accent enchanted Ruby. To her and Jack's astonishment he treated them as if they were members of the royal family, ceremoniously ushering them out of Zane Publishing and into a limo as though they'd never had to open a door for themselves in their lives. His first task was to take them to their hotel and when he learned that they'd have to go to the rig first to collect their things, he acted as if this was perfectly normal and all the classiest people drove to Sydney in forty-foot rigs.

At the hotel he glanced about their rooms in a slightly worried way as though fearing the place was not up to their standards, while Jack and Ruby simply stood and stared. The foyer of the luxury hotel had given them an idea of how grand the place was but they were still astonished, nonetheless. Their rooms were huge, with vast beds and large ensuites with spa baths. But what really amazed both of them was the view. From the windows of their rooms they could see across Sydney Cove to the Opera House and beyond to the hills and bays of the eastern suburbs. For the first half hour that they were in their rooms all that Jack and Ruby did was stand and admire their million-dollar outlook.

Afterwards Jack undid his suitcase and laid out his meagre belongings. A couple of crushed checked shirts; two pairs of jeans; underwear with donkey motifs which he had failed to notice when he bought them at Thrifty's in Broken Hill; one tie; a white shirt and a suit, era 1979. He thought the suit still looked sharp – a subtle pinstripe took it away from the every-day black and blues that blokes were wearing in the street. A tad wide at the collar perhaps, but it wasn't bad.

'Bugger it!' he swore, noticing a stain on the sleeve left there from Alf Bell's drunken wedding in Dunedo some eighteen months earlier. He immediately trudged off to the bathroom and searched through the array of three-inch plastic bottles in the hope of finding something that would clean suit fabric. Shampoo for normal hair? Perfect!

There was a knock on the door.

'Coming.'

He placed the suit aside and opened his door to reveal Eugene, the limo driver, standing there in a state of distress.

'Oh, Mr Willis, sir . . .'

'What's the matter?'

Eugene glanced at his watch. He was definitely troubled. 'It's Miss Ruby, sir . . .'

'What?'

'You gotta come, sir. She's in a right dreadful state.'

Jack tucked in his shirt and walked quickly down

the corridor towards Ruby's room. Eugene ran to keep up.

'She has an appointment in ten minutes, at three p.m. I ring her room, there's no answer. I go to knock on the door and I hear tears. There's something not right, Mr Willis.'

'Call me, Jack, will you?'

'Yes, sir – Jack.'

They reached Ruby's door. Jack knocked. No answer. He knocked again, then placed his ear to the door.

'I tell yer, it's cryin', sir,' whispered Eugene. 'I know cryin'. My good wife, God bless her soul, does it all the time.'

'Shhh!' Jack tried to listen. Still nothing.

'Ruby,' he called. Now he could hear crying. Then a crowd applauding. 'Eugene, get someone up here.'

'Yes, sir.' The little Irishman ran from the scene totally relieved that someone else was now dealing with the catastrophe. Jack noted that Eugene had a penchant for drama.

Jack had tried to stir Ruby a few more times before an ardent-looking young woman whose name badge said Ms M. Garfield charged from the elevator armed with another keycard to Ruby's room. Ms M. Garfield, naturally, felt obliged to knock again.

'She won't answer,' said Jack.

'Definitely tears . . .' repeated Eugene.

Ms M. Garfield opened the door. Eugene was right. This was Niagara Falls after the rainy season.

'Look, Miss . . .'

'Melissa Garfield – assistant to the manager.'

Jack smiled gratefully. 'I think I should take it from here, thanks,' suggested Jack.

Ms. Garfield looked relieved. Tears clearly were not her bag. 'Should you need me, I'll be downstairs in my office.'

Eugene glanced nervously at his watch again.

'Eugene,' said Jack.

'Yes, sir – Jack.'

'Go and ring the make-over people – whatever they're called – and put Ruby's appointment off till four.'

'Good idea.' Eugene left with Ms Garfield.

Jack hadn't actually opened the door more than two inches. Ruby was crying buckets and the television was blaring. Oh, Christ, he thought. This was not a good sign.

Jack slowly opened the door to reveal Ruby seated cross-legged on her huge bed dressed only in panties and bra. Beside her on the bed were two boxes of tissues.

'Ohhhh, – J-J-J-J-Jack . . .' She could barely speak through the jerks of her hysterical tears. Jack entered, closed the door behind him and made his way hesitantly to the edge of the bed.

'Ruby, they tried to . . .'

'Oh, G-G-G-God! – There's this . . . poor . . . woman . . . who didn't know . . . they lied . . . they bloody lied to her . . .'

'What?' Jack inquired, gently. 'Who, Rube? Who's lied?'

Ruby grabbed another four tissues and pointed to the television. 'Thirty years . . . her son. Look! There's her son!'

Jack turned and looked at the television. An afternoon audience show revealed a large, suburban woman in her fifties hugging her thirty-year-old son.

Jack smiled. His relief was monumental. 'Oh, I see . . .'

'No – you don't,' cried Ruby. 'She was tricked to give him up . . . when he was born . . .'

'Why?' asked Jack.

'Low self-esteem,' she sniffled. 'She tried to . . . find him . . . they said . . . he was . . . in America somewhere. She had . . . to live a . . . a lie, Jack.'

'And now she's got him back. That's great!'

Ruby just looked wondering how he could be so insensitive.

'Rube, it's three o'clock.'

'Oh, Jesus . . .'

'Rube, it's a TV show.'

'But it's real! We're the . . . same, Jack. We didn't . . . have mothers.'

'Yours lives in Wagga Wagga,' said Jack.

'That's not – the point.'

Jack tried a different tack. 'What's this show called?'

Ruby settled a little and sniffled, *'We'll Help You Find Your Loved Ones'*.

'Bugger me,' said Jack. 'A whole show about people finding each other?'

'It's – wonderful.'

Jack moved up closer to Ruby on the bed and eased the channel changer from her grip. Without even a look back to the television, he switched it off. Silence.

'Ah, that's better, eh? You okay?' he asked. Ruby nodded and blew her nose. Her face was red and tear-stained. At least she'd stopped crying. Ruby looked down and realised that she was scarcely clad. It hadn't escaped Jack's eye. Ruby suddenly rolled off the bed, walked into the bathroom and closed the door. God, he thought, cherishing the memory of the curves of her hips and her bottom for a moment in his mind.

'I'll tell Eugene you're gettin' ready,' he yelled.

There was no answer from the bathroom. Jack got up off the bed and left the room.

9

The pre-Christmas reception at the Art Gallery turned out to be an extremely glamorous affair. Before it, Ruby was whisked away from her hotel for her re-scheduled make-over, which gave Jack time to organise his rig into a safer parking space. Fortu-nately, he found just what he needed in a city construction site. The construction workers were on strike, so the security officer permitted Jack to park his rig while the trouble was being dealt with.

In the lead-up to the event, no one at Zane gave Jack a second thought. Ziggy assumed that he would appear at the reception dressed in something appro-priate – hopefully a rented black dinner suit. As far as Ziggy was concerned, it didn't matter if Jack chose plastic buttons instead of studs or even a coloured clip-on tie. As long as he kept out of the way, she would be happy.

Jack had been to exhibitions at the Art Gallery but had never been there for an occasion like this, and was slightly worried about finding his way. However, when he reached the solid old Victorian building he saw a group of people in evening dress making their way up the central stairs, and he joined them.

He didn't notice the startled looks they gave him. He did observe that everyone about him seemed to be very flashily dressed – the women in long gowns and the men in black dinner suits – but this didn't make him think how he must look in his twenty-year-old suit. Clearly there were times – weddings, funerals and grand parties like this – when you had to wear a suit, and Jack thought he was lucky to have inherited one in such good condition from his father. 'A wonder he never pawned it,' he said to himself, as he offered up his invitation card to a uniformed person at the door who was standing before him in what seemed to Jack a rather confrontational manner.

The man looked at the invitation carefully, looked at Jack again in some surprise and murmured something before stepping out of his way.

The interior of the gallery's foyer was tastefully decorated with just enough Christmas colour to blend with the current exhibition of modern art. Waiters and media people shuffled between guests – everyone was either searching for attention or, if that wasn't forthcoming, for a drink.

Jack always felt like a 'fifth wheel' at any occasion that required him to dress up. In the bush, most dos were weddings, buck's parties or the infamous annual Bachelors and Spinsters balls held mostly at the local showground pavilion. Party-goers would drive hundreds of kilometres dressed in their finery to attend these affairs. Many country districts would try to out-do each other by putting on bigger bands or laying out more kegs of beer. Young men in the bush didn't have the opportunity to party like their city counterparts, but when they did they made up for lost time. The aim, first and foremost, was to get plastered with their mates. Then later, using whatever charm they had left, they would try hard to get laid. This sometimes happened in the back of some dusty utility truck or in the cattle stalls of the neighbouring pavilion. The women were known to party as diligently as the young men but, for most of them, romance just meant an unsatisfying grope behind the tank stand. Jack was fond of woolshed dances. They were less casual affairs. He used to like the smell of the sheds. He remembered old Mr Reece's shed, one of the oldest in the district, opened up every New Year's Eve to the haunting sound of bagpipes. Who could forget that Scottish tradition, hogmanay, tinged with the aroma of wool lanoline? Or the dark, shiny timbers where thousands of sheep had rubbed their fleeces? Jack had fond memories. It was a time when his parents laughed and danced their hearts out. Those were the good years.

None of this experience had equipped Jack for Zane Publishing's Christmas reception. He'd never seen so many people and, what was worse, it wasn't organised like a social do in the country with men occupying one end of the room and the women the other, the younger ones coming together for dances and the older ones inevitably talking about that never-ending rural topic: the weather. As he gazed at the mass of people before him, Jack realised that things were a lot simpler in the country. There he knew that if anyone came up to him at a party – or at a wedding or a funeral – they'd always start the conversation by saying 'Been dry' – or, very occasionally, 'Been wet.' In response, Jack would give a bit of a nod, take a sip of his beer and reply, 'Been real dry.'

As Ruby would have said, even someone as quiet as Jack could manage this sort of approach but, as he looked about him at Zane Publishing's other guests, he knew it wouldn't work here. In any case it didn't look as if he was ever going to get a chance to find out, for everybody else seemed to know each other. People were kissing each other and exclaiming how well each other was looking and cameras were flashing and waiters were somehow negotiating the crowd with glasses of champagne and not losing a drop. All too fast for me, thought Jack, peering into the mass of people trying to locate a familiar face. He was conscious that he was late – getting the rig stowed away, getting back to the hotel, getting dressed and getting to the gallery had all taken much longer than he had expected.

Anxious to find Ruby he began to edge his way through the crowd, noting as he went that to qualify as a successful guest at a Zane Publishing Christmas party you obviously had to be able to do half a dozen things more or less simultaneously: kiss an acquaintance lightly on both cheeks while saying how wonderful he or she was looking and introducing whoever you were with to whoever they were with while accepting a glass of champagne and – this was clearly the clincher – keeping your eyes moving rapidly around the room in case you were missing anyone more important. He was thinking, 'I'll bet Ziggy can pull it off when he heard her say, 'Here he is.'

'Sorry I'm late –' Jack began.

'Nice suit.'

Jack knew she was having a dig but couldn't think of anything to say. He fingered his tie nervously. Ziggy was thinking that while his suit was daggy, he looked great – she'd never noticed how handsome he was – and even with his nervousness, and the fact that the suit could have done with a good press, he had style.

'Kind of – retro,' she said, with a smile.

'That's it.' Jack was looking around anxiously for Ruby. Ziggy smiled again and gestured casually. Jack saw a beautiful woman in a red, backless dress, her dark hair elegantly drawn back. Her face was turned away from him.

'Ruby!' Ziggy called.

Ruby turned. Jack caught his breath. She looked utterly gorgeous. Grinning at him she asked, 'What do you think? Oh, apart from the colour.' Ruby's red dress was totally distinctive.

Was this the annoying eight-year-old that had always tagged after him? The exasperating girl who pretended to drown in the swimming hole? Or the obnoxious young woman who dumped superphosphate all over his rig just for the fun of it?

'What do I think?' Jack answered feebly. He had never imagined Ruby could look so beautiful.

'Amazing what a designer and a little suffering'll do,' Ziggy commented, before moving away to greet someone and leaving some distance between Jack and Ruby. A press photographer took immediate advantage of the situation and intruded without warning. He stung Ruby's surprised eyes with a light-bulb flash.

Jack closed the distance between them. 'Sorry I'm late.'

Ruby nervously slipped her arm through his. 'You were meant to come with me in the limo.' Another camera flashed. 'Damn!'

Jack eased his finger under his tight shirt collar to ease the blood supply to his head. He looked back at Ruby and shook his head.

'Don't gawk, Jack.' He made her feel self-conscious.

'I'm not!' he replied, under his breath.

Noticing that his tie was now askew, Ruby reached up and made the necessary adjustment. 'Merry Christmas,' she smiled.

'It's November,' replied Jack.

Ruby leant forward and whispered close to his ear, 'So, you're a Wilbur Smith of the love jungle . . .'

Jack pushed her hands away just as they were approached by a tall, good-looking journalist with a moustache and an east London accent.

'Merry Christmas, Ruby,' said the journalist, with a confident smile.

'It's November,' quipped Ruby.

'Well, this lot like to show-off before anybody else.' He then produced his hand. 'I'm Wesley Clarkson from the *Mirror*. I thought your book was great!'

'Thanks,' said Ruby, nervously shaking his hand.

The journalist glanced at Jack with an inquisitive smile.

'Who's this then?'

'This is Jack. He's my . . .' Ruby was about to say 'manager' but the journalist dismissed the introduction completely.

'Pleased to meet you,' he said, then turned his full attention back to Ruby. 'I didn't think you'd be so young. I thought, you know, romance writer, maybe fifty-something!'

Jack chuckled. 'You wanna drink, Rube?'

The journalist turned to Jack. 'Yeah, yeah, feel free – go ahead. I'll have a scotch, no ice.'

As Jack wandered off, Ruby wondered how long she could keep up the charade. 'Where you from?'

'London. Have you been there?'

'Not lately.' Oh Christ, thought Ruby. Why did I say that? Haven't I got enough to hide?

'Well, I must say I've been through the outback,' said Clarkson with a smirk, 'and I've no idea why anyone would actually want to live there.'

Ruby's hackles began to rise. 'Oh, where have you been?'

'Let's see. Alice. That was depressing. All those poor Abos hanging around waiting for their welfare cheques. I did a story on Ayers Rock . . .'

'It's called Uluru.'

'Yeah, that's the Aboriginal name.'

'No – that's what it's called.' Ruby took pleasure in correcting him. 'While you were there you must've seen King's Canyon or Simpson's Gap?' she asked.

'No.'

'What about Kakadu? There are colours up there close to heaven.' Ruby smiled. 'Didn't you make it up to the north of the Territory?'

The journalist paused a beat before he replied. 'No, I didn't really have that much time.'

'Well, Wesley, I don't think you've seen much at all.'

He smiled. He liked this young woman. 'Maybe you should show me around?'

Ruby smiled back. 'Take the tour.'

Across the room, Errol held court with Ralph and Ziggy while carefully observing Ruby and her apt handling of the journalist.

Ralph topped up his glass with water from a large Perrier bottle, which he insisted drinking at every boozy occasion. 'Jesus, what are we gonna do with the Lone Ranger?' Ralph had taken an instant dislike to Jack.

'You were much more humorous before AA, Ralph,' sniped Ziggy.

'Why didn't you know Jack was her manager?'

'He's some trucker here for the ride.'

Errol smiled at his bickering employees and expertly replaced his empty champagne glass with a full one from a passing waiter's tray.

'Whoever he is, get this girl signed for her next two books. Ruby Vale's going to make us a fortune.' Errol surveyed the room with an expert eye. 'Is there anyone here from *Who Weekly*? Surely we can get a cover story out of this?'

'I've already spoken,' Ralph said, with a sting meant

for Ziggy. Ziggy looked back at him with her intense eyes.

'On your behalf, naturally,' Ralph added, with a smirk.

Ziggy smiled and leant forward, close to his ear and said, still smiling, 'Don't fuck with me, Ralph,' before slipping away into the crowd of elegant guests.

Errol saw the flicker of rage that crossed Ralph's face and asked, 'What'd she say?'

Ralph thought for a moment trying to find an appropriate translation. 'Ah, good luck to me – you know, for the partnership?'

'How gracious.' Errol didn't believe a word of it but kept the irony out of his voice.

Ralph moved closer to him. 'What's the latest, Errol? Any decision from up above yet?' Ralph chuckled nervously. 'Up above' meant the board who were thinking of enlisting a senior employee to the board of directors. Both Ralph and Ziggy were strong contenders.

'What are you after, Ralph, the inside track?'

'Do I look like a betting man?' asked Ralph, lightly.

'My dear boy, all I can say is that whoever signs Ruby Vale for her next two books will greatly impress the members of the board. Merry Christmas.'

Errol drifted off leaving Ralph to ponder his future. Another waiter passed, offering champagne. Ralph accepted one and, carrying two glasses and his Perrier bottle, set off to find Ruby.

Ralph wove his way expertly through the crowd of publishing executives – many from other houses – accompanied by their wives, their husbands, wannabe scribes and other freelance folk loosely associated with the publishing world. It was the time before Christmas when the spirit of the festive season was celebrated. So what better time could Zane have chosen to show off its success?

'Excuse us, friend,' he said, as he expertly eased his way in between Ruby and the handsome journalist, who was still trying to make a move on her. Pulling Ruby aside, he asked, 'How's it going?'

'You saved my life – I think,' Ruby said, with a genuine sigh of relief.

'You didn't say too much?'

'What do you mean?'

'Watch these guys, Ruby. They're smooth. Never give too much personal stuff away.'

Ruby had thought the journalist was trying to chat her up rather than con her, but she supposed Ralph knew what he was talking about.

'I'll remember that.'

'Think of me as your guardian angel.' Ralph leant towards her confidingly then waited a moment before asking, 'How's Jack working out?'

'Okay . . .' Ruby didn't know what to say.

'Ruby, believe me,' Ralph said, jumping in swiftly, 'your life's about to change for the better.'

'Better than this?' Ruby had realised what Ralph was on about and was becoming more and more amused. All these city slicksters thought they were so smart. The idea that she and Jack could put one over them had not even crossed their minds.

'Rube, you gotta have a smart team around you. Know what I'm saying?' Ralph was now about to make his big move. 'I mean, I handle international promotion, back-end sales, merchandising . . .'

'You know this stuff?' asked Ruby, looking up at him with large dark eyes and seeming really impressed.

'Hey, I wrote the book.'

To Ralph's delight Ruby seemed to think that really funny; she was still laughing when Jack reappeared a minute or so later with the drinks. He had a champagne for Ruby, a beer for himself and a scotch for the journalist.

'Where's numb-nuts?' he asked, looking around.

'Ralph pissed him off,' Ruby said, casually.

'No, Ruby . . .' Ralph corrected her carefully, 'I eased you away from his clutches. You see people, we need journalists – they must remain our friends.'

'Well, you can give him this,' said Jack, as he passed him the glass of scotch.

Ralph took the glass gracefully, and said, 'I was just telling Ruby, I'm trying to help her evolve. She's gotta shed her skin like a . . .'

'A snake?' suggested Ruby, with her serious impressed look. This caught Ralph unawares.

'Well, more like a butterfly, you know. You gotta fly, Ruby. You gotta fly.' With that, Ralph took a well-earned gulp of Perrier water and turned to Jack. 'It's a dog-eat-dog world out there.'

'Yep!' said Jack.

Ralph then felt another opportunity. 'Being with Zane's a good thing. Being with the right person is even better.' Ralph leant close to them both. 'I could be your man.'

Ruby thought about this over a sip of champagne. 'That would give us a nice cozy feelin', Ralph.' She turned to Jack. 'Wouldn't it, Jack?'

'Sure would.'

Ralph chuckled, and gave Jack a playful punch on the arm.

Ruby handled the remainder of the evening with the aid of her newly acquired taste for Moët champagne. It was her first experience of the intoxicating bubbles of the 'good stuff'. The Lucktown pub often had bottles of something sweet 'n' bubbly on the shelf, but Ruby knew that old Artie would never consider buying any expensive champagne in case it wasn't purchased. The sight of those bottles just sitting there on the shelf would drive him crazy. In any case, beer was considered good enough for most weddings and family celebrations in Lucktown.

For those around her at the reception, it was Ruby's sheer beauty that was intoxicating. She'd never had such attention. When possible, Jack tried to cut down on her Moët. He knew what Ruby was capable of sober. He didn't want to find out what she could get up to drunk.

'Like flies on a carcass,' Jack said.

Ruby turned up her nose and looked at him. 'What?'

'This lot. I haven't met one person that actually does anything.'

Ruby laughed. 'This is how the other half live, Jack.'

'More than half!'

Ruby touched his face with such fondness. 'Are you gettin' drunk, mister?'

'On imported beer? You gotta be jokin'.'

******

It was getting late, about ten forty-five p.m., when Jack, Ruby and Ziggy finally left the Christmas reception at the gallery. It was a relief for Jack to be in the limo driving safely back across town to their hotel. Ziggy was flipping through her Filofax, straining to see with the aid of the interior courtesy light. Ruby leant her head back against the seat, and Jack gazed out into the city lights that seemed to flash past his window like an aurora. Far too much alcohol, Jack thought, as the limo turned right into George Street off Park Street. They were heading for The Rocks, an historic part of the city that had been workers' cottages and wharves years ago, but was now renovated and full of tourists. Glamorous hotels flourished amid tourist shops, bars and cafes.

'Tomorrow's huge,' Ziggy said, breaking their silence. 'We have an eight-thirty a.m. radio talkback . . .'

'Talkback?' Ruby looked anxiously at Jack.

'You got a lotta fans, Rube,' answered Jack. He couldn't hold Ruby's narrowing stare so he turned to Ziggy. 'That right, Zig?'

'Growing by the minute,' Ziggy said, without looking up from her Filofax. Jack gave Ruby an enthusiastic thumbs up.

'I could be a one-shot wonder,' Ruby said, shooting a meaningful glance at him. Jack looked at her.

Vaguely aware that something was happening but too busy to be bothered about it, Ziggy asked, 'May we go on?'

'You're doin' a great job,' smiled Jack, warmly grateful for her intervention.

Ziggy glanced up to him, appreciating the compliment. 'Thank you.'

Ruby sighed, leant back into her seat and peered out of the window. 'What else's happening tomorrow?' she asked, with no hint of enthusiasm in her voice.

'We've got a ten-thirty a.m. appearance at a bookstore in Parramatta. Lunch with the mayor and his wife . . .'

'The mayor?' gasped Ruby, again.

'Yes,' replied Ziggy, 'his wife's your biggest fan.'

'Why don't we ask them up to your weddin', Rube?' Jack was feeling mischievous, but his teasing fell on deaf ears as Ruby suddenly remembered Hamish. Hadn't she promised to call him as soon as she arrived in Sydney? And now look at her: she'd been too carried away with all this big-city glamour to speak to her fiancé.

'Oh, fuck!' she cried, and suddenly remembered her pledge to watch her language. 'I'm sorry, I mean . . . shit, I forgot to call Hamish.'

Jack rolled his eyes. 'Do it when you get back.'

'It'll be too late. Oh, damn!'

Ziggy was leaning towards the limo driver. 'Eugene, could you drop me at the Neptune?' Eugene glanced up into his rear-view mirror, concerned that Ziggy was about to be alone in this part of the city late at night.

'Shall I wait for you, Miss Keane?'

'No, you take these two back to their hotel. I've got to catch up with another author. I'll get a cab.'

'Right you are,' said Eugene, obviously not happy with the arrangement.

'When do you go to bed, Ziggy?' chuckled Jack.

'I'm an insomniac,' Ziggy said with a smile, as the limo pulled up outside the Neptune Restaurant. 'Fortunately, so are some of my authors. Goodnight, everyone. Eugene will pick you up in the morning.'

Ziggy climbed out of the limo, gathering her dress as she slid across the seat.

'Night,' said Jack. He caught a glimpse of her beautiful legs as she stepped out. They were breathtaking. In heels Ziggy stood nearly five-foot-ten. Her height was accentuated by the trim toning of her athletic body. Jack was impressed – nails, hands, eyes – Ziggy must spend hours grooming herself, he thought, as he watched her sweep off into the night.

The limo lurched forward as Eugene took advantage of the first space between traffic. Jack smiled and looked back at Ruby, only to be met with a grim face.

'What?' asked Jack.

Ruby had been watching Jack eyeing Ziggy and telling herself that it was about time that he was finally showing interest in a woman. Ziggy was not right for him, but she certainly was pleasing to the eye. Ruby decided on a change of topic.

'I shoulda got you into one of those dickie suits,' she said.

'Nah,' said Jack, dismissing the idea. 'You look nice – that's all that mattered.'

Ruby nervously touched her hair. She knew she looked good tonight but, let's face it, Ziggy Keane looked good all the time.

'What do you think of her?' continued Jack.

'Who?'

'Ziggy.'

'Not your type,' she mumbled, now wondering what 'type' he really went for.

Jack threw his head back with a chuckle. 'Maybe you should put a good word in for me.'

'You don't even like her,' Ruby protested mildly.

'Yeah.' Jack sighed and sat back deep into his seat but Ruby knew he hadn't stopped thinking about Ziggy. 'What's there to like, I suppose,' he added.

'That's what she said about you,' said Ruby.

Nothing more was said for a while as the limo made its way on through the thick midnight traffic. The streets were narrow in this old part of town. The sort of streets that tourist brochures often refer to as 'charming', while those who use them find them congested and annoying. Ruby was thinking about her future life with Hamish. Although she was looking forward to living somewhere new, Lucktown would always have a place in her heart. It was where she and Jack shared so many childhood memories. It was where her father had taught her to fly.

'Do you ever get the feelin' life's just one big trail of – emotional debris?' she said, with her cheek pressed against the window.

Jack stared at her. He'd never before heard her use such an expression. Before he could speak though she asked, 'Jack, how many girls have you known?'

'None o' your business.'

'Suzie reckons you're too shy and Hamish said you couldn't impress any girl.'

'Is that right?'

'Yeah.' Ruby then looked away again and sighed deeply. 'And you write all that great stuff.'

'I'll tell you something . . .' groaned Jack, 'finding the right woman out there's not easy.'

'Not meant to be,' Ruby answered, with slight condescension.

Jack replied with a scoff. Ruby figured he was too tired and drunk to make further comment, but after a moment she slid closer to him along the seat and looked directly into his blue eyes. 'I have a question.'

He hadn't seen her in a mood like this before and asked, 'Are you drunk?'

But Ruby was thinking of everything she was leaving behind. She smiled. 'Am I ever, ever going to see you again?'

Jack had rarely felt so confronted. He calculated that this was pre-wedding nerves and too much to drink. He had to lighten the mood. 'No, never, ever again.'

'Jesus, you piss me off.' Ruby's response startled Eugene. His eyes hit the mirror in the hope of catching more of what was brewing in the rear of his limo.

'You'll be in Queensland,' Jack pointed out. He was half expecting Ruby to slug him.

'I'll come home once in a while,' she replied softly.

'What, so you can dump birdshit on me?' Jack grinned, which completely disarmed the tension they had between them.

'I only wanna remember the great times,' Ruby said, then leant forward and kissed him on the cheek.

'What was that for?' Jack said feebly.

'For not calling me "kiddo".' Ruby had made the first move without thinking about the consequences. A kiss on the cheek was harmless anyway – people at the party had been kissing each other all the time. What she didn't realise was that Jack was not aware he'd stopped calling her 'kiddo'. Her face was turned up towards him. The next moment his lips were on hers. It was a fabulous kiss. Ruby found her eyes closing. Her heart had begun to race. Their lips parted. Ruby exclaimed startled, 'Damn! Jack, can you hear that?' The pounding in her chest was so intense she felt as if everyone in Sydney could hear it. Jack stared at her, not sure what to say.

Eugene's strong Irish lilt cut through their moment like a blade. 'Here's your hotel, folks.'

Jack looked out of the window and felt the sway of the limo as it entered the forecourt of the Regent Hotel. He knew he was in no mood to go upstairs calmly to bed. He turned back to Ruby, 'You wanna play pool?'

Ruby's face lit up.

Jack leant forward. 'Eugene, could you take us to a pool hall? Do you know any good ones?' Eugene decided that this young couple needed some exercise in the fresh air.

'A walk from here, sir. There'll be a pub with pool tables just down the street. Try the Orient or the Lord Nelson.'

'That'll do,' said Ruby. 'Good night, Eugene.' Ruby had the limo door open in a flash. She grabbed Jack by the hand and pulled him out with her.

Ruby's spirits lifted as she walked with Jack through the narrow, charming streets of The Rocks. Music wafted from every window as they ambled past quaint old pubs with young drinkers crowding the footpath out the front, and sitting in the gutters. The place was throbbing with life. People were gathered to listen to live jazz being played in the corner of one tiny bar that was so small there was barely enough room for the musicians to perform. Italian and Thai restaurants competed to impress young Japanese tourists who wandered the street, perplexed by the varied and boisterous crowds around them.

Ruby felt overdressed in her red evening gown as Jack escorted her into an Irish pub on the next corner. Jack had already removed his tie. Although it was a rowdy bar, with European football playing silently on a number of monitors, as Jack and Ruby walked in everyone's attention was focused on a large, bearded man with a warm smile. He was standing on a makeshift stage in front of a three-piece band. Coloured lights gave his beard and face a reddish hue.

'Come on, folks, how can we have a talent night without talent? There's gotta be more of you out there that sing!'

A few drinkers applauded him. Jack spotted a

number of mid-size pool tables at the back of the room, grabbed Ruby's arm and led her through the crowd.

'You should do the Big O for them, Jack,' said Ruby, in earshot of a drunken man with his face in a jug of beer. The man chuckled, and took another swig.

'Don't be stupid, Rube,' replied Jack, as he slapped coins onto the first available pool table.

Back upon the makeshift stage, a contestant had been encouraged by his mates to climb up into the coloured lights and sing Billy Joel's 'Just the Way You Are.' Unfortunately, it was a poor rendition. Ruby turned up her nose in disgust and opened their first game with a smashing cue shot. She had already sunk two balls.

'You wanna talk about your new book?' she asked, with a cheeky grin.

'No!' replied Jack, waiting for Ruby's next shot.

Ruby lined up again with confidence and sank another ball. She then inspected the tip of her cue and exchanged it for another hanging on the wall. 'I got some good ideas,' she said, lining up yet again.

'You don't even know what my next story's about. Anyway, who's the writer here?'

'You're gettin' fussy for someone who doesn't put his name on anything.' Ruby missed her next shot. 'Shit!'

'Serves you right,' said Jack, moving forward to play his first ball.

Meanwhile, the Billy Joel contestant moaned on through his song.

'Jesus, no wonder Christie Brinkley walked out,' said Ruby, just as Jack played his shot. This caused him to laugh and miss the ball completely.

The drunk who overheard Ruby's earlier comment about Jack singing a Roy Orbison song, had quietly taken a fancy to Ruby in her gorgeous evening dress. During their pool game he moved closer to gawk at her. 'Why don't you sing us a song, missie? You're dressed for it.'

Ruby slowly straightened and turned towards the drunk.

'I just might,' she said, staring coolly at him.

The drunk turned towards the stage and yelled out to the ailing 'Billy Joel'. 'Get off, yer mug! Give someone else a go.' Other rowdy patrons soon joined in, eager to get rid of this wailing bore.

'Rube,' said Jack.

'What?'

'Play pool,' he insisted firmly.

Unfortunately, the drunk was not going to give up on his quest. 'There ya go, missie. What-are-ya-gonna sing?' he asked in a menacing tone.

Ruby walked straight up and confronted him. 'It's a catchy little number called, "You're an arsehole when you drink".'

Jack rolled his eyes and moved forward quickly to halt further escalation. He grabbed Ruby around the waist, lifted her and walked backwards towards the pool table. 'You are nothin' but trouble,' he said quietly, as he dumped Ruby down.

The drunk decided to have another go. 'Yeah, missie, listen to yer big brother before I slap yer one.'

Ruby's face burnt with anger. 'I could take him, Jack.'

'No you won't,' he said, and grabbed her arm.

By this time, the drunk believed that he was on a roll. He turned to face the stage again. 'Hey – this mug over 'ere reckons he can sing like Roy Orbison.' His remark caused an uproar of applause. Jack glanced at the drunk with a sarcastic smile.

'Get him up here,' yelled the large, bearded man under the red lights. Jack had no intention of doing such a thing.

'Go on, show the bastards, Jack,' she said. This was followed by a barrage of encouragement from the patrons within earshot. Everyone turned to him. All Jack could feel was a sea of faces yelling for him to 'have a go!' Ruby stood there smiling, daring him to sing like Orbison.

'Show 'em, Jack,' she said, softly.

Jack gave a long look at Ruby before he reluctantly moved off towards the stage. Why was she able to get to him with such perfect timing? He couldn't see that Ruby had both her fingers crossed.

As he moved forward through the swelling crowd Jack, passed close by the outspoken drunk. 'Here's yer chance to be a Flying bloody Wilbury,' the drunk said, almost slobbering into Jack's ear. The sharp elbow-jab to the man's solar plexus was most effective. He fell like a stone. Jack bent over him. 'That's "Traveling" Wilbury, okay?'

The drunk was unable to do anything but nod as he lay there pained and breathless on the floor. The yelling soon subsided as Jack nervously took the stage. He squinted up into the red spotlight, then smiled down at the sea of faces.

'What are yer gonna do for us?' asked the large, bearded man.

'Ahhh . . .' said Jack, then turned to the guitarist and whispered something in his ear. The guitarist shrugged his shoulders and nodded. Jack faced the crowd.

'I'm gonna sing, "Crying".'

The crowd erupted. Ruby made her way closer to the stage as Jack cleared his throat for the third time. He then nodded to the guitarist for him to commence. After a short strumming intro, Jack leant closer to the microphone, spluttered the opening lyrics, and coughed, nervously. 'Sorry, I'll start again.'

A whistle from somewhere in the crowd made him smile. The guitarist started again. He figured the crowd, for some reason, was on this guy's side, and was prepared to be helpful.

Jack's second attempt was more confident, and after just a few lines the audience started singing along. They were a tough crowd and Jack wasn't sure whether this response was an endorsement of his singing or not, but it was good-humoured. Suddenly Ruby stepped up onto the stage beside him and leant into the microphone, and together they sang the chorus: 'Cryyyyying over you . . .'

The crowd was elated by Jack and Ruby's presence on the stage. As their confidence grew, they sang their hearts out – their eyes never left each other as Ruby's surprisingly strong voice supported Jack all the way through the duet.

As the love song ended, the huge crowd of onlookers gave them a rowdy standing ovation.

10

Early next morning just outside Lucktown, Lance, who was riding in the back seat of Hamish's Land Rover, became extremely excited as Hamish turned off the dusty main road and onto the rough track that led to the airstrip. Lance remembered that this was where he'd last seen Jack. A small flock of emus took fright as the Land Rover approached and raced off through the low mulga bushes. Suddenly the stench of an animal carcass permeated the interior of the vehicle. Hamish quickly rolled up his window as he saw a flock of jet-black crows rising from a carcass on the side of the track. It was so far decayed that it was difficult even for Hamish to tell what the unfortunate animal had been. Probably a roo, he thought, slowing down to peer at it. Spot-light shooters had been reported a few nights ago. They were kids who drove out from the mines – usually after a drinking binge – armed with high-powered rifles and ready to kill anything that moved. And for that matter, anything that didn't move. Signposts, oil drums, car bodies, even satellite dishes. Nothing escaped the drunken eye of a seventeen-year-old with a Remington rifle. Over the years, Hamish had had to extract bullets from quite a number of prize livestock. Merino sheep were favourite targets. When they were hit, they leapt straight in the air and fell like a rock. These incidents were reported, but nothing was ever done until the mayor's kid accidentally shot his best mate in the leg. The high-velocity bullet ripped a great hole in his thigh. There was not a lot of sympathy in the district.

Hamish pulled up outside the aircraft hanger and waited a moment for the fine dust to pass him before opening the door. Even at this early hour, the sun was burning his pale Celtic skin. Hamish grabbed his hat, told Lance to stay put, and walked into the hanger.

Inside was no cooler. Mack Milson, the aero-mechanic, a robust fifty-year-old, was servicing Ruby's biplane as it sat proudly in the centre of the corrugated iron building.

'G'day, Mack,' said Hamish.

'Mornin' Hamish. Bloody hot already, eh?' Mack replied, dabbing his temples with a dirty rag. 'How's Ruby?'

'Good, I think.' Hamish hesitated. 'Haven't heard from her yet . . .'

To Hamish's relief, Mack didn't seem to notice his slight pause. Hamish himself had been very surprised not to hear from Ruby and had double-checked his pager several times, first for messages and then to make sure it was working. Ruby had left two days ago, had travelled hundreds of kilometres and had now spent the night in a strange city. And still she hadn't called him – not even just to tell him she was all right and to make sure that he was all right, which, considering how bruised he was from his buck's night, would have been the sort of thing you'd expect your fiancé to do. It was behaviour, Hamish had told himself several times, that would stop when they were married.

Apart from being in love with Ruby, Hamish also thought she was perfect – except for one thing, which he called her 'wild streak'. But he didn't think this wild streak was her fault. He blamed her father, the late George Vale, for her passion for flying, for her fondness for playing pool and for her constant swearing. In Hamish's opinion it was no way to bring a child up – regardless of whether it was a boy or a girl – marooned in a one-horse town hundreds of kilometres from anywhere, learning how to speak from overhearing truckers talk and being taught aerial acrobatics in an ancient biplane by your own father. It was amazing that Ruby was as wonderful as she was.

Inevitably he'd heard about her before he met her. In a place like Lucktown, unless you're a recluse, you hear about everybody in the first two weeks. But getting to meet them in a district of huge distances was another matter unless, in Hamish's case, they had sick animals. As it was, even though he lived in a cottage behind the Lucktown vet surgery, it was weeks before he met Ruby because every animal in the district took his arrival as a sign to get sick or to injure itself. His first days – and nights – in Lucktown were spent hurrying from one property to another: inserting thermometers, giving injections, setting bones and swatting flies.

One evening, returning to Lucktown near dead with tiredness, he'd seen a woman emerge from the Boomerang Cafe and thought to himself, 'That must be Ruby.' He had been a bit surprised, though, because it had been made clear to him that the local men thought Ruby was very attractive, and the woman he saw, though pleasant-looking, was nearer to fifty than twenty. Obviously in the outback, he thought, they like them mature.

It hadn't been until he went to the Boomerang for breakfast that he realised his mistake. The older blond-haired woman was Suzie, the publican's wife. He was gorging on an excellent hamburger when Suzie called out, 'Rube!'. From the corner of his eye Hamish had seen a slight figure in overalls detach itself from the rowdy group playing pool. As she crossed the room her eyes scanned the cafe and came to rest on Hamish. Their eyes met and Hamish felt a thrill down his spine. With her pale oval face, thick, dark wavy hair, bright dark eyes with shadows under them, she really was beautiful – if a bit too thin in the face. She had a dash of black grease on her temple, and faded grease stains all over her overalls. 'That's the woman,' he had said to himself, 'I'm going to marry.'

Now, for a happy few seconds, Hamish imagined their future in Goondiwindi. All these long hours of work would stop. He would have a nine-to-five job in a practice with two other vets. While Ruby – instead of

169

working from dawn at the Boomerang and crop-dusting for farmers in her biplane – would be busy setting up house. Soon there would be babies, who would quickly replace their mother's interest in flying.

Mack had straightened his back and was watching Hamish with a grin. 'The old groom-to-be, eh?' he said, as if he knew the marriage was on Hamish's mind.

'Less of the "old" thanks, Mack.'

'Big day's loomin', mate.'

'Yep!' Hamish smiled.

'You here for Ruby's stuff?'

Hamish glanced around the service bay. 'Sure am.'

The mechanic dropped his tools and wiped his hands on the same dirty rag. He pointed to a cardboard box under a workbench.

'Over there, under the bench. Just leave her logbooks; she'll need those.'

As Hamish headed for the box, Mack walked over to a small metal table that doubled as an office desk.

'I got something else for you.' He picked up a number of handwritten pages from under a heavy, metal ashtray. 'Joe Buckingham found these scattered out on the edge of the highway, when he was checking after the spotlight shooters.' Mack held up the pages between two of his cleanest fingers. These were the very same pages that had blown out of Ruby's window while she was travelling with Jack in the rig. 'The title says *Bird in the Hand*. Pretty schmaltzy stuff. Must be Ruby's, eh?'

Hamish, carrying the box to his chest, walked towards Mack. 'Stick 'em on the top, mate.'

Mack did so, carefully trying not to make the pages dirtier than they already were.

Hamish secured them by holding them down with his chin and headed for the door.

'Thanks, Mack.'

'I should have the old plane serviced by the end of the week,' Mack called out, as Hamish reached the door of the hanger.

'Good, we'll be pleased to be rid of it.'

Mack looked bewildered as Hamish walked outside. Sell the biplane? That was the first he'd heard of it. Mack picked up his dirty rag and rubbed the two pilot names that had been painted just forward of the cockpit. The names read *George Vale*, then directly underneath, *Ruby Vale*.

Outside, Hamish struggled to keep his chin on the loose pages so they wouldn't blow away while opening the rear of the Land Rover with one hand and a booted foot. Eventually he manhandled the box inside, and picked up the pages to study the scrawl. To his surprise, although the handwriting looked familiar, he was sure it wasn't Ruby's. Lance moved closer and whimpered. He could smell Jack on every page.

'Stay there,' Hamish ordered, without taking his eyes off the pages. A deep anxiety began to build as he read. He knew the pages must be a part of the novel – even the title of Ruby's book was scrawled on the cover page. Hamish closed the rear door of the Land Rover and climbed into the driver's seat. Still puzzled by his find, he dived into his old leather briefcase and sifted through a pile of papers containing bills and medical orders. Eventually, he found a note that had been slipped under the windscreen wipers of his Land Rover some time ago. The note read: *Hamish, if you're passing by Saturday, could you call in and give Lance his shots? Thanks.* The note was signed by Jack. The scrawl was identical to the one on the pages. Hamish looked out the window.

'Bugger me,' he said, with a deep sigh. He started the engine and roared off away from the airstrip towards the Fergusons' place where an important patient – the Fergusons' prize-winning quarter horse – was waiting for him with a broken leg.

******

Barry Ferguson and his son, Jeff, helped soothe the quarter horse while Hamish administered a pain-killing drug. Fortunately, the leg was not a bad break. Hamish set a splint and noted there was no evidence of any infection. Barry Ferguson was first to notice that Hamish was not his usual jovial self. He had worked on their horse for some time without even saying a word. There were no bad jokes, and no inquiries about the Ferguson family. Usually a vet was like a family doctor in these parts, eager for all the news.

When Hamish had finished and was packing up his Land Rover, Mrs Ferguson suddenly emerged from the homestead calling out something about Ruby. The closer she came to the stockyards, the greater her excitement became.

'Ruby's on the ABC! Ruby's on the ABC!'

She sounded to her embarrassed husband as if she'd just heard radio for the first time. 'Settle down, love,' said Barry.

'What did you say, Betty?' asked Hamish, stopping and looking at her.

Betty Ferguson took a few deep breaths to help calm herself. 'I've just heard Ruby on the radio doin' a talkback show in Sydney.'

Everyone looked perplexed.

'Well . . .' she continued, 'get yourself over to our phone an' call her up.'

Hamish looked to Barry. He just shrugged, which was his way of saying 'Help yourself.'

Hamish put down his veterinary equipment and strode quickly back to the homestead, Betty following in his tracks.

'Sounds like she's havin' the time of her life!' she announced smiling, unaware of Hamish's anxiety. Betty steered him into the kitchen where every bench top was covered with freshly baked cakes and bis-cuits. These were her contribution to a fundraising for the local church. Three thousand dollars were needed to repair the old church hall, which had recently been scorched while the volunteer fire brigade were demonstrating how to deal with a small grass fire. The irony of the situation had not been lost on the district.

The kitchen radio was blaring over the screams of a baby in a highchair.

'Excuse the mess, love.' She went quickly to the

phone. 'Look, I've written the number down.' Presenting him with a slip of paper, she said, 'I'll leave ya to it.'

As Betty grabbed the screaming baby and left the room, Hamish picked up the phone in the kitchen and started dialling Sydney.

******

Ruby was a guest on the ABC's morning show. Ziggy knew that talkback radio had the influence she needed to help promote her new young writer. This show in particular had a huge audience at this hour of the morning.

Jack and Ziggy stood outside a glassed radio booth while Ruby answered inane questions from a man phoning in from Coogee. She was surprised that men were responding to the book so strongly – traditionally romance novels were the domain of women readers. By the time the third or fourth caller was through, Ruby was handling herself well. Her confidence was growing and, to make things easier, most of the questions were pretty similar.

First up, the announcer would ask the callers to identify themselves.

'Hi, Ruby,' the next caller announced, 'my name's Harmony and I think your book's wonderful.' Harmony had a nasal tone with a huge inflection at the end of all her sentences.

'Thanks, Harmony . . .' replied Ruby. But before she could elaborate Harmony was back on air.

'Yeah, Virginia and Brian are really brave characters. I reckon only a woman could write such beautiful, romantic stuff.'

Ruby glanced up to Jack who kept a poker face, then gave her a smile. 'I think you're right!' said Ruby, firmly.

'Well, I'm lookin' forward to your next book. What's it called?'

Ruby gave Jack another look. This time he didn't return a smile, but more of a glare. Ruby didn't feel threatened. '*Love in Africa*,' she answered, proudly.

Jack's response was contained. He had to be careful in front of Ziggy. A roll of the eyes was enough to show his disapproval. After all, he was Ruby's manager.

While the radio announcer accepted the next caller, Ruby noticed Jack lean over and whisper something into Ziggy's ear. As she watched, Ruby felt unaccountably annoyed. But the laugh Ziggy responded with pissed her off even more. What could be that funny? Jack never made anyone laugh – much less a stuck-up city girl who, it was obvious to Ruby, disliked him.

Ziggy touched Jack's arm and indicated that she must move off to other appointments. Jack smiled and gave her the 'thumbs up', assuring her that he could take care of everything.

'Ah, hello – it's me.' Ruby heard a man's voice in her headsets. 'Hello there – hello!' he continued.

Ruby prised her eyes from Jack, cupped the headsets in her hands and listened once more for the caller's voice.

'Hello, Ruby?'

'Sorry, who's this?' Ruby asked, aware she hadn't been listening properly.

'It's Hamish.'

'Hamish?' she repeated, breathlessly. 'Where are you? Jesus, I've been tryin' to phone you.'

Why Ruby lied at that point she couldn't explain. The fact was, Ziggy had her locked into a near impossible schedule. Also, they had only arrived yesterday. Yet Ruby was overcome with anxiety. There was a seemingly endless pause in their conversation.

'Are you well?' she asked, unable to think of what else to say.

'I'm at the Fergusons' place . . .'

'Oh, give my love to Betty,' Ruby burst in. 'How's she doin' with her cakes?'

'Betty heard you on the radio. Rube, have you been tryin' to call me?' he asked, hopefully.

'Oh, God, when I can, you know, we're really busy – signin' this an' signin' that!' A long pause. Ruby could tell that Hamish was not himself. Or was it just her guilt?

'Have we had any offers on the Boomerang?'

'No,' replied Hamish. 'Suzie was gonna buy it but Artie told me they can't afford it.' He then continued as if trying to get something off his chest: 'Rube . . .'

Already Ruby's mouth was drying up. 'Yeah?'

'I got something important to discuss with you.'

This was it, thought Ruby. Here was the moment of truth.

'Hamish, I can't really talk now!' she said, nervously tapping a pencil on the desk.

'Isn't this supposed to be talkback radio?' Hamish questioned, with an odd laugh. The announcer was looking at her with concern.

'Yeah . . .'

'Rube, I found some handwritten pages of your novel . . .'

Ruby immediately covered the microphone with her hand and looked over to Jack with a horrified face.

'Are you there?' persisted Hamish, over the air. Jack quickly stepped forward and rapped on the glass to get the producer's attention. Jack instructed him to cut the call.

'Thank you, sir. We have a lot of calls waiting here for Miss Vale . . .'

Before the announcer could add anything further, Ruby had ripped off her headset and was shooting out of the sound booth. Panic started in the studio as the producer scrambled for the station ID.

'Ruby!' yelled Jack, as he took off after her. He saw her running for the elevator and caught up just as the doors were opening and she was stepping inside. Jack leapt in after her as the doors closed.

'Rube . . .' he began, in an urgent whisper. Behind them was an elderly woman and a number of young executives.

'Shit, what have I done?' Ruby was wailing. 'He's found out. Oh, Jesus, there goes my marriage. I shoulda told him. Why'd I listen to you? Everything's a lie!'

Jack leant towards her. 'These aren't lies.'

'No?' she replied angrily, and span around to face him. 'Well, I looked it up: "Any untrue statement made deliberately" it said.'

Jack stifled a grin. 'You looked it up?'

'Yes!'

Everyone else in the elevator, apart from the elderly woman, was making feeble attempts to appear not to be listening. They were glancing at watches and studying paperwork.

'Jack, I just wanna settle down, have a life with Hamish an' fly my plane. If none of this happens, I'm blaming you.'

'Might as well, I guess,' replied Jack with a sigh.

Ruby quickly wiped her eye of a growing tear. 'I don't know what to believe any more.'

The elderly woman lent forward, prizing her stout body between them. 'Love!' she said firmly.

Ruby looked around at the woman with bewilderment.

'Anger and confusion, young lady. It seems to me that you're capable of creating the most beautiful, poetic work. However, it's obvious that you're at a complete loss regarding your own heart.'

Everyone was silent in astonishment for a moment, then Ruby declared indignantly, 'I am not!' As the doors opened the old woman just smiled knowingly, and stepped into the foyer of the building.

Ruby called out after her, 'My life's as good as my book. Better!' she added, suddenly inspired, but all she heard in reply were heavy footsteps as the woman disappeared across the tiled floor and out onto the street. 'Who does she think she is?' Ruby demanded, staring after her uselessly.

Ruby started pacing the foyer. Everything was closing in on her. How could she have let this situation get so out of hand? She knew the charade was succeeding but she wondered whether Jack was worth it. It was infuriating how much control he seemed to be able to exercise over her life. She felt it stifled her.

'Guess who's got a spot on the *James Allen Show*?' Ziggy's sudden appearance in the foyer was not a welcome sight. Ruby just dropped her head to her chest and aimed for the street. Ziggy looked to Jack for an explanation.

No longer the cocky manager, he hesitated before answering. 'Ruby's a little upset.'

'Well thanks, Jack. I thought it might have been the coffee,' scoffed Ziggy.

'I'll find her.' Jack took off without another word.

'Am I to assume we've finished upstairs?' Ziggy called out, as Jack went through the doors.

There was no answer as Jack was swallowed up by the crowd on the footpath.

11

Speeding vehicles were a rarity in Lucktown, but occasionally an emergency would send some local at high speed through the town. Heads would turn as the driver rushed down the main street, past the shops and the pub and the cafe, to the doctor's surgery. By the time the vehicle had reached the surgery more often than not the locals would have identified the driver and worked out, more or less, what had happened. Usually it was a baby arriving early, or a farm accident.

On this occasion heads turned as Hamish's Land Rover roared up the main street and all the locals immediately thought the vet had been injured – one of the cows must've kicked the poor bastard. However, to their surprise the Land Rover did not go to the surgery but skidded into a four-wheel drift outside the Boomerang Cafe. The next second Hamish got out, dressed in his best moleskin trousers and crisp checked shirt, clearly uninjured, and dragging Jack's old dog on a rope.

In all his long life Lance had never been treated badly. Everyone in the Boomerang stared as Hamish strode in with Lance on a short piece of rope behind him. He was pulling the old dog hard, and Lance was cowering. He knew Hamish was angry and he knew it was somehow connected with him and with the bunch of pages that Hamish was carrying in his other hand. Lance could still smell Jack on the paper.

Upon reaching the counter, Hamish slammed down the manuscript pages in clear view of Suzie. She was immediately suspicious. 'What's that, Hamish?' she asked.

'A bloody conspiracy!' he snapped. 'That's what it is. Why am I always the last bloke to know anything 'round here unless some bloody animal's got a disease?'

Suzie lit a cigarette and glanced down at the pages. She knew exactly what they were. 'You want coffee?' she asked casually, conscious the whole room was watching the scene.

'That's Jack's scrawl, isn't it?'

Suzie glanced down again, this time using the glasses that usually hung around her neck. 'Think so,' she replied, after peering at them for a bit while trying desperately to think what she could do.

'Bloody oath it's his writing. Our Mr Quiet-one, our Mr Loner. He's been movin' in on my Ruby. Sly bugger – I thought he was too shy for girls. I thought he was a mate.' Hamish turned to address the few truckers seated around him. 'I'll give you blokes one guess who writes schmaltzy romance novels.'

'Not you – that's for bloody sure,' was the reply he got from somewhere in the crowd. This was followed by a round of laughter from everywhere else.

Suzie walked from behind the counter holding a cup of coffee. 'Hamish . . .'

Hamish spun around. 'Don't you protect him, Suzie. Jack's been lyin' and he's in Sydney with my fiancée doin' – God knows what.'

'Maybe Ruby's just doin' him a favour,' she said.

'Ruby's always doin' him favours.'

This response brought another round of laughter from the truckers. Hamish was so embarrassed by the inadvertent sexual innuendo that he turned back to Suzie to hide his red face.

'I reckon you're jumpin' to conclusions, love,' Suzie said gently, as she offered up the coffee.

Hamish thought about this for a moment, then picked up the pages from the counter. 'I gotta go. Will you look after Lance?'

Suzie nodded. She knew this man wouldn't give up Ruby without a fight. Hamish handed her Lance's rope and left the Boomerang without saying another word.

******

It was late afternoon by the time Jack and Ruby headed back across the harbour to the city on a ferry. After leaving the radio station, Jack had caught up with Ruby and talked her into going with him to Bondi Beach for a sumptuous meal of fish and chips. Jack knew that if he didn't engage some damage-control at this point the whole operation could blow up in his face.

'God, I could just live on this!' said Ruby, as she reached over and stole a huge handful of Jack's chips. Out of loyalty to Suzie she'd never say it, but Ruby knew that the fish and chips Suzie served up at the Lucktown pub on Friday nights was nothing like this. Jack pushed her away, causing her to laugh and fall back onto the soft grass. She chewed off half a chip and threw the remainder high into the air to tempt a bird. Suddenly, out of nowhere, hundreds of squawking seagulls converged upon them. Throwing food was a mistake as these aggressive birds are always on the alert, eager to pounce upon unsuspecting visitors. 'Bloody hell,' screamed Ruby, as she dived at Jack for cover. 'I feel like Tippi Hedren.'

Jack laughed, as he held her protected under his jacket. His mind flashed back to an evening years ago when Artie had just purchased a video recorder – the first in Lucktown. Artie was always up on new technology. As Jack was on the road a lot he was delegated to bring in movies on video for viewing at the Lucktown pub. In most country towns, the choice was never good, but on this occasion, Jack had managed to find Hitchcock's *The Birds* tucked away in the 'classic movie' section of a television repair shop in Dubbo. Everyone in Lucktown saw *The Birds* that night.

Jack loved Bondi Beach. Fond childhood memories flooded back – warm days spent with his mum and dad as they surfed and ate fish and chips on the sand. That was when his father was filled with dreams, and intoxicated everyone with his enthusiasm. Jack always remembered his father telling him, when he was seven, that Bondi Beach was synonymous with good fish. He loved the sound of that word 'synonymous' even though he didn't know what it meant. It was then that Jack realised there was a special connection between him and words.

Jack turned away from the powerful, crashing surf that was sending a fine salt spray across the entire beach. He pointed to an ageing apartment building on the corner of Beach Road and Campbell Parade. His family had lived there for a time during one of his father's lucky phases. The block, originally built as a residence for wealthy single gentlemen, had once housed a ballroom. 'Not in my day,' he explained to Ruby, 'but back in the 'twenties and 'thirties – they were Bondi's glory days. My Dad told me about being brought here to visit when he was little, and seeing ladies sweep by in long dresses with stoles and men in dinner suits with bow ties.'

Ruby raised her eyebrows. On the footpaths, where stylish couples had once paraded their finery, kids on skateboards raced each other.

'A bit of a waste being down here now in your best clobber,' she said with a grin.

Her quip broke Jack's train of thought. He glanced down at her and smiled. She was right, of course.

'Don't stop now,' Ruby said, regretting interrupting his reminiscences. But Jack remained silent until they were back on the harbour heading towards the city. They had chosen the slow way home by catching the ferry from Rose Bay wharf. Even though it was late in the afternoon the warm sun was quite high in the summer sky and the harbour was a mass of sailboats. Sydney was famous for days like these.

As the ferry drew closer to Sydney Cove Ruby stopped noticing the spectacular views about her and started to worry about the consequences of what she'd done. When he'd caught up with her after her mad dash from the radio station, Jack had said, 'Rube – you're panicking. Calm down. Come on – you've been in some tight spots in your plane and you've kept your head.'

She had stood staring up at him, 'What'll I do?'

'What we'll do,' he'd said, 'is get out of this madness and go off to Bondi Beach – look at the waves and eat fish and chips.'

He'd been right, of course. Nothing was improved by getting hysterical, but now she thought about it, Ruby noticed how quickly she'd let herself be persuaded by Jack. Why hadn't she gone and tried to ring Hamish? He must have expected her to call. It struck her then that nothing was happening as expected. Up until now, her life with Hamish had been all laid out. But now she'd lied to him – well, she certainly hadn't told him the truth. And it was all her fault; Suzie had warned her. Yet she'd let herself get talked into Jack's charade and she knew that a part of her had been thrilled by the idea, had just enjoyed the sheer mischief of becoming such a superior know-it-all type as Ziggy Keane. After all, she'd said to herself, she wasn't doing anybody any harm. 'Except Hamish,' she now thought, and a sudden clear memory of that kiss with

Jack came back to her. 'Too much champagne,' she told herself quickly, but she felt guilty and her eyes filled with tears.

'Jesus, it all ends here,' she said. A couple of tears made their way down her cheek, but Jack didn't notice.

'Yep, isn't it great? Four thousand kilometres the way the crow flies.' He was turned away from her, admiring the panorama of the harbour.

'I'm talkin' about my life, you idiot,' she snapped. 'Come on, Jack, you're the romance writer. What am I gonna do?'

'Nothin',' he answered calmly, his eyes still on the Harbour. 'You an' Hamish will get married, move to Queensland, have lotsa kids and live happily ever after.'

He turned and looked at her and saw her tear-stained face. He smiled and gently rubbed a dash of mascara off her windswept cheek. 'Hey,' he continued jovially, 'I'm the best man, Rube. I'll straighten him out.'

Ruby wrapped her arms around him. The ferry blasted its whistle as it fast approached the wharf at Circular Quay.

'Jack, what if he says no?' she murmured into his jacket. 'What if he doesn't trust me any more?'

'You walk.'

Ruby pulled away. 'Walk?'

Jack held Ruby firmly at arm's length. 'Look, Rube, why do you want to marry Hamish?'

'Stupid question,' she answered quickly.

'There you go.' Jack let go of her and stood back as the ferry crew started their preparations for docking.

'He's sweet,' Ruby explained. 'And he's made something of his life and I think we're really good together . . .'

She stopped, remembering her first date with Hamish. He'd thought it was a disaster because they were on their way to a woolshed dance, but Hamish had had to stop and see a sick mare first. It had turned out that the mare was foaling prematurely and Hamish had had to stay. So she had drunk cup after cup of tea, which the grateful farmer kept supplying, and eaten a small truckload of biscuits so as not to offend his wife. While Hamish kept his eye on his patient they'd talked. About hundreds of things. She'd admired his kindness and his skill. After a couple of hours she'd realised that it was the first time since her father's death that she'd felt happy.

Jack saw that a gangplank was being slid directly towards Ruby. Preoccupied with her memories, she had not noticed the crew moving around. Jack grabbed her by the arm and pulled her back,

'Listen to me,' he said, 'Hamish is not gonna call it off.'

Ruby's face lit up with a smile of relief.

'Well, not straight away,' added Jack.

Ruby turned on him like a demon. With a thump upon his arm, she yelled, 'Jesus, I hate you!' The crowd of passengers that were now gathered around the gangplank smiled at one another and dismissed what they thought was a lovers' tiff.

******

Hamish's anger had subsided somewhat by the time he caught his plane to Sydney from Broken Hill. During the flight he sat beside a talkative salesman with unfortunate breath.

'Everything we make is plastic,' were the first words that this man uttered as he clipped fast his seatbelt and flipped up his sunshades to reveal thick glasses underneath. 'What do you do?'

'Corporate espionage,' replied Hamish, with a poker face. Hamish had already gulped two scotch whiskys while waiting for the plane, and he wasn't in the mood for company.

'Oh,' was the reply. The salesman settled back into his seat after deciding that it might not be advisable to ask further questions. Very soon he was asleep and Hamish was left to his own devices.

Corporate espionage? thought Hamish. What a brilliant way to stop a conversation. He twisted the top off his fourth mini-bottle of Johnnie Walker and devoured his pre-packed lunch.

Hamish peered out the plane's window. He could see evidence of the city they were approaching – the urban sprawl of red tiled roofs; all those little Aussie dreams fighting for square-footage in between the Blue Mountains and the Pacific Ocean. Hamish loathed the city. He could never come to terms with the mentality of city people. No one really cared about each other – the city was just a collection of soulless people fighting over who could earn the most money. For Hamish, Sydney meant six years of hell while he was at boarding school. All he could ever remember doing was praying to get back to his country town. Fortunately, he was bright at school and his academic prowess had won him a university scholarship. He'd spent a further five years in the city studying to be a vet. But he would have preferred to have been a farmer. Eighty thousand sheep on fifteen thousand acres. Yes, he said to himself as he finished his scotch, that would have suited him splendidly. Maybe it was still possible, if Ruby—. He stopped himself thinking about that and became aware that all that grog had made him hungry.

The man next to him was still asleep. Hamish eyed the man's pre-packed lunch, which sat untouched on his fold-down table. He carefully reached over and swapped his empty tray for the full one. Just as he successfully manoeuvred the tray into place, an air hostess swooped in and removed it.

'Thank you. Tables up, sir, we're landing.'

It was not a good day for Hamish. As he brought his seat into the upright position he saw Mr Plastic looking at him disdainfully. He knew he was drunk and his flushed face grew heavy and solemn as he started to wonder if Ruby would be beside him on the flight home.

******

Ziggy was furious as she paced the foyer of the busy Regent Hotel. Never before had an author gone missing for so long. It was obvious that Jack was not a manager – certainly not one to be relied upon. 'Babes in the woods,' she murmured to herself.

189

She had already made excuses to the mayor's office regarding Ruby's scheduled luncheon appointment. The book signing in Parramatta would also have to wait.

******

A strong wind whipped up street dust and papers around Jack and Ruby's feet as they crossed George Street and ran up into the forecourt of the hotel. Jack was anxious about being away for so long, but at least he'd convinced Ruby to play out the remainder of their charade. Tomorrow, he had promised, would be their last day.

'Where have you two *been*?' demanded Ziggy, as she strode across the marbled foyer.

'Uh, oh. In-coming!' murmured Jack.

'You're AWOL!' She turned to Ruby. 'We're spending a fortune getting your career launched, and you've missed two appointments!'

Jack tried to butt in, 'None of this is Ruby's fault . . .'

'And you call yourself a manager?' Ziggy snapped. She glanced to her watch. 'Come on, we've got a television show to do.'

Ziggy started pushing them back out towards the main entrance acting rather like a school teacher with a couple of misbehaving five-year-olds, Ruby thought.

She asked, 'What about my wedding plans, then?'

'They're coming along.'

'So is Christmas!' Ruby replied dryly.

At the door Ziggy quickly gestured to Eugene to bring his limo up to the front. Eugene threw out his cigarette and started the engine of his sleek, black machine.

******

Hamish was quick to leave the domestic terminal, jump in a cab and ask for the Regent Hotel. Sydney cabbies were a breed of their own. Depending on which rugby team you supported, and provided your destination wasn't over the Harbour Bridge at peak hour, they were quite possibly the most helpful folk in the world.

The alcohol hadn't worn off by the time he trudged into the foyer of the Regent Hotel.

'May I help you, sir?'

Hamish turned and looked over the reception counter at an attractive Asian girl staring at him with a professional smile.

'Yeah . . .'

'Are you checking in?' she asked.

'Ahh, no. I'm – a big surprise for Ruby Vale.'

'Yes, I'm sure you are, sir.' Although the girl's eyes shifted nervously the fixed smile was still very much in place.

'I'm her fiancé!' Hamish added impatiently.

The receptionist turned to engage the assistance of her senior manager, who stepped forward calmly to intervene.

'Ruby Vale is not here at present, sir,' he said politely. 'Perhaps you'd like to wait in the foyer until she returns?'

'Where is she?' demanded Hamish.

'Doing *Clive Rooney*, sir.'

Hamish stared at the male receptionist, regretting that he'd consumed so much scotch.

'And who's Clive Rooney?' he asked quietly, after taking a slow deep breath.

'A television show, sir.'

Hamish immediately turned on his heels and marched back out across the foyer of the hotel. Now, he thought, he could test a Sydney taxi driver.

12

The *Clive Rooney Show* was, in fact, the most popular late-night television show in Australia and Ziggy had been thrilled to get Ruby on it. Recorded late afternoon and beamed out across the continent every evening. The proven formula was simple: famous guests, a cool live band and a stable of comedy writers to keep the show one step ahead of the late-night pack. The guests this night were an eclectic bunch: a popular but ageing rock 'n' roll star who'd successfully started a stand-up comedy religious show on cable; a prominent sex-change surgeon; a surprise American action hero in Australia to promote his latest 'theme park' movie; and Ruby Vale, romance writer from the bush.

Ziggy led Ruby and Jack at a frantic pace down the corridor from the green room. 'Just be yourself,' she instructed Ruby, as she hurried them along. 'Relax. Don't try to impress anyone. Just be yourself.'

'Oh, Jesus!' exclaimed Ruby, who was feeling less like herself with every second.

'And remember, sweetie,' Ziggy went on, 'This is

television. You can't say "Jesus" – "fuck" – "shit" – "damn" – "bloody" or discuss sexual organs.'

'That's a lot to remember.' Ruby glanced at Jack with a grin.

Ralph suddenly joined the troupe from a side corridor. 'Sorry I'm late. How's it going? Everyone happy?'

Everything Ralph said made Ziggy's skin crawl. She thought it better not to answer him as she pushed on through the next swing door. Unfortunately, Ralph's position for the return swing left him vulnerable. The heavily sprung door flew back and hit him in the face, giving him an instant nosebleed.

'Ohhh, fuck!' yelled Ralph, as he threw his head back to stop the flow.

'Can't say "fuck" on TV, Ralph,' quipped Jack. Ralph was not amused.

Ruby moved forward pulling toilet tissue from her carry-bag. 'Here, Ralph – stuff this up your nose.' Ralph was grateful as he grasped at lengths of tissue. Jack thought he resembled a well-dressed walrus with tusks of tissue protruding from his nostrils.

'Sorry, Ralph,' Ziggy said. She'd felt obliged to stop but was nervously tapping her fingers on the back of her clipboard. Turning to Ruby, she said, 'We've got to go.' She took off without waiting for a response; they were still some distance from the production set and time was running out. Ruby clasped Jack's arm, shrinking back at the sound of applause coming from within the theatre. 'Sounds like thousands of people,' she said weakly.

'Piece of cake, Rube,' he whispered so confidently that he almost believed it himself.

'You're a terrific writer, you know?' Ruby said suddenly, in a nervous voice Jack had never heard before. He smiled at her as she continued to grip his arm. 'I just wanted to tell you that,' she went on in a loud whisper.

'Thanks,' he glanced ahead at the others but neither Ziggy nor Ralph seemed to have heard. Talking was Ruby's only relief from her nervousness.

'You know,' she said after a moment, 'I've been thinkin' . . .'

'Not now, Rube.' He knew what was coming.

'You gotta be able to say what you feel in your heart.' It was time, she felt, for everyone to start telling the truth.

'Can we talk about this later?' Jack interrupted firmly.

Ruby stopped walking. She couldn't believe he was treating her this way. 'Damn, you're a stubborn bastard!' She glared up at him.

'Rube . . .' Jack pleaded, 'we've almost finished.'

'What? My life as we know it?' she asked, raising her voice. 'Jack, I'm not goin' out there.'

Overhearing this, Ziggy stopped dead in her tracks and turned and walked back towards Ruby, wearing a gentle smile. Ruby stood with her arms folded. Having Jack own up to being the author of the book was going to be a healthy start to the sensible lives she was determined they were both going to lead in the future.

Ziggy maintained her smile. 'Sweetie, we all get nervous . . .'

'You don't seem to, you silly bitch,' snapped Ruby. 'And stop callin' me "sweetie" – I bloody hate it.'

Ziggy had to think quickly. Ruby's interview spot on the show was just minutes away. Luckily, Jack stepped forward.

'Rube – why don't we just calmly . . .'

Ruby spun around on Jack, 'It's all right for you, nothin' in your life has to change!'

Ziggy leaned against the wall as if she had all the time in the world, but she was feeling very nervous. 'What's happening here?'

Hamish's voice suddenly reverberated down the corridor. 'Ruby!'

Everyone turned to see him standing by a fire door held firmly by two huge security men. After being refused entry at the main entrance, Hamish had stumbled around to the alley at the side of the building just as a pizza delivery car pulled in and parked by the stage door. Hamish was kind enough to hold the door open for the delivery boy as he struggled with eight large pizza boxes. Hamish was inside.

'Who the hell is that?' Ziggy called out to the security men.

'Hamish!' cried Ruby. She turned to Ziggy. 'Let him go. That's my Hamish.'

Hamish was free. He shook himself and walked towards them straightening his clothes in the most dignified way possible under the circumstances.

'Hello, Ruby,' he said, very formally.

'What are you doin' here?' asked Ruby.

Hamish turned to Jack and looked at his friend with complete disdain, the sort of look that was supposed to send daggers into a man's heart. Jack realised immediately that Hamish was drunk, so he decided to hear what he had to say.

'I thought I'd come an' save you before my old mate, Jacko here, led you completely astray.'

'Hamish, I'm not leading anyone astray,' Jack said, calmly trying not to aggravate the situation. Hamish was bigger than he was, and thicker set. Jack had never known Hamish to be a brawler – but then again, he'd never seen him so upset before.

Hamish pointed his finger dangerously close to Jack's face.

'*You* are a liar!' he drawled, taking his time over every word.

Ziggy felt obliged to take charge and gestured to the security men. 'Please, will you remove this drunk?'

'He's my fiancé,' said Ruby firmly. Ziggy extended her hand to Hamish and smiled.

'Oh, *that* Hamish. Welcome to Sydney. We'll talk wedding plans straight after the show.'

Hamish smirked at her as they shook hands. 'Hope you're the kinda gal who likes changin' horses midstream,' he said.

'What are you talking about?' she asked.

Hamish knew he was going to enjoy this. He glanced around at each face to punctuate the moment. 'Ruby's not your romance writer, is she?' he announced, with deep satisfaction.

Ziggy looked to Ruby, then back at Hamish. Surely Hamish wasn't the writer? Oh, God forbid, no! Ziggy felt squeamish.

'It's him!' said Hamish, pointing to Jack.

'Oh, God.' It was difficult to determine from Ziggy's expression whether her exclamation was the result of horror or relief.

'My old mate here,' Hamish went on, 'has been livin' in some sorta self- . . . ummm . . .' he started to flounder, 'self-denouncement.'

'Denial?' inquired Jack, unable to stop himself.

'Yeah, that's it – denial,' Hamish nodded.

'Who's in bloody denial?' Jack had gone suddenly from being amused to being angry.

'You are, you dumb bugger!' yelled Hamish. 'You haven't got the balls to tell people, have you?'

'Tell 'em what?'

'That you write romance novels. Don't worry, I just did it for you.' Hamish then turned, looked at Ruby and started back down the corridor, yelling, 'Come on, Rube, let's leave 'em to it!'

No one moved. Ruby gave Jack a furtive glance.

'Hamish,' she called out loudly. Hamish turned, surprised to see that Ruby hadn't followed him.

'You coming?' he asked firmly.

Ruby looked back to Jack, desperate for him to intervene.

'What do I do, Jack?'

'Go with him.'

These three words tore at her heart.

Hamish sensed trouble. 'I'll be in that cafe across

the street for as long as it takes me to have a cuppa tea.' With that, he turned and walked away.

Ruby looked up to Jack again, her face full of confusion.

'He needs you, Rube,' said Jack softly.

'And what about you?'

'I think we're all wrapped up here, Rube,' he said. There was a slight pause. A hesitation so brief that afterwards Ruby was not sure she hadn't imagined it, then Jack turned to Ziggy and said, 'That right, Ziggy?' His tone was casual.

His words went through Ruby like a shock.

'You're bloody kiddin' yourself,' said Ruby.

Jack looked back at her. 'Is that right?'

'All that writin' is rubbish to you, isn't it? Well, you don't know it yet but most of it comes from there!' She pointed to his heart. This time it was Ruby's tone that was casual as she added, 'It's all right, Jack, you always thought it was on the other side, anyway.'

Without another look, she turned and left. Before Ziggy could realise what had happened Jack was leaving too. She had to chase off after him calling out, 'Jack, please – where are we going?'

Jack turned to face her. 'I dunno what *we* are doing – I'm going home.'

'Oh, this is great!' said Ralph, as he secured the wads of toilet paper hanging from his nose, and moved up to join them. 'Who's gonna buy a romantic novel written by a dumb trucker from the outback?'

Jack's fist was decisive. Ralph fell like a horse with

a bullet to the head and lay spread-eagled on the dirty carpet.

Ziggy was still gasping when a perky stage manager popped his head through a door. 'You guys are on straight after the break.' The stage manager then noticed Ralph out cold on the floor. 'Shit, what happened to him?'

'Fainted,' said Jack and Ziggy in unison.

'We've got a little problem,' smiled Ziggy anxiously at the stage manager. 'We'll have to re-schedule Ruby Vale.'

The stage manager sighed. 'The man won't be pleased,' he said with a pained expression, as he retreated back into his production hole.

By the time Ziggy looked back to Jack, he had disappeared out the exit door. It was rare that Ziggy was stuck for words; her personality wouldn't allow it. But for once she was utterly speechless. She had a successful book to promote, except now she had no author.

She felt nauseous as the thought of Errol's reaction flashed through her mind. Her promotion into the board of directors was looking marginal, at best. At worst, she could lose her job. Wouldn't Ralph love that? 'Oh, fuck it!' she exclaimed, as she took one look at her colleague who was coming to with toilet paper hanging from his nose.

******

The afternoon was ushered in by a cooling southerly wind, or 'southerly buster' as it was more fondly referred to by locals. This wonder of nature literally turned the climate around in an instant. What usually followed was rain. Heavy, subtropical rain. Lightning would crease the darkening sky as a deluge filled the footpath gutters and sent sheets of water across the streets so rapidly that pedestrians would be trapped before they could seek the cover of shop awnings and bus shelters. Still, the thunderstorms provided relief from the humidity of Sydney's sweltering summer days.

Ruby stood in the pouring rain outside the television studio for what seemed like an eternity. She was watching Hamish sip tea in the small, crowded cafe across the street. Soaked to the skin with tears and rain cascading down her cheeks, Ruby closed her eyes and lifted her face to the heavens. The Sydney sky seemed to echo her grief. But the heavy rain disguised her tears. Ruby knew that if she crossed the street her life with Hamish would be restored. From that moment on, there would be no turning back.

Inside the cafe no one noticed the soaked, waif-like figure across the street. Hamish glanced at his watch and signalled an elderly waitress to order another pot of tea.

'Why won't yer have some cake?' she asked, with a thick drawl. 'I make it meself.'

Hamish felt obliged. 'That'd be nice,' he said, with a sad smile. He was sobering up now and his normal good manners had returned.

The old woman waddled off. Hamish glanced aimlessly around the cafe. It seemed to him that most people were there because of the rain. He hoped that

Ruby would burst through the door at any moment and give him one of her huge, affectionate hugs. Then they could leave together on an evening flight back to Broken Hill. He felt sober but very confused about what to do next. Perhaps there was nothing more he could do but pray.

Ruby gave herself a moment longer while the rain withdrew and the skies started to clear above her. The last gasp of afternoon sun burst through the receding rain clouds and threw a shaft of brilliant light upon the crest of the Sydney Harbour Bridge. The image caught Ruby's eye. It was quite magical and reminded her of the photograph that Jack kept in his rig, the one his father had given him.

'Don't you ever forget me, Jack Willis,' she said out loud.

She pulled back her wet hair, wiped her face with her sleeve and walked across the street towards the cafe.

Hamish was so relieved when she entered that he jumped up, bumping the table with his huge, clumsy frame and spilling tea everywhere.

'Christ love, what are ya doin'?' yelled the elderly woman, making her way heavily back towards him with a dishcloth. Hamish heard none of this as he watched Ruby come through the cafe towards him.

'Make that two pots of tea, please,' said Hamish, grinning at the elderly woman as she started to swab at the table.

'You are gonna drink it?' she checked, before committing herself to the return trip to the counter. He nodded, still grinning.

Ruby smiled and walked into Hamish's arms.

'Did I act like a mug in there, Rube?' he asked quietly.

'Possibly.'

They sat down. Hamish attempted to clean up the mess on the table. 'I'm sorry.'

'I reckon we both did, Hamish,' Ruby said, taking his hand to stop him fidgeting.

'What did Jack say?' asked Hamish, as a fresh pot of tea arrived.

'Wished us luck.'

There was no comment from Hamish other than a slight raising of an eyebrow. He suddenly remembered he had brought something for her. He drove his hand into the pocket of his sports jacket and withdrew Ruby's walkman.

'Bet you were missing it, eh?' he asked with a grin. Ruby took the walkman from him and thought about his question for some time. To her surprise she realised she hadn't missed it at all.

'I didn't bring any music,' added Hamish, 'other than what's in it.'

Ruby opened the cassette player. The REM tape was the last piece of music she was listening to. It was from that night in the cafe when Jack had come in while she was dancing on her own.

13

Ziggy found Jack in a bus shelter. After he'd gone she'd hurried down the many corridors to the front of the building expecting him to show up there where he could hail a cab. When he didn't appear, she took out her mobile and started phoning – first, the hotel; then Eugene, the limo driver; then Ella on the desperate off-chance she'd heard something. But there were no reported sightings of Mr Jack Willis, lately revealed to be the true author of Zane Publishing's current bestseller, *Bird in the Hand*.

She was standing there, holding the mobile and trying to decide what to do, when she saw him. Two buses had pulled away from the bus stop across the street, emptying the shelter of its evening crowd of commuters, but leaving one person sitting there alone.

Ziggy closed her mobile phone, opened her briefcase, inserted the phone neatly in its assigned space and closed the briefcase with a decisive snap. Hope was surging up inside her. She wouldn't have said she was a public transport type of person but she understood the basic principles: you waited at bus stops, buses came along, you got on. People who waited at bus stops but didn't get on a bus, either didn't know what they were doing, or didn't know where they were going. Ziggy suspected that both these things were true of Jack Willis.

He said nothing when she sat down beside him, gave no sign of being aware she was there. This didn't surprise her. What she was really worried about was that he would get up and leave. But he didn't move. Ziggy's confidence grew. Half an hour ago in the studio corridor, she reckoned her chances of surviving this sudden career setback were nil. Now it was occurring to her that she couldn't be held responsible for what had happened. Who could have guessed that Ruby Vale, hot new romance writer from the outback, would turn out to be a thirty-four-year-old truck driver? In fact, it was a great story. It would boost sales. Ziggy already knew the publicity spin she could put on Jack's predicament. In her imagination she could see television talkshow hosts in half a dozen countries announcing to their viewers: 'How would you feel if you had a big talent and a big dream but you lived in a community where you knew everyone would laugh at you if you told them about your dream? Well, our next guest tonight, from the Australian outback, is Jack Willis, a truck driver who . . .'

'So,' said Ziggy, 'are you a writer who drives a truck, or a truck driver who writes?'

'Take your pick.' He spoke flatly, staring ahead. Ziggy surveyed him. He really was good-looking, she thought. He needed a decent hair cut and a bit of sprucing up, but all the basics were there – she and Ella could handle the packaging.

'Either works for me,' she said calmly. He looked at her. She continued, 'They'll go for you, Jack; ten per cent of romance novels are written by men.'

'Yeah – but I'd be the only one stupid enough to put his name on the book.'

You're a writer who drives a truck, thought Ziggy, looking at him – correction: *drove* a truck. I know about writers. Writers are my business.

'Come on,' Ziggy stood up, 'I live around here. Let's have a drink, Mr Willis. You won't have to say a word.'

Jack was startled but found himself admiring her as she stood there in front of him with her long legs and her smart designer suit and her fashionably casual hair. Half an hour ago she'd been totally undone and near hysterical. He didn't know that much about Ziggy's professional life but he could see that what had happened to her in the space of those five min-utes – from discovering the truth about her new hot author to seeing her colleague knocked unconscious – would be enough to unnerve most people. Yet here she was looking completely gorgeous and fully recov-ered and – it was now becoming clear to him – utterly determined to launch his career as a writer.

'You don't waste any time, do you?' he said, half teasing, half impressed.

Ziggy gave a wry chuckle, 'Just a drink – I never cook.'

As they walked in silence through the lower part of the city and towards The Rocks, Jack thought, of course, Ziggy would live somewhere like this – in one of the big terrace houses that still rose in tiers above the hilly streets in this old section of Sydney. The area was unusual, elegant, historic – everything that would appeal to Ziggy.

However, to his surprise they didn't go into the residential area of the Rocks but followed around the harbour until they reached a big pier warehouse. She waved her hand at it proudly: 'Home,' she said. 'Well, I have an apartment in there.' He stared at it, astonished.

'The location's fantastic,' he said, to allow himself time to recover. She was looking at him expectantly. The location *was* fantastic – Ziggy's unexpected home was set out upon the water facing the western side of the bridge. The view was unimpeded right across to the northern harbour shore. The lights of North Sydney and Luna Park were reflected in the darkening water like stars in a black liquid mirror.

The warehouse, constructed before the turn of the century, was all timber. Beautifully honed hardwoods that had endured saltwater and the ravages of time. Now, no longer used for shipping and storing, these ash-coloured monuments had been converted into apartments, theatres and restaurants.

'What do you think?' asked Ziggy excitedly, as he gazed in silence.

'A big wooden shed?'

'Warehouse, Jack. A warehouse!' She grinned, 'Big enough to park your rig in.'

******

'The lift's broken.' Ziggy's voice echoed through the building as she called down from the top landing on the steel fire escape. Jack trudged up the remaining stairs to join her at an oversized door that led into her apartment. Ziggy fed a key into the lock and put her shoulder to the door.

'Help me push.'

Another shove from Jack and the door opened to reveal a huge living space. Large windows overlooked the wharves. Everything was oversized and industrial, with exposed air-ducts and beams. Areas had been divided off with artwork and screens to give some semblance of habitation. A lonely red leather couch and table were dwarfed by the huge space. Jack wandered inside, bewildered by it all. He couldn't believe that someone so precise and proper could live somewhere so . . .

'Liberating, huh?' said Ziggy, as she kicked off her heels, removed her jacket and walked a good thirty metres across to the fridge.

'It's different!' called out Jack.

'I've still got some stuff to get.'

Jack peered up into the rafters. He'd only ever seen buildings like these used for wool storage. The timber work was awesome. Huge hand-cut beams had been sawn from trees that must have stood one hundred feet tall.

Ziggy slammed closed the fridge with her foot and, holding two glasses of wine, motioned for Jack to sit on her leather couch.

'What happened to coffee?' he asked.

'I ran out,' said Ziggy, passing him a glass and climbing into the opposite corner of the couch. 'Cheers!' Ziggy took a sip then asked, 'That photo you have of the Harbour Bridge in your truck.'

'What about it?'

'You said your dad took it?'

Jack thought for a minute. 'Yeah, he was a journalist, novelist, miner, gambler – alcoholic.'

'In that order?' asked Ziggy.

'Yes, unfortunately.'

Ziggy paused, then raised her glass. 'Well, I'm going to make him proud of you.'

The moment they clinked glasses she knew that Jack was weakening. It was only a matter of time before she had him accepting his own fate. Jack was a fine writer and promoting him was going to be a cinch.

'My mother eventually called him a loser,' he said, as he tried to make himself more comfortable on Ziggy's stiff leather couch.

'Maybe he was just . . .' Ziggy tossed words around in her mind, '. . . unlucky?' She rose and fetched more wine from the fridge, and refilled their glasses.

'You sure need a lot of luck out there, huh?' she said to get him talking again.

'My mum used to say luck was only for people who didn't believe in God.'

Ziggy chuckled.

Jack smiled. 'Needless to say, the old bugger didn't!'

Their laughter broke the melancholy.

'What do you need to know about me?' asked Ziggy brightly.

'Not much more!'

She laughed – drifting off into a genuine giggle, helped by the alcohol. Jack had never seen her so relaxed.

'Ziggy's not my real name, you know,' she went on, 'I was born "Catherine". I hated it with a passion.'

'I like it.'

'You do?'

'Yeah, Catherine Keane. Has a ring to it.'

'Really?' Ziggy stared at him for a moment as they sipped their wine. Jack was still quite distracted by the extraordinary interior of the warehouse. There were three huge modern paintings hanging by wires from the rafters that created a division between the bedroom and the living space. One of these was by Aboriginal artist, Dini Campbell.

'I was born in London, which you've already guessed. Lived with my father until I was thirteen, was sent to an appallingly strict school, completed a degree at university, joined Zane Publishing, reinvented myself completely and . . . bingo!'

'Self-made woman,' Jack said, without taking his eyes off the Aboriginal painting.

'Something like that.'

'You've got a Dini Campbell,' said Jack, and turned back to her.

'Yes, you know of him?' she smiled, rather impressed by his display of culture.

'It's upside down.'

'No it's not!' Ziggy looked at the painting. There was the faintest tone of doubt in her voice. 'What makes you think that?'

'I see his work all the time.'

Ziggy now started to seriously doubt herself, which was not a familiar feeling for her. What if he was right? A painting hung upside down. God forbid!

'The art dealer man said the squiggly bits go to the top.' Ziggy regretted saying it that way, but couldn't think of any other.

Jack shook his head. 'He's wrong.'

Jack allowed Ziggy's embarrassment to linger a moment before he put her out of her misery. 'Well, he wasn't completely wrong,' he added with a grin.

'What do you mean?'

'These are painted flat on the ground. The artist walks around and works from each side. They used to be on bark, now it's mostly canvas.'

Ziggy tilted her head as she studied the painting.

'There's no real top or bottom. So, I reckon, for you, it's the right way up.'

Ziggy couldn't tell whether Jack was still pulling her leg. 'Okay, Mr Know-all, let's talk about you. Mr Writer Willis.'

Jack looked at her with a smile. He had been waiting for this.

'Come on,' Ziggy persisted. 'We've been on the road together – we've seen blood.'

Jack suddenly remembered that he had brought something in his pocket to give her. Ziggy watched him curiously as he searched.

'What are you doing?' she asked.

Jack grinned as his hand fell upon a Polaroid photo. He pulled it out and straightened the dog-eared corners before presenting it to her. Ziggy was stunned. The photograph was of the little emu they had hit in the rig that day while travelling to Broken Hill.

'He's not dead?' Ziggy asked with a squeak in her voice.

'Nope – the little bloke's up and about.'

Ziggy sighed with relief and touched the photo with her fingers. She could see that the bird was bandaged but standing.

'Oh, God.'

'You saved a life,' said Jack.

This was all too much for Ziggy. She suddenly flung herself forward and gave Jack a huge hug. She then flopped back into the couch and held the photo tight to her chest.

14

It was unlike Ziggy to be late for work. In fact, her assistant, Ella, could not recall a single day when Ziggy was not in her office and on the phone before any of her colleagues had arrived.

Thursday morning was important. Errol always demanded a meeting in the boardroom before all other work resumed. This was his way of 'keeping in touch with his people'. Everyone knew that Errol wasn't interested in problems, only results.

Errol strode along the corridor with two other executives and an assistant. Ralph and Ella trailed behind.

'Where on earth is Ziggy?' Errol called out. He was irritated that his team wasn't already assembled.

'Travelling, sir,' Ella replied tactfully. 'Something about her car.'

'Haven't we just given her a new one?' he asked.

'Yes, a Honda,' said Ralph, with a wry smile. 'Very reliable.'

Ella flashed him a hostile look but said in a pleasant tone, 'It was a tyre problem.'

Ella was telling the truth about Ziggy's tyre. It was

as flat as a pancake. Vandalism was rife in Sydney, especially around The Rocks. Drunken youths would take their fill at the pubs, then proceed west around the harbour's edge destroying phone boxes and scratching coins along the paintwork of expensive cars.

Jack had stayed late. Into the very small hours they talked about their childhoods, parents, careers, animals, food and music. The more they drank, the more they revealed. For Ziggy to let herself be so open about her feelings could only mean she was in the company of someone quite exceptional. She was determined to make it her quest to get the 'country' out of Jack and, get 'Jack' out of the country. Either way, she felt, this task was not going to be difficult. In the past, she had dealt with a variety of authors – some had been awe-inspiring, while others were tiresome. Now she'd decided that Jack was going to be her paperback hero.

'Here I am. Sorry I'm late,' Ziggy called out brightly, as she raced up the corridor to catch up to Ella and Ralph. 'No doubt Ella has filled you all in,' she added.

'I have,' said Ella.

'You sound particularly perky this morning, Ziggy,' commented Errol, not glancing around at her as he marched down the corridor rapidly ahead of his troops.

'You betcha!' Ziggy replied, administering eye drops into her eyes, but not losing pace as she did so.

Ralph threw a wry look to Ella. 'Christ, she even talks like him now.'

Errol reached the door of the boardroom and opened it to allow his team to enter. He observed Ralph's black eye.

'What on earth happened to you?' he asked in a droll monotone.

'Squash ball.'

'Excuse me, Errol.' Ziggy pushed forward. 'I must have a pee before we do all this.'

'Ziggy . . .'

She stopped. 'Yes?' Ziggy knew from Errol's expression that he was about to be condescending.

Sure enough, he smiled. 'That was more information than I needed to know.'

'Oh, thank you, Errol,' she responded, unfazed. With that, she moved away pulling Ella by the sleeve in the direction of the women's toilet. Errol rolled his eyes and wondered why it always required two females for one to go to the toilet.

Ziggy dragged Ella excitedly into the rest room and closed the door.

'Let me guess. You've had sex with him,' said Ella, in her usual laconic manner.

'No, no . . .'

'You do remember how it goes?' But Ziggy was too excited to react to her comment.

'Oh, you've no idea, Ella. We talked for hours about our lives and books and animals . . .'

'Really?' Ella was droll. She glanced at her watch.

'Oh, but there's work to be done,' Ziggy was about to burst. 'We've got to get clothes on this man's back.'

'We?'

Nothing was going to halt Ziggy's excitement. 'And – guess what?'

Ella looked at her fearing the worse.

'We have a new author.'

Ella smiled at the uncharacteristic squeak in Ziggy's voice. 'Ziggy,' warned Ella with a firmness, 'we won't have anything unless we get to the boardroom.'

Ziggy was not listening. 'We – that is, you and me – are going upstairs into directorship! The view's the same,' said Ella.

Ella had no intention of bursting Ziggy's bubble, but she was genuinely concerned about Errol and his ritual Thursday morning meeting. She grabbed Ziggy by the arm and dragged her towards the door. 'Please!'

'Ella, believe me, Jack Willis will look perfect by the time I'm finished.'

15

Back in Lucktown Ruby and Hamish settled back into their life as it was before Ziggy's arrival, but with one difference. Ruby's participation in Jack's charade had made Hamish realise that she really did want to have a proper wedding and, on the plane back from Sydney, he'd told her that he thought they should have a wedding reception and as many of the trimmings as they could afford. However, he did not tell her how he intended to pay for it. A chat with the auctioneer at Mr Reece's sale had put him in touch with one George West. George West collected old aeroplanes. So their marriage plans were in full swing. Cost was definitely an issue, of course, but they had managed to talk the Flying Doctor Service into allowing them to have their reception in their new hangar outside Broken Hill. Hamish would have much preferred the Lions' Club Hall or the RSL, but if celebrating in a hangar meant that much to Ruby, why fight it?

Ruby and Suzie had chosen a lace and white chiffon fabric for the wedding dress. Ruby wanted a simple and elegant design. She thought that wouldn't be easy to find. Judging by the displays in most bridal shops in the region, elaborate gowns were very much in vogue.

Ruby was flying again. She was no sooner home than she was scheduled to crop-dust a number of properties farther east. There had been rain, and all along the Darling River crops were flourishing. Her first job was to dump fertiliser on a huge Japanese cotton farm some twenty kilometres out of Bourke. The next job was crop-dusting irrigated fields about one hundred kilometres away, not far from the township of Menindee situated on the Darling River. Ruby was thrilled to be back in the cockpit of her Stearman. She didn't care where she had to fly, just as long as she was airborne.

******

Hamish, Lance and George West, a middle-aged, dumpy man, pulled up in the Land Rover at the Lucktown airstrip. It was rather late in the day and storm clouds were building from the north-west. A thunder roll caused Hamish to gaze up and ponder the severity of the coming storm.

'Looks like hail,' said George, peering up through thick horn-rimmed glasses.

'Yeah,' murmured Hamish. He was worried about Ruby still flying over Menindee. Lance whimpered softly, his nose pressed against the window in the hope of being released from the Land Rover for a run.

'Stay there, you mongrel,' said Hamish, in a low,

almost threatening voice. There was no love lost between these two. Hamish had only agreed to take the dog back from Suzie at Ruby's request.

George West was from Brisbane. Hamish had called him out of the blue about the sale of the biplane. George thought that if this aircraft was as good as Hamish described it, it was an opportunity too good for him to miss. Hamish lead the way into the hanger where Mack was soaking carburettor parts in an old biscuit tin full of petrol.

'G'day Mack. Has Ruby called in?' he shouted from the door.

'Yeah, twenty minutes ago,' replied Mack. 'I reckon she's got about two more runs.'

'I don't like the look of the sky.'

'Ah, that'll be a while off,' Mack said casually.

Hamish turned back to George, who was already poking through a bin of old aircraft spare parts. 'Mack, this is George West. He's come to take a look at the biplane.'

George turned and smiled at Mack through his thick glasses. 'Hello,' he said, and walked towards him offering his small podgy hand.

'I didn't know Ruby was selling,' said Mack, as they shook hands.

George held his grin. 'Well, I'm buyin'!'

Mack turned to Hamish for an explanation. Hamish was quick to say, 'George is just gonna give us a price, you know, see if it's worth our while.' Hamish felt uncomfortable as he picked up the microphone on the two-way transmitter.

'Hamish, you did say the Stearman was for sale?'
George West spoke clearly but Hamish pretended not
to hear him, as he listened to voices on the receiver
and fiddled with the frequency knob.

'So – George, are you a flyer?' interrupted Mack, as
he removed another engine part from the biscuit tin.

'Not really. Just a collector.'

'So you're just gonna stick Ruby's ship in some
shed an' charge people to look at her, eh?'

'Yeah, it's history,' smiled George, and pushed his
glasses higher up onto his nose in a frequent habit
that annoyed everyone and was soon getting on
Mack's nerves.

'History, eh? Aren't we all?' asked Mack.

Meanwhile, on the two-way receiver, Hamish was
making contact with Ruby.

'Ruby, is that you? Do you read? Over.'

Ruby's voice filtered back to him across the air-
waves. 'Yeah. How's my big Celt? Over.'

Hamish smiled to himself. 'Rube, I'd get back here
soon if I were you. Those storm clouds look like they
could be hail. Over.'

Ruby's voice came back to him. 'Piece o' cake,
Hamish. I'll be home as quick as I can. Hey . . .'

'What? Over.'

'What are we gonna do for fun tonight, big boy?
Over.'

As George let out a dirty little chuckle, Mack
dropped an engine part back into the petrol tin. The
splash caught George on the sleeve, leaving a large
oily mark. 'Bloody hell!' he gasped.

'Sorry, George,' said Mack, trying to muster a little sincerity.

Hamish was back on the microphone before Ruby could say any more. 'Let's not discuss it now, Rube. We've got company. Over.'

Ruby laughed. 'Sorry. Okay, see you soon. Over.'

Mack wiped the oily petrol off his hands and turned to George. 'What have you got in your museum then?' he asked sarcastically. George removed his thick glasses, oblivious to Mack's antipathy, and began to polish them on his shirt tail.

'Let's see,' he thought. 'I gotta De Havilland Fox Moth; coupla Sopwith Camels – one I'm rebuilding; a Swordfish; a Curtis Jenny – only seven of those left in the world,' he grinned.

'Eight!'

'You know of another one?'

Mack thought better of it. He couldn't have this little man grounding every vintage aeroplane. 'Nah, maybe I'm wrong.'

George thought more about his collection. 'A Stearman Junior and this one of Hamish's is a converted trainer, isn't it?'

Mack nodded. 'Yeah, Model 75. But it's not Hamish's – it's Ruby's.'

'Oh!' George shrugged.

'Her dad converted it to a duster about twenty-odd years ago.'

George grinned with anticipation. 'I'll soon rip those phosphate bins out,' he said, pushing his glasses back up his nose.

Hamish, meanwhile, made himself busy by sorting through Ruby's personal effects on the desk. The conversation was making him uncomfortable. 'Well, George, let's get outside and wait,' he said, and strode off towards the door.

George felt his coat pockets for his wallet. 'I'll give you a business card, Mack.' Finding his scuffed brown wallet in an inside pocket he pulled out a card, 'Never know, you just might see another plane out here that takes my fancy.' He winked. 'Could be something in it for you.'

Mack took the card. 'You know what, George? I could be your eyes 'n' ears.'

George smiled, pushed up his glasses and headed for the door. Mack flicked the business card straight into the waste bin, half hoping George West would look round for some reason and see him doing so.

******

There was a definite chill in the air as Ruby banked and flew one more superphosphate run across the hundred-acre field. Normally, over a freshly ploughed field, the rising warm air gave her biplane that extra lift after the load was released, but today was different. The cold air of a storm front was moving in fast. The darkening sky now looked more threatening as lightning streaked across the horizon.

The single-engine Stearman struggled under the weight of a full load of superphosphate. Ruby pulled hard on the bin-release and felt the plane lighten as she laid a cloud of pellets upon the field below. This was the time Ruby loved best. Now free of the extra weight, she could feel the plane respond eagerly to her demands. She opened up the throttle of the 450-horsepower engine and raced for home just ahead of the storm.

Spread out below her the beautiful Menindee Lakes covered the harsh earth like a stepping-stone of glistening mirrors, each lake reflecting the last of the afternoon sun. She could see pleasure crafts still sailing on the water below. A goods train on the Orange to Broken Hill railway line had pulled into the town of Menindee. From the air, the train and the houses below looked like toys.

A huge flock of sulphur-crested cockatoos lifted from a gum tree and flew parallel below the biplane. A smile was permanently etched on Ruby's face as she banked to the left, pulled slightly back on the stick and headed, full-throttle, due west towards the Lucktown airstrip.

With the help of a strong tailwind, Ruby was heard approaching the strip about forty minutes later. Hamish was relieved when he heard the familiar drone of the powerful Pratt & Whitney engine, relieved even more than he cared to admit. Hamish, in fact, was desperate for the day when Ruby would give away all this flying about in an antique biplane.

George squinted up into the sky as he watched Ruby bank once more, and prepared for her downwind approach. 'She sure looks good from here, Hamish.'

Hamish grunted and moved further away from the hangar for a clear view of Ruby's landing. Lance began to bark furiously in the Land Rover, while he pawed at the driver's door window.

'Lance – settle down,' roared Hamish. 'Bloody dog!' he murmured. Lance quietened but still went on pawing the window. It opened on a slide and there was a crack.

From up above, Ruby could see the strip clearly – the hangar and Hamish and some other man standing not far from the Land Rover. This welcome brought a different expression to her face. What an opportunity to buzz the strip and impress the onlookers! Ruby quickly glanced at the space around her, hit the throttle and dive-bombed Hamish and George. The engine screamed over their heads like a fighter-plane. The pass was so low that Hamish and George threw themselves to the ground. Mack raced to the door of the hangar and peered out with a grin from ear to ear. Lance didn't bark – he had his nose through the crack now and he knew to be quiet.

'You show 'em, Rube,' Mack yelled, and disappeared back into the hangar.

Hamish stood up, cursed and dusted off his moleskin trousers.

'Sorry about that, George,' he said, giving him a pull to his feet.

George was visibly shaken as he tried to re-adjust his glasses. He glanced back up into the air in search of the attacking biplane. 'Does she always do that?' he asked nervously. 'I thought she was gonna hit me.'

Ruby made her steady approach towards the strip – almost a glide as her engine powered back sounding as if it were only just turning over.

Lance, meanwhile, had managed to slide the window of the Land Rover fully open. He leapt out and bounded off in the direction of the biplane.

'Lance . . .' screamed Hamish. 'Come back here!'

Lance had had enough of Hamish. All he wanted to do was get to Ruby. He had flown in the plane once. He didn't recall much of the trip but remembered the excitement and pride Jack had had for him when he landed still securely strapped into the seat in front of Ruby.

Hamish watched in horror. He couldn't do anything to stop Jack's old dog from running straight for the biplane. It wasn't until Ruby's undercarriage was about to touch the ground that she caught sight of Lance directly on the landing strip in front of her. Ruby fought desperately to abort her landing position. Her Stearman was now well below its required air speed to lift back up into the air.

Lance was dangerously close. Fortunately, he was too low for the prop but the undercarriage wheels could snap his back like a dry stick. Ruby knew her only hope was to hit the brakes and rudders hard and attempt to slide the aircraft off to one side. Ground speed was still too high for such a manoeuvre but she attempted it anyway. The biplane pitched against the wind and veered off the strip towards a drainage channel.

'What's she doin'?' gasped George.

Hamish was speechless. All he could do was watch.

Ruby again fought for control of her aircraft. She knew Lance had safely run under the wing-tip so now she had only herself to think about.

The drainage channel was cut deep at the edge of the strip to halt the flow of water in the rainy season. It was full of long grass, making it look shallower than it was.

The biplane's left wheel first caught deep in the trench and spun the aircraft like a top. The right wing then fell under with the momentum, swung around and dug violently into the bank. This literally pivoted the biplane into the air, rolled it over and threw it onto its back.

'Oh, bugger me!' Hamish yelled, as he charged off across the airstrip.

'Ruby . . .' he screamed. He could see no movement in the upturned cockpit. 'Oh, bloody hell!'

Hamish was breathless when he arrived at the tail of the biplane. He grabbed it and with all his strength tried to lift the fuselage, but to no avail. He dived on the ground underneath the cockpit.

'Ruby, Ruby . . .' Hamish was desperate. He clawed at the hard earth to make a space to crawl in on his belly.

'Ruby!'

'What?' Ruby yelled out angrily.

Hamish's relief was instant. He peered up into the cockpit. 'You okay?'

Ruby hung upside-down in her seat harness. 'Shit!' she cursed.

'Thank God, you're all right.'

Fortunately, due to her small frame, she was able to duck down below the top of the cockpit as the biplane flipped onto its back.

'I think I've broken my bloody leg,' she moaned.

George and Mack arrived at the wreckage just as Hamish stood up and proceeded to kick violently at the fabric of the plane. He was attempting to make a hole big enough to drag Ruby out the side.

'What are you doin'?' screamed Ruby from under the biplane.

'Leave it, Hamish,' said Mack. 'You'll never get to the straps from there. Let's lift the bugger.'

All three men took hold under the tail of the aircraft and with one mighty lift, hoisted it five feet into the air. Then, while Mack and George held the tail in position, Hamish scrambled under and released Ruby. She fell with a thud when her harness was released.

'Jesus, now you've broken my back,' she said.

As she was dragged well clear of the biplane Ruby saw the extensive damage for the first time. 'Oh, Hamish, look at my plane.'

'What's left of it,' sighed George, pulling at the damaged fuselage.

'Who are you?' asked Ruby.

'Never mind him, Rube,' Hamish intervened quickly. 'George, you go an' phone the Flyin' Doctor. Mack an' I'll carry her over to the hangar.'

'Righto.' George pushed up his glasses and jogged back across the field.

Mack bent down beside Ruby and smiled. 'That was a nice little piece of evasive action, Pilot Vale.'

'Oh, Mack – reckon you can fix it?' Her eyes were filling with tears at the sight of her Stearman.

'No bloody way,' groaned Hamish. 'Come on, Mack, let's carry her across.'

'I reckon we shouldn't move her, Hamish.'

Hamish bent down closer. 'How's the back, Rube?'

Tears started to pour from Ruby's eyes.

'Yeah, maybe you're right, Mack.'

Lance moved ever so slowly up to Ruby, crouched down beside her on the ground and licked her hand. Hamish grabbed the old dog firmly by the collar and pulled him away. He then took off his jacket and placed it under Ruby's head.

'Comfy, Rube?'

Ruby nodded. Her eyes were fixed on Mack who was checking massive alignment damage to the biplane.

'Think you'll need a new prop, Rube,' he called out, poker-faced.

A smile appeared through the tears on Ruby's face.

16

'Don't think about it, Skip,' Boult's rear gunner had said two nights ago over the aircraft intercom, 'Just get in there and open your mouth – something's bound to come out.' There was laughter in the rear gunner's voice as he issued his instructions. A minute later, he was dead, strafed by a German night-fighter.

'Well, at least he died fast,' said Jack to himself. He hadn't liked killing off the rear gunner who was witty and light-hearted and very confident with women – the best dancer on the base – but he'd known from the start that the rear gunner was going to die. Rear gunners had the highest mortality rates among bomber crews.

Now Pilot Officer Boult was gearing himself up to take his dead friend's advice. He was at a dance in the officers' mess and Susanna Langton had just walked into the room. Boult had met her a month before when he was driving back to the base through a heavy storm. He'd come upon a group of English pilots and military

nurses trying to shelter under a tree. Their jeep had bro-
ken down. He'd offered them a lift into the next village
and there were introductions as they all crowded laugh-
ingly into his car. His eyes had met hers. Beautiful deep
blue eyes, golden hair drawn back, high forehead, a
gravely lovely face with a wonderful warm smile. One of
the pilots, a tall handsome golden-haired young man,
was her brother, Guy. The trip to the next village had
lasted only a few minutes, but somehow Boult had man-
aged to tell them all that there was going to be a big
bash in the officers' mess at Waddington next month.
He knew he was in love for the first time in his life. But
he hadn't expected her to come to the dance tonight. A
couple of weeks before he'd heard that Guy Langton had
been shot down over France.

Yet she was here.

Jack got up from his desk and drew the curtains closed
across the windows with their panoramic view of the
city. He'd decided that the view distracted him. There
was too much going on. His attention got caught by
the ferries on the harbour. He became curious about
all the people he could see in the windows of the distant buildings. It was very different from driving
through miles of countryside with Lance sleeping
deeply beside him on the front seat of the rig.

Back at his desk Jack focused on the scene. The
officers' mess. Young men in uniforms gazing across
the room at the young nurses sitting around the
walls. Dancing started to the sound of Tommy
Dorsey. The room is thick with smoke and there's

Susanna looking so beautiful . . . The trouble is that Pilot Officer Boult is shy. He's a great skipper. His men respect and trust him and, because he knows that, his first duty is to keep their confidence up. They think he's brave, but he's tongue-tied around women.

I ought to be able to do this easily, thought Jack – should be a pushover imagining a shy bloke trying to approach the girl of his dreams. But even as he was thinking this it was occurring to Jack that he'd met so many people lately he'd been too busy to be shy.

Ziggy had been perfectly right when she said that people would accept the truth about Ruby Vale's identity. Two days later Jack had appeared on the *Clive Rooney Show* and told the full story. It hadn't been as bad as Jack had expected. Clive Rooney had interviewed him so expertly that everything had flowed out naturally. Jack had come across as a shy, modest, good-looking country bloke and his fans, after their initial shock, had been very enthusiastic. They were mostly women after all and the truth – Ruby taking part in the charade to help out an old friend and to pay for her own wedding – struck them as romantic.

The rest of the media had reported the story in an amused but sympathetic fashion with lots of 'she's a he' type headlines, and within hours Ziggy realised that the whole thing had been a major publicity coup. She was getting calls from every television channel, radio station and newspaper, all waiting to interview Jack Willis. After the first couple of interviews Jack found that all the questions he was asked were much the same; and his only real problem was concealing from interviewers that his next novel was not about the Boer War. Fortunately, most interviewers were sympathetic to the idea that writers are superstitious when it comes to talking about books they're writing.

At the same time Jack knew he ought to tell Ziggy the truth, but he hesitated. The problem was that the book was still only half written. In the few spare hours he had between interviews, books signings and publicity appearances, he'd stay in his room to work on *Blood on the Moon* because he felt that Ziggy would be happier with the truth if she was given a new, completed manuscript at the same time. But he was finding writing in his luxurious hotel room with its lavish array of pens and paper far more difficult than writing in the rig with one eye on the road and Lance snoring beside him.

'It's just a matter of what you're used to,' he said firmly to himself, and returned to World War II where Pilot Officer Boult was sipping a mouthful of beer to boost his courage to approach Susanna.

In his mind Boult heard the gunner's words again. They brought back other memories. For an instant he could hear the drone of his aircraft, the screaming of his men and the ear-splitting rattle of the machine gun fire . . .

'Then what?' thought Jack. He got up and went to the window and opened the curtains again. Across the street he could see a small figure at a window desk.

Jack peered and eventually decided it was a young Japanese woman with very short hair. As he watched, the woman got up, and swung her bag over her shoulder. He realised it was lunchtime and he was meant to meet Ziggy at a restaurant overlooking Sydney Cove.

She was already seated when he arrived, and she watched admiringly as he crossed the room towards her. He was wearing a new Armani jacket that he'd bought under her direction, and it made him feel uncomfortable. He thought it was an astounding amount of money to spend on a piece of clothing. He also noticed that some people looked at the jacket as if they knew exactly how much it had cost.

Ziggy smiled at him as he took his seat.

'I'm dying to get pictures of your gorgeous face,' she said.

'This?' inquired Jack, pointing to his face, as if she must have confused it with someone else's.

Ziggy opened his napkin and slid it into his lap. 'You've no idea.'

A perky waiter walked up carrying a tray with a beer and one glass of wine. Jack was quick to accept his stubby and immediately clinked it against Ziggy's glass of wine.

'Here's to us, eh?'

'How's the new book progressing?'

Jack took a quick swig and lied. 'Terrific!'

Ziggy smiled, took Jack's beer from his hand, whipped a glass off the waiter's tray and proceeded to pour the beer into the glass. 'Jack . . .' she started slowly, 'How do you . . .'

Jack waited for Ziggy as she searched for the right way to ask her question. He also hoped that she could pour a beer without creating too much froth.

'Tilt the glass as you pour it,' he said.

'Oh.' Ziggy obeyed, poured the beer and handed the glass to Jack. Jack took it with a forced smile.

'Thanks,' he said, 'that'll make the beer a tad warmer.'

'Jack, it's much nicer out of the glass.'

He took his first sip. Jack was unaccustomed to being taught how to drink beer. Ziggy leant closer to him. She had something on her mind. 'Do you actually know any of these characters you write about?'

'Sure.' Jack said matter-of-factly.

'Okay, I mean – apart from the fact that you've completely over-romanticised their personalities to give the necessary quality of adventure and heroism.'

Jack looked at her with a puzzled smile. 'You don't know any romantic people?'

'Jack, I live in a city.'

Jack threw his head back with laughter. Ziggy hadn't heard him laugh before. It was a loud and generous laugh. The kind that turned heads and make people feel that they were missing out on something. She took a sip of wine.

'You just send me up the whole time, don't you?' she said.

The perky waiter reappeared holding a small notepad. He looked at Jack. 'I thought so.'

'What?' Jack inquired.

'I saw you on TV. You're that Ruby Vale bloke.'

'That's me!'

'Actually,' intercepted Ziggy, 'his name is Jack Willis. What are today's specials?'

'Emu pie . . .'

The words hit Ziggy like a brick. 'Forget it,' she snapped.

'Why? asked the perplexed waiter. 'It's fresh.'

Ziggy turned on him. 'Have you ever seen their faces?'

The waiter paused, then shrugged before answering, 'No, not on the rotisserie.'

Ziggy stood up causing her chair to fly back onto the floor. 'Let's go, Jack.'

The waiter was totally bewildered. How could he have upset this woman so much?

'What about fish?' Jack called out, as Ziggy stormed away from the restaurant. He handed the waiter a ten-dollar note. 'Will this cover the drinks?' The waiter nodded.

******

Lucktown had never had a hospital. If medical help was required, a local family doctor dealt with the usual aches and pains of the small community. Anything more serious took patients into Broken Hill, which had one of the best hospitals in western New South Wales and was backed up by the famous Flying Doctor Service. Everyone admired the 'flying angels' who, ever since the late thirties, had cast their network of medical care across four hundred scattered outposts. Lucktown was one such place.

Ruby didn't remember a great deal of the flight to

Broken Hill. She recalled a young doctor murmuring something to Hamish about her ankle as they eased her carefully onto a stretcher. Her ribs were hurting, too. Then she blacked out.

Hamish stroked her hand gently as Ruby stirred and opened her eyes. She realised she was in hospital. When she tried to move, it hurt.

'Damn!'

Hamish grinned at her exasperation, knowing she was on the mend.

'Hello,' he said softly.

Ruby looked around the hospital room trying to orient herself to the plain room, painted pale blue to match the hospital blankets. A noisy truck roared by outside the window causing her to flinch. Hamish got up and closed the window.

'I tried to get you a room facing the courtyard, but there's been a few births in the last twenty-four hours.'

Ruby glanced down to her suspended leg, in plaster to the knee.

Hamish moved back to the bed. 'Doc said an ankle and two ribs.'

Ruby turned her head to the side, half-burying her face into the pillow. Hamish said, 'Lance wouldn't have jumped out of the Land Rover if you had just landed the first time.'

Ruby didn't move. 'I'm sorry.' Her apology was muffled. A tear fell from her eye and stained the white pillow slip under her face.

'You don't sacrifice a plane for a stupid dog, Rube,' said Hamish quietly.

Why was he doing this? Ruby looked back up to him with tears still wet on her cheeks. 'And you call yourself a vet?' She wiped off her face, more out of anger than anything else.

Hamish smiled and moved closer to her along the bed. 'Look, Rube. I know I'm not Sir bloody Lancelot or Richard Gere or whatever his name is . . .'

Ruby stopped him right there by placing her finger to his lips. His anger subsided with this gesture. They looked at each other for a moment.

'You're very sweet, that's what you are, Hamish,' said Ruby softly.

'Really?' he replied. Ruby assured him with a smile and a nod.

'Sweet, eh?' asked Hamish. 'Doesn't sound very sexy, does it?'

Ruby held out her arms to invite a hug. 'Come here, you big lug.'

Hamish moved in, careful not to touch her ribs.

'This place in Queensland,' she continued, 'Is it anywhere near Camelot?'

Hamish laughed with his face in the pillow. 'Yeah, just out past Goondiwindi.'

'Has it got an airport?'

Hamish straightened his large frame and pointed his finger at her with a playful gesture. 'There'll be no more shenanigans from you.' Ruby said nothing as he went on. 'You know what? As soon as you can walk we'll pack up, make a fresh start and get married in Queensland. What do you say?'

Ruby paused. 'Hamish.'

'What?'

She reckoned on the headlong approach. 'That funny man with the glasses . . .'

'You mean George?'

'Yeah, George. Was he a buyer?'

Hamish's face turned red immediately. She knew she was right. He was about to tell her that this was how he intended to pay for the wedding but it didn't seem the right time.

'I gotta get out to the Barnes place before two,' he said, getting off the bed.

'You were trying to sell the Stearman, weren't you?'

Hamish's eyes scanned the hospital room. 'Look, Rube, all I was doin' was makin' inquiries . . .'

'Inquiries?' asked Ruby, raising her voice. 'Jesus, Hamish, thanks for discussing it with me.'

'We had to do it sometime . . .'

'What?' yelled Ruby. She tried to sit upright but a sharp pain shot through her body. 'Oh, Christ!' she moaned, and lowered herself carefully back onto the pillow.

'H-e-l-l-o,' said a voice from outside. Suzie poked her head around the door of the hospital room.

Hamish rolled his eyes and reluctantly turned to greet her. 'G'day, Suzie.'

Suzie entered the room nervously. It was obvious that she'd overheard what had been said. In one hand she held a bunch of wildflowers and, in the other, a *Women's Weekly* magazine, which she placed on the bed.

'How're you feelin', love?' she asked Ruby, with a warm smile.

'She's doin' fine,' said Hamish, before Ruby could reply.

'She's doin' fine!' repeated Ruby in exact imitation of Hamish.

After a pause in the conversation, Hamish glanced at his watch again. 'Well, I gotta be goin'.' He leant forward and kissed Ruby on the forehead. 'I'll come by an' check on you later, Rube.'

'Bye,' said Ruby solemnly.

Hamish left without another word. Suzie busied herself by pouring drinking water into a glass vase and arranging the flowers.

'Well then . . .' she probed.

'Well, what?' asked Ruby.

'These walls are thin, you know.'

'Well then, you've already heard that he tried to sell my biplane.'

'I gathered that much, love.' Suzie completed the floral arrangement and sat it proudly on the bedside table.

'Still,' she continued, 'the bugger can't do it now, can he?'

Ruby started to laugh, which only brought on a giggle from Suzie. Soon the two of them where rolling about until Ruby's ribs hurt.

'Stop it, Jesus, Suz – please.'

The two women look at each other.

'That's the best medicine I know, love,' said Suzie softly. The women looked at each other knowing how much they were going to miss one another when Ruby went to Queensland.

'Anyone inquired about the Boomerang?' asked Ruby hopefully.

'No, not yet. I hope whoever it is wants to keep me on,' she said brightly. Ruby just smiled.

'Have you heard from you-know-who?'

'Christ!' said Ruby, 'are you kiddin' me?' Ruby suddenly noticed the *Women's Weekly* placed carefully within her reach. She picked it up without opening it. 'Tell me he's not in here!'

Suzie just grinned.

17

It was now well and truly past their lunch hour, Jack had to literally jog along the street to keep up with Ziggy as she strode purposefully along in search for a more suitable cafe. Thai, Japanese – no. Finally she pointed to a health-food cafe called Inner Healing.

'You're vegetarian now?' Jack gasped with disbelief.

'Absolutely,' Ziggy announced proudly.

'Since when?'

'From now on, I won't eat anything that's had a mother.'

Jack laughed and threw his hands into the air. 'Bloody hell, Ziggy, a fish doesn't know its mother.'

Ziggy stopped dead and turned to face him. 'You know this for certain?'

Jack sighed. He couldn't believe that he was having this conversation. He was about to turn away in exasperation, then said, 'Ziggy, I'm just hungry – that's all.'

Ziggy glanced at her watch. 'Oh, God. Now I'm late.'

'Okay, you jump in a cab and I'll get something to

eat.' Jack raised his hand to attract a taxi cruising some distance away. Ziggy pulled his arm down.

'Was I a real pain in the arse when you first met me?' she asked quietly. She was still holding his arm.

Jack paused longer than he should have.

'I was, wasn't I?' Ziggy smiled, and shook her head. 'Well, I'm sorry.'

'No need,' he said casually.

Ziggy looked up to him, exploring his eyes. She then leant forward and kissed him on the cheek. She was hesitant at first, but then threw her arms around him and kissed him on his lips.

Her fragrance filled Jack's head. He felt overwhelmed. His arms went around her. The third and fourth kisses were soft and sensual, almost nibbles around the corners of his mouth. There they were, standing in the middle of George Street, kissing as if they were in the privacy of a bedroom.

'God,' breathed Ziggy as she broke free, unaware of the people around them. She took a breath to steady her nerves. What was she doing, kissing a guy passionately in the middle of George Street? 'Will you still be hungry tonight?' she asked. She smiled suddenly, not having intended the innuendo, but the double meaning pleased her. Never before had she even considered having a liaison with an author; this was exactly how women ruined their careers.

'I just thought if you weren't writing – maybe, I mean, we've got to eat.'

'We'll never do it if today's any indication.'

Ziggy laughed and hugged him once more. She caught sight of another cruising taxi.

'Taxi,' she yelled, and ran out into the street to claim her ride. 'I'll meet you in the hotel lobby at half-seven.' In a moment she was gone. Jack watched her taxi join the thick flow of traffic. 'Zane building – quick as you can,' ordered Ziggy.

'Righto, Miss,' mumbled the cab driver.

As the taxi manoeuvred through the narrow streets, Ziggy took out her compact and checked her face in the mirror. Her lipstick was smudged and her cheeks were red. Her heart was pounding. She felt joyful and shocked all at once. She closed her eyes and said, 'Shit!'

'Now, if only,' said Jack to himself, gazing after the departing taxi, 'it could be that simple for Pilot Officer Boult and Susanna.'

'Maybe it can be,' he added a moment later, 'maybe it can. They can just go into a clinch on the dance floor. Hell –' he was grinning so broadly, people were looking at him, '– I did it in George Street.'

******

Jack knew how important his novel was to Ziggy's career. She rarely complained about the pressures of life in Zane Publishing, but when she arrived at a publicity event or one of their increasingly more frequent lunches or dinners there would often be a telltale set to her mouth. It would disappear as soon as they started talking, and she relaxed. But he'd realised that the spectacular success of *Bird in the Hand* had improved her prospects of becoming a director and thus the competition between her and Ralph.

At the moment it looked as if she had the upper hand, but Ralph was doing everything possible to undermine her. Whenever Jack made a light mistake in an interview, answered a question badly or got temporarily tongue-tied, he'd see that set look appear about her mouth. She never criticised any of his slip-ups but he'd seen enough of life in Zane Publishing to know that each of these minor errors would be pounced upon eagerly by Ralph. Ralph had two ways of playing the situation: either he'd imply that Ziggy was mishandling Jack and not preparing him prop-erly for his public appearances or he let her know that he thought the popularity bubble was soon about to burst for Ziggy Keane's outback trucker-cum-romance-writing superstar. Both strategies really got under Ziggy's skin although there wasn't the slightest evidence of either strategy materialising. Indeed, Zane was getting lots of requests for Jack to start doing publicity tours overseas, as his book was being released in other countries. Ziggy was eager for Jack to go overseas, but Jack was not thrilled by the idea . . . He was having a difficult enough time trying to write *Blood on the Moon* in his room at The Regent. He could not imagine how he could write at all while going from one strange city to another in half a dozen other countries. He was therefore very relieved when he learned from Ziggy that Errol Ruben didn't think

Jack should commit to any overseas tours until his second book was finalised. But Ziggy had soon set him right about this: 'Oh, Errol's not at all concerned about your writing,' she said dryly. 'He thinks he'll get better deals overseas if he's got one hit novel actually in the bookshops and a second one at the printers.'

Jack couldn't help grinning at that. He knew it was true. Underneath all of Errol's public charm and graciousness was total ruthlessness. In fact, it was Errol rather than Ralph whom Jack blamed for the stress Ziggy was experiencing. He was sure that Errol was deliberately stringing out the decision about the directorate so that his two ambitious colleagues would be driven to compete even more intensely, so as to out-perform each other. Jack was sure Errol knew the price that Ziggy was paying. It had been immediately obvious to Jack that despite her smooth professionalism, Ziggy was repelled by Ralph and found him very difficult to work with. Jack was confident that Errol was fully aware of it too. Jack had often wished that he could do something to help Ziggy and, as he was heading back towards his hotel after their passionate lingering kiss, he became determined that he was going to do the one thing that really could help her – finish his next novel.

He knew it was just that one scene that was stopping him. If he could get Pilot Officer Boult and Susanna together – if he could get that moment right so the reader knew that they were meant irrevocably to be together – then he was sure that the rest of it would flow. It was all so clear in his head and now he knew he had the moment. He raced the last short stretch of street and up the fire escape to his room, where he pulled the curtains closed against the million-dollar view and sat down at his desk to write.

That was it – they didn't say anything to each other. She just stepped towards the dance floor as he approached her. Without a word they were in each other's arms, and she was dancing with her eyes closed . . .

Jack stopped for a moment. The room felt closed in, claustrophobic. He jumped up and quickly jerked the curtains open. In the break Susanna and Pilot Officer Boult go outside for some air, and suddenly Boult finds himself talking. He's telling her everything he has to fight so hard to hide from his men, so much so that he's hidden these things even from himself. For once, he is scared and vulnerable. He'd had a tough time growing up. His father, turned sour and abusive by failure and alcohol, had mistreated his wife and humiliated his son when he learned of his son's dream to be a pilot. Boult's father had been a famous World War I pilot . . . 'No,' said Jack to himself, 'not too much about him wanting to fly as a boy here. I'll come back to that again in the air battle over Nuremberg when, for a moment, he really loses it. First I've got to get him to Nuremberg.' As Jack stared over the desk trying to set the scene at the dance in the officers' mess again in his mind, he decided that the view of the city was distracting him and jumped up once more to close the curtains.

Pilot Officer Boult was telling Susanna that this coming mission was the fortieth operational attack for him and his crew of six. His rear gunner had been killed on their last raid and the rest of them had been utterly stripped of their courage. Their next mission to Nuremberg, their deepest probe into Germany, was to be the last in this tour of duty.

On their worst night over Berlin, the Luftwaffe – backed up by ferocious anti-aircraft fire – had downed seventy bombers. Lancasters, Halifaxes and Mosquitoes; well over four hundred men had perished in one catastrophic night. He sat for hours relating his horrific stories to his Susanna . . . about the heavier armament carried by the German night-fighters and how, due to the freezing temperatures, the breech-blocks of their own machine-guns would lock in the forward position. 'Sometimes,' he said, 'all we had was evasive flying to break the advantage of the angry German Tiger.'

Susanna just held his hand as she listened. She knew she was in love with him and she knew that during every second he was in the air, she'd be praying for him. But she knew she had to hide her fear so as not to destroy what little courage he had left.

Boult's fingers folded more tightly around her own as he started to tell her about Dave, his rear gunner. He remembered him joking over the intercom, then the silence, then the sound of strafing fire and the realisation of what it meant. His mate, Dave, was now just part of that terrible debris of burnt metal and human flesh that would be trailed all over the ground below.

Skipper Boult had gone chill with horror but kept his hand steady on the controls, he . . .

'Did what?' asked Jack of himself. 'What did he do then?' He gazed blankly at the drawn curtains for a moment and then thought, Do it logically – what would a pilot do now? It occurred to him that he really didn't know what a pilot would do at this point for a very good reason: he hated flying. He was practically phobic about it. In the vast inland where air transport was the only means of reaching anywhere in less than a day, he never ever went near a plane – hadn't flown since he'd once been taken to Broken Hill in the Flying Doctor Service when he was a kid. Yet here he was – a writer who was scared of flying, writing a book about a bomber pilot. He couldn't believe that he'd never noticed the absurdity of it before. How Ruby would have laughed if she'd known.

The closed-in room was oppressing him. He wished he could be back home again in Lucktown, in the outback, with thousands of miles of space. He rose again and opened the curtains and stared with hostility at the million-dollar view. He then jerked the curtains shut again to the complete bemusement of Ms Matsuko Harigawa who worked in the building opposite. Matsuko, a slender, bright-eyed twenty-year-old, was spending this year in her firm's Sydney office. She'd often noticed lately that the curtains in this particular room of the hotel opposite were pulled open and shut in quick succession at irregular intervals. Now she was thinking that it was almost as if someone was trying to send a message. Perhaps it was morse code. A ransom victim trying to signal 'Help'? Turning back to her computer screen, she shook her head to herself. Her family was right – she really did have an over-active imagination. But privately she thought this was a very good thing. One day she intended to write a novel.

Jack, meanwhile, had decided to call it a day. There was a satisfactory pile of scrawled pages on his desk and his mind kept wandering from Boult and Susanna and World War II to Ziggy Keane and her long legs and her shapely body. All pressed up against his as they'd been for a long delicious moment in George Street. They were to meet each other in two hours time at Mario's Trattoria, a smart restaurant in the Little Italy strip on the eastern side of the city. The old suburbs of Darlinghurst and Paddington lay just beyond. Jack decided he'd set off early and go for a walk around this historic part of Sydney before dinner.

He spent the next couple of hours contently wandering up and down the winding streets admiring elegant rows of terrace houses and little workers' cottages, now restored – despite their nineteenth-century facades – into smart residences for inner-city professionals. He was pleased to see *Bird in the Hand* prominently displayed in bookshop windows, but what gave him the greatest thrill was the billiards shop.

He discovered it by accident. He was hurrying down a side street, aware that it was getting late, when he passed a dark, narrow shop. What he registered as he was passing was that he couldn't work out what sort of shop it was, so he paused and went back and pushed open the door.

The first thing he saw was a handwritten sign, which said, *You Touch, You Buy*. Then he saw what must have been thousands of pool cues. Every inch of wall space was covered. If it wasn't a cue, it was an accessory or a photograph of some bloke in a 'sixties dinner suit standing proudly beside a tournament cup he'd just won. Jack had to walk sideways to slip between the floor displays.

'You want something?' an old man's voice barked suddenly from the back of the shop. Jack shook his head and took a last regretful look around before threading his way quickly but carefully to the door. He didn't need a pool cue and the sight of them was bringing back memories of that night in the Boomerang when he'd come in from the rain and found Ruby dancing with her eyes closed around the pool table.

Mario's Trattoria was buzzing. It was known as a media industry hangout and that night everyone who was anybody seemed to be there for dinner. Every table was occupied, and the aisles between were full of people table-hopping, blowing kisses, saying hello and shaking hands. Waiters manoeuvred their way expertly through this busy throng bearing trays and drinks, opening bottles and fanning out table napkins over laps, while at the same time intoning the evening specials.

In all the hum of conversation and haze of cocktails the waiter assigned to the bank of tables by the windows paid only minimal attention to the couple at table thirty-two. He'd sized them up within minutes of their arrival and decided that they weren't here for the food. They weren't here for the wine either, though they were downing their bottle of chianti pretty quickly. But it was perfectly obvious to the waiter that they were so hot for each other that they'd scarcely noticed what they were drinking. They were completely oblivious to anything except each other.

When he'd gone to take their order, the woman, who was tall and gorgeous, had asked for a pasta alfredo with no cream and no garlic. The waiter wondered what she expected to receive as their alfredo sauce consisted mostly of cream and garlic. But at least she'd made the effort. Her date, mesmerised by the woman's lips while she was speaking, had not even looked at the menu. When he muttered something about ordering later, it was the woman's eyes that became transfixed on her companion's lips. The waiter had thought of saying, 'Look, I know what you both want for entree, dinner and dessert, and it's not on this menu,' but instead he nodded agreeably and moved away. For the rest of the night the couple was engrossed completely in each other's body language. They were so excited by each other that they couldn't meet each other's eyes.

It came as no surprise to the waiter when Ziggy declined dessert.

'Why don't we just have coffee at home?' she suggested, leaning closer to Jack.

Jack drained his glass and smiled. 'I think we'll have the bill, please, mate?'

'Yes, sir.' The waiter collected Ziggy's scarcely touched pasta and walked away.

'Funny, I wasn't very hungry, were you?' asked Ziggy innocently.

Jack leant forward and placed his hand on her thigh beneath the table. Ziggy was burning. She figured no one could see under the tablecloth. She glanced around anyway. A sea of faces – laughing, talking. Ziggy gently parted her legs as Jack played with the hem of her mini-skirt. The skirt rose slightly as she slid forward in her seat. Jack's warm hand caressed the inside of her thigh.

'Tear the panty-hose . . .' she whispered.

'Are you sure I can't get you anything else, sir?' Oh, shit, they both thought, the waiter was back with the bill. Ziggy looked up to him with a demure smile.

'Do you sell chianti by the glass?'

'Yes, ma'am.'

'Two please, mate.'

The waiter nodded and left. Ziggy looked directly to Jack.

'You stop an' I'll kill you,' she whispered.

Christ, thought Jack, what if she screams out? But he was unable to stop himself.

Ziggy slid her chair closer to make it a little less obvious that Jack had his hand between her legs. Two more glasses of wine arrived. Ziggy now had something to do with her hands above the table other than scrunch up the napkin. She picked up her glass, took an appreciative sniff and sipped it.

'This is madness,' Jack whispered.

'Why, is it illegal?'

'I don't think so. No,' he added, with a nervous smile.

'Illicit, perhaps?'

He chuckled. 'Maybe.'

Ziggy was moving closer and closer to orgasm. 'Good material for a novel?' she asked, sounding a bit breathless.

'Christ –' Jack was getting breathless himself.

'Well, just remember, you started it.'

Ziggy's body beneath the tablecloth tensed and writhed gently. She stared at him with such intensity. Then, when the moment was upon her, closed her eyes and smiled. The next moment, tears flowed but she was still smiling.

Jack withdrew his hand from under the table. He wasn't sure where to look. He picked up the bill.

Ziggy dabbed her eyes with a napkin.

'Well,' he said nervously. 'I'd better get you home.'

'And not a minute too soon,' thought the waiter to himself. He'd been perfectly aware of what was happening at table thirty-two. It'd been quite a performance, though he didn't think anyone else in the restaurant had noticed. By way of showing his appreciation, he hadn't charged them for the extra two glasses of wine.

18

Any sign of rain soon disappeared as heat from the midday sun burnt the main street of Lucktown. Suzie stood in the doorway of the pub and gazed out at the man wearing a huge hat, who once again was hammering the 'For Sale' sign outside the Boomerang Cafe. Every strike of the sledge-hammer made her flinch. She'd always known she would miss Ruby, but it wasn't until Ruby went into hospital and the Boomerang was closed that she realised how much of a void Ruby's leaving would make in her life.

Suzie had offered to keep the doors open while Ruby recovered, but Ruby had insisted the workload would be too much for her – especially since Suzie still had to work nights at the pub.

Artie pushed his way through the door armed with a hand-pump flysprayer. He noticed his wife gazing at the cafe and proceeded to douse the environment with the hideous spray.

'We can't afford it, love,' he said between squirts. Suzie could hear the satisfaction in his voice beneath the pretend sympathetic words.

'The bank manager said . . .'

'I don't give a bugger what he said,' interrupted Artie, 'we owe too much money on this place without payin' out on somethin' else.'

Artie decimated a few more flies before continuing. 'Anyhow, that place is only popular because of your little friend.' Artie spoke with such a patronising smile that Suzie turned to him slowly, 'Oh, that's a steamin' pile of wisdom.'

Artie responded with his stern raised finger. 'I'm not tryin' to have an argument with you,' he warned, 'I'm just not gonna pay a penny for a dump like that.'

'Everything's a dump to you, isn't it Artie?'

Artie looked up proudly at the facade of his pub.

'This place isn't,' he said.

'I've got news for you, love.' Suzie turned and quietly walked back inside.

'Oh, that's great, isn't it?' he yelled. 'Why don't you bite the bloody hand that feeds ya?' Artie resumed his spraying with quick, violent strokes. He would've sprayed it directly into his wife's face if she'd been near. 'Fuckin' flies!'

The man with the huge hat had long gone by the time Ruby pulled up beside the sign in Hamish's Land Rover. Still with her lower leg in plaster, she hobbled out from the driver's seat and, with a thick felt pen, wrote 'sold' across the face of the sign. She then tried to pull the sign from the ground. It wouldn't budge, so she climbed back into the Land Rover, slammed it into gear and ran the sign to the ground. Afterwards she climbed out of the Rover, picked up the sign now a bit worse for wear, and carried it over her shoulder towards the pub.

'Suz?' she called out, as she entered the cool darkness of the public bar. Two drinkers murmured something and pointed to the back room.

'Suz?' yelled Ruby again.

'That you, Rube?' Suzie's face popped around through the swing door.

'Who else do you think it is?'

Suzie's face brightened. She was delighted to see Ruby and hurried forward wiping her hands on her apron.

'You should be restin' that leg . . .' Suzie stopped dead. She saw Ruby was holding the real estate sign with the word 'sold' written across it with a pen.

'Oh, dear,' was her first thought, but she smiled for her friend's sake. 'Who bought it, Rube?'

A grin broke out across Ruby's face. 'You'll be pleased to hear that it was a really nice person.'

'Will they want me to stay on – do you think?' The answer meant everything to Suzie. A decision on her life.

'Absolutely!'

Suzie smiled. 'That's the way Jack would say it, wouldn't he? Absolutely!'

Ruby shrugged casually. Any remark about Jack brought floods of images through her mind. She dreamt about him last night. A stupid dream.

'Well, then – when do they open up?' Suzie asked hopefully.

Ruby passed the real estate sign to Suzie. 'Any time the new owner wants to.'

'Yeah, but who is it, Rube?'

Ruby reached into the rear pocket of her overalls and pulled out a property deed. She held it up.

'You.'

Suzie stared at her friend, too overwhelmed to speak.

'Look, all legal,' insisted Ruby, 'got your name on it an' everything.'

Artie, who was coming through into the bar room carrying a refill can of flyspray, overheard the conversation.

'We don't want your charity, Rube,' he said. A chill went through Suzie's body.

'It's not charity,' said Ruby. 'Suzie can pay me something when she can afford it.'

'What if she doesn't want it? What if we . . .'

'Yes, I do,' interrupted Suzie. This uncharacteristic burst of confidence brought a vicious glance from Artie.

'I'd love it, Rube,' she continued. 'Would it really be mine?'

Suzie took the paperwork from Ruby.

'That's what it says there,' said Ruby.

Tears swelled in Suzie's eyes. 'Thank you. This is the happiest day of my whole life . . .'

The embrace that Suzie gave Ruby literally lifted her off the ground. Artie paced a little to try and control his anger.

'Oh, that's just great,' he said. 'Who's gonna work the bar at night?'

Suzie turned to Artie and stared at him. Suddenly, for the first time, she felt detached from this man who'd lost her love long ago and she realised she was no longer afraid of him.

'You can, Artie,' she said, with a gentle smile. 'You can look after the bar. Now, if you'll excuse me, I've got a cafe to open.'

Suzie held the For Sale sign to her chest and walked straight out of the bar into the street. Artie was horrified.

'Well,' said Ruby, turning to him with a smile, 'I gotta pack. See you when I see you.'

With that, she pivoted on her plastered leg and exited into the hot sun. A heavy cloud of anger hung over Artie as he moved up to the door to watch the women walk away.

He tried his ultimate weapon. 'This could be divorce, Suzie,' he screamed.

Suzie stopped half way across the street and slowly turned to him. 'Artie, that's the only decision I'll leave up to you,' she called back.

Neither of them noticed the satisfaction on Ruby's face as she climbed back into the Land Rover.

19

A bright moon and unexpected clear skies meant that the stream of bombers were sitting ducks on every navigational leg of the flight to Nuremberg. Just short of Cologne it started. For two straight hours the aircraft were continuously under fire from night-fighters. Cannon tracer could be seen in every direction. These attacks were so precise, Pilot Officer Boult told his crew, that the Luftwaffe pilots must have been 'sitting-in' on their operation briefing. Nobody grinned. They all knew that over 760 Lancasters and Halifaxes had been shot down in the first twelve weeks of 1944. Why should tonight be any different?

Boult ran his gloved finger over a smiling photograph of Susanna dressed in her nurse's uniform. His wireless operator caught the gesture and smiled. 'You're doin' well for yourself there, Skip,' he said over the intercom.

Boult had no time to reply before two more kites, on his starboard side, exploded and plummeted to their fiery grave. More cannon tracer – streaks of blue, green and red lit up the sky around them. The mid-upper gunner shot off a burst into the night but it was like

shooting at shadows. Behind them, on the ground, an
incendiary trail of burning aircraft clearly marked their
route to destruction. It was deathly cold at 20 000 feet.
All Boult could do to keep his head was to recall the
wonderful moments he'd had with Susanna.

Jack read the opening lines to the chapter that led to
the climax of *Blood on the Moon* again, and decided
that yes, they were fine. The trouble was that they
were all he'd written of his big chapter. The other
afternoon when he'd written of Boult's reunion with
Susanna it had all flowed effortlessly, but in these last
three days all he'd written was – he did a quick calcu-
lation – two hundred and five words, give or take a
few. And it was wrong to say it'd taken him three days
to write that small amount. In fact, he'd written that
in a wonderful exhilarated fifteen minutes after coming home from his first night with Ziggy. Since then
he hadn't written a word.

For a while he'd rationalised this by thinking he
was just too tired from long nights of lovemaking
with Ziggy, but then he'd remembered times when
he'd written pages and pages after having spent a day
and a night on the road. Ziggy distracted him and it
was true that he'd scarcely recovered from one night
when he started looking forward to seeing her again.

Ziggy was an easy lover. The rules of discretion were
simple. No one at Zane, apart from her confidante,
Ella, must know of the affair. They always meet at her
place – never at his hotel.

'But she's only a distraction,' Jack said to himself,

'because you want her to be.' Whenever he made himself stop thinking about Ziggy to focus on his book, he'd hear, reverberating in his mind, that question he'd asked himself the other afternoon: how come a writer who's scared of flying is writing a book about a bomber pilot on the most dangerous flying assignment of them all?

And after that he'd hear another question being asked. A real one this time. He'd hear Ruby's voice exclaiming, 'Why the hell didn't you use Suzie's name or Tina's from the hairdresser's? Why did you use mine?'

He hadn't answered that morning, though he'd thought he knew the answer. Using a real person's name made the book seem real and, as the author had to be a woman, who better than Ruby Vale? It would appeal to her sense of mischief, she needed the money and, as she was about to get married, leave Lucktown and disappear out of his life, there wouldn't be any awkward consequences. But now he'd begun to realise he was wrong. The real reason why he'd used her name on his first novel was the same reason why his next novel was about flying. He wrote his books for Ruby.

Jack sighed and glanced at the tiny dictaphone sitting on his desk. He picked it up. The size of the mechanism intrigued him when he first received it from Ziggy. He had pulled out the batteries, inspected the micro-cassette and tested its sensitivity at various distances around the room – anything to avoid trying to use it for writing.

Jack threw it onto the bed and picked up the phone.

Ziggy took his call from her speaker phone. 'Yeah?' she said, assuming the call was coming from Ella in the outer office.

'I'm stretched out on the bed completely naked . . .' To her alarm Jack's voice rang out through her office. She reached for the privacy button and picked up the receiver, then swung her chair around to face the Harbour Bridge. A huge, golden sun was setting behind the clouds.

'Oh, God, where are you? What are you doing?' she asked.

'I told you.'

'No, really,' Ziggy giggled.

'Trying to work with a bloody dictaphone.'

Ziggy stretched out her long, elegant legs and rested her feet on the low windowsill. The phone was cradled in the nape of her neck. 'Should I bring over paper and pencils?' she asked quietly.

Jack loved the sound of her voice on the phone. It was low and smooth and seductive.

'I don't suppose . . .' he began quietly.

'What?' asked Ziggy.

'I don't suppose a fuck's out of the question?'

Ziggy burst into laughter as Ralph cleared his throat at the door. It was rare that he caught her so completely off guard.

Ziggy spun around in her chair and ended her call in a businesslike manner. 'Ahh, yes, that'll be fine. I'll set something up with you later.' Ziggy placed down the phone and composed herself, smiling at Ralph leaning on the doorjamb. 'Don't you ever knock?' she inquired.

Ralph was holding a copy of *Who Weekly* magazine with Jack featured on the cover. A slow grin crossed his face. He was watching her closely. 'You've really pulled the sheets over his eyes, haven't you?'

Ziggy remained calm. She gave him a look that said she had no idea what he was talking about.

'Well, there you go,' Ralph continued. 'If it gets you upstairs in the firm, it's all worthwhile, eh?'

Did he know or was he just guessing? Ziggy took an anxious moment to reorganise papers on her desk while she thought of an appropriate reply.

'Ralph, if I remember correctly, you weren't ever interested in romantic novels. "Tedious rubbish" was what I think you called them.'

Ralph threw the *Who Weekly* onto Ziggy's desk to land directly in front of her.

'I did say that. However, unlike you, I'm here for the firm.' Ralph maintained his grin as he turned and left her office.

Ziggy felt furious with herself. How could this man upset her so much?

It was now getting late and the last of the sun's rays glittered off the Opera House roof, turning the sails a deep yellow.

Ella slipped inside the office holding a glass and a can of Coke. 'Don't worry, we've all thought about killing Ralph for years. Just a little push as his train enters Town Hall station . . .'

263

She held up the Coke. 'Want some?'

Ziggy smiled. Tears were welling up in her eyes.

'Don't let him get to you,' said Ella as she filled the glass and offered it to Ziggy.

'He's not,' said Ziggy taking the glass. 'God, he thinks I slept with Jack just to get a contract.'

'A woman's work is never done.'

Ella's quick response caused Ziggy to look up in horror.

'That's called a joke!' said Ella, raising her eyebrows.

Ziggy swivelled her chair around and stared back out the window towards the setting sun. 'Boy, am I getting too sensitive?'

******

'A game of squash?' Ralph suggested.

'Never played in my life,' answered Jack on the phone.

'Good for stress, great way to lose weight.'

Had Ralph forgiven him for punching him out off-stage at the *Clive Rooney Show*? There was no doubt that Ralph was thick-skinned and manipulative, but a game of squash? Perhaps, Jack thought, it was Ralph's way of getting back at him. At least the exercise would take his mind off his problems.

It didn't surprise him, however, to find that Ralph was a power player. His skilfully placed shots soon had Jack charging about the court like a madman in pursuit of a blowfly. They slugged it out – backwards and forwards rapidly across the court with Ralph yelling instructions each time he played a shot.

The score was eighteen–two, in Ralph's favour. He served again – a smashing shot that sent the little black ball straight back into Jack's face. It seemed to hit him like a stone.

'Jesus!' yelled Jack, as he dropped his racquet and held the side of his aching face.

'Sorry, mate.'

'Guess I deserved this, eh?' smiled Jack.

Ralph flicked his racquet high into the air and caught it by the handle. 'Nah, water under the bridge. Come on, you gotta really throw yourself into this.'

'Oh, so that's what's wrong,' said Jack dryly, and picked up his racquet.

Ralph's self-satisfied smile spread across his face. 'Maybe you an' Miss Ziggy are gettin' too much bed and not enough sleep?'

Jack looked over to Ralph, who was leaning against the wall waiting for a response. The evening had been bearable until this moment. Jack had felt he was picking up on this game of squash and even enjoying the exertion that it took to keep up. 'Serve the ball,' he said, determined not to react, as he positioned himself within the receiving area of the court.

'That's my man!' Ralph served, smashing the ball as hard as he could up high against the front wall. The ball rose up and fell deep in the right-hand corner. It was a trick that meant the ball had eluded Jack many times. Jack lashed out in the desperate hope of connecting with it but his racquet hit the wall and the ball fell square into the corner.

'Tricky one, that,' commented Ralph. 'You should

try and get to it earlier.' Ralph didn't try to hide his complacency.

'Earlier?' puffed Jack, 'I'm having enough trouble seeing the bloody thing.'

Ralph chuckled and served again. 'Ah, I wouldn't want to be a woman in this business,' he said casually.

'What?' asked Jack, after he hit the ball out. He could tell Ralph had something on his mind. He kept dropping these comments like little annoying barbs.

'We're hitting the new millennium, Jack. People don't have loyalty any more.'

'What are you gettin' at?' Jack wiped his face with the bottom of his T-shirt.

'Jack, this might sound outta line but Ziggy has a reputation for pulling out the stops . . . to get what she wants. Know what I mean?'

Jack tried to look as if all this had nothing to do with him.

'The directors have frowned on this for some time.'

Ralph served again. This time Jack returned with a swift lunge into the air sending the ball right out of Ralph's vision. 'Good shot,' he was forced to say. Ralph continued while awaiting Jack's serve. 'You know, mate, your deal goes right down the toilet if she's asked to leave.'

Jack held back on his serve. 'Ziggy, asked to leave?' he said, unable to pretend any more.

'You didn't hear this from me.'

Ralph's mobile phone rang. 'Shit, who's this?' he said, as he rummaged through his BMW sports bag tucked in at the front of the court. He pulled out his cell-phone.

'Yeah – What? – Who? . . . hang on.'

Ralph sighed, and looked over to Jack. 'Some chick called Suzie?'

Jack shrugged. Ralph put the phone back to his ear. 'He doesn't know a "Suzie".' Ralph rolled his eyes at Jack. The woman was being persistent.

'From Lucktown?' he asked as if his time was too precious to be dealing with personal calls.

Jack looked up. 'Suzie?' Of course he knew Suzie. He took the phone from Ralph. 'Suz, I'm sorry . . .'

She was sitting in the Boomerang Cafe. The place was empty but that suited Suzie. There was something she had to do.

'I know you must be busy, love,' she asked.

'Never too busy to talk to you, Suz. Pour a beer for me while you're there.'

'Oh, I'm not in the pub,' she said lightly.

'Don't tell me old Artie gave you the night off?'

'Jack – Ruby an' I have come to an arrangement. I own the Boomerang now.'

A smile lit up Jack's face. 'Fair dinkum?'

'Yep,' she said.

Ralph rolled his eyes again. He couldn't believe people still say 'fair dinkum'. He started to run on the spot to stay warm.

'Well done, Suz,' said Jack. 'I won't ask what Artie thinks.'

'No, I wouldn't do that,' she gave a quiet laugh. There was a note of victory in her voice.

'How's Lance?' Jack asked.

'He's right here with me.' Suzie held out the receiver to Lance. 'Say hello, boy.'

Lance barked once. That was enough for an old dog who needed his rest and who'd been unaccountably deserted for weeks.

'Everyone misses you, Jack,' said Suzie. Jack's brief silence told her what he was feeling. Meanwhile, Ralph, in the background, could not make head nor tail of the conversation.

'How's Rube?' The question sounded friendly and casual, but Suzie smiled to herself. She knew that that would be the next thing he'd ask.

'That's why I've rung, love,' Suzie was choosing her words carefully. 'She's had a bit of an upset with her plane.'

'What do you mean?' he asked quickly.

'She's okay. One rib and an ankle in plaster . . .'

'Jesus,' Jack exclaimed. 'What happened?'

By this time Ralph was so bored he was running furiously on the spot and counting rapidly, 'One, two. One, two.'

'Ralph . . .' yelled Jack. Ralph stopped and looked at him. 'Will you knock it off?'

Ralph got the message, gave him the thumbs up and started doing silent knee-bends.

Suzie resumed. 'Hamish and some bloke, who wanted to buy the plane, were at the airstrip and, well, Ruby didn't land so well. She's okay, that's the main thing.'

'She in the hospital?' asked Jack. He was thinking

Ruby, selling her Dad's biplane? It didn't make sense.

'No, you know what she's like. Limped outta there soon as she could.'

'Suz, why was she selling the biplane?'

'Well – I reckon there was no place for it in Queensland.' She paused, then added, 'So Hamish said.'

Jack took the phone away from his face. 'Bloody hell!' he swore. Ralph pointed to his watch and gestured that they should resume their game. Jack ignored him and placed the phone back to his ear.

'When are they getting married?' he asked.

'The accident has changed things a bit. They're lookin' to do it in Queensland now.' Suzie paused a beat. 'You should come up.' Suzie was about to burst. Why couldn't she just say what was on her mind? God, she'd just put Artie in his place after twenty-seven gruelling years of marriage. It was clear to her that someone had to guide this young man towards his destiny.

'I'm hardly the best man, Suz,' Jack said dryly.

Suzie sighed.

Right, she thought – in for a penny, in for a pound. 'Jack' she said, after taking a deep breath, 'I've had too many years of listening to inane crap an' never bein' able to say my piece. Well, things have changed, I'm layin' down some truths.'

Jack had never heard Suzie laying down the law. Ever. 'You okay, Suz?' he said, finding it difficult to conceal his amusement.

Suzie felt patronised. One more breath and she was into it. 'Our Ruby is about to marry Hamish. Now, we all know he's a good bloke. He's steady and reliable . . . Trouble is, Ruby's in love with someone who's not steady and not reliable.' Suzie now felt that she was on a roll. 'Ruby an' Hamish are headin' over the border day after tomorrow on Highway Thirty-two. Now, if this "someone" has the guts to do something about all this – I'll love him forever! Day after tomorrow. Highway Thirty-two.'

To Jack's surprise the conversation suddenly ceased. He stood staring at Ralph's little mobile, expecting to hear her voice again, but when he put it back to his ear the line was dead.

'Lord!' Suzie was saying back in Lucktown, 'You'll give me a heart attack.'

Ruby was standing in the doorway. 'He won't come.' She added as she limped into the room, 'He won't come to the wedding.'

Suzie reached out for a cigarette while she recovered herself. She thought her performance with Jack had been just right – she'd rehearsed it several times with Lance as her audience. But she had not reckoned on Rube walking in like that just when she was about to finally tell Jack Willis what he ought to be doing.

'I was just –' she began, suddenly feeling guilty, but Ruby wasn't taking any notice.

'He's irritating, selfish, insensitive, pig-headed, irresponsible –'

Now that Ruby was closer to her, Suze could see marks of tears around her eyes. She knew it wasn't the most appropriate thing to say to a young woman who was going to be a bride herself shortly, but she felt a diversion was important.

'Look,' she said and held up her left hand. There was nothing but a faint red line circling her fourth finger where her wedding ring once was. Ruby smiled.

******

Meanwhile in Sydney Jack switched off the phone and threw it back to Ralph. 'Hey.'

Ralph dropped his racquet in a panic to catch his airborne phone. 'Jesus.' Ralph did not relax until he had it safely packed away.

'My serve.' Jack threw up the little black ball and whacked it into the wall with a furious stroke. One bounce off the wall and it flew straight back into Ralph's other eye.

'Oh, fuck,' exclaimed Ralph, as he bent over in agony. Now he would have two black eyes.

'Sorry, mate,' said Jack.

'I'm fine – I'm fine. Happens all the time.'

'That's all right then,' said Jack, smiling grimly.

'Just to show you there's no hard feelings,' said Ralph at the end of the game, 'let me buy you a drink.'

Jack dearly wanted to be on his own. His dislike of Ralph had grown with every minute in his company and, more importantly, he wanted time to digest Suzie's surprising phone call. But while he was trying to think of a polite way to extract himself from the situation

Ralph added, 'And you'll be wanting to celebrate your big news, of course.'

It was immediately obvious to Ralph that Jack didn't know what he was talking about and he went on smoothly, 'Oh, hasn't Ziggy told you yet? Zane's office in New York has been talking to Errol and they want you to go over for the American launch . . . they're planning a big coast-to-coast author tour. Apparently outback truckers who write romantic novels are very promotable in the US. And then there's London . . .'

As Ralph went on talking, spouting dates and deals and expected print runs while they had a beer in a nearby bar, Jack kept going over and over Suzie's phone call. Those specific instructions – so specific that they were like orders – and that abrupt ending; no good-byes, nothing. It was as if she'd nerved up to ring him and then hung up once she'd gotten her words out. In the middle of one of Ralph's seemingly interminable speeches, Jack suddenly realised that Suzie thought it was a mistake for Ruby to marry Hamish.

'And she's not married,' he said to himself, 'she's *not* married.' He still couldn't quite believe that. Ever since that night that Ruby had left Sydney with Hamish, Jack had tried not to think about her. 'She's made her choice,' he thought, 'she loves him.' I told her he needed her and she went to him. I thought it was what she wanted. Hell, she'd been panicking about him all day, thinking he was going to ditch her. She and I have been fighting all our lives – until just recently . . .

'Want a lift back to the hotel? It's on my way.' Ralph was asking him a question.

Jack looked at him blankly. 'Sure mate,' he said absent-mindedly. He was feeling both confused and exhilarated. She wasn't married to Hamish – yet.

'Got a big night planned?' Ralph asked, as he swung into the kerb in front of the hotel.

For the first time in the hour or so that he'd spent with Jack Willis since their game, Ralph felt like he had the other man's complete attention.

Jack turned and looked at him as he was opening his car door, 'Yeah,' he said. 'A very very big night.'

'Going somewhere special?' persisted Ralph.

Jack smiled at him, 'Somewhere very special.'

'Well,' said Ralph, who was very curious but unable to think of a way to elicit any further information, 'Make sure you get some sleep.'

'Won't have time for that,' said Jack, as he closed the car door.

******

There was a cool breeze coming off the Harbour by the time Jack arrived at Ziggy's warehouse apartment. He climbed the steel staircase slowly; each step he took seemed to echo throughout the vastness of the building.

'You're late,' Ziggy stood at the door wearing nothing under her red silk kimono, completely open at the front. The silk fabric fell in one line from her shoulders, across the very tips of her nipples and down to the floor. Ziggy had never before greeted a man this way. But right now that moment of vulner-ability turned her on. Ziggy wanted Jack immediately, anywhere he chose.

Jack's gaze fell upon her with such uncertainty that she automatically closed the front of her kimono.

'Good thing I wasn't the gas man,' he smiled.

'Where have you been? Your game with Ralph was over hours ago,' Ziggy asked.

'Just took a walk for a bit.'

'What's wrong, Jack?' She searched his eyes, sensing something.

'Nothing.' Jack entered and closed the door behind him.

'I gotta surprise for you,' Ziggy couldn't stop herself. She was so excited.

'I think I've already seen it.'

'Shut up and close your eyes,' she insisted.

'Ziggy, I don't feel like . . .'

'Jack, men don't get headaches.'

'Okay, they're closed – they're closed.'

Ziggy led him forward and around into the main part of her apartment. Jack shuffled along over carpet and bare boards, fearing the worst. The thought of an elaborate sex machine crossed his mind. He wouldn't have put it past Ziggy. Somehow he envisioned an apparatus of pulleys and canvas love seats criss-crossing the rafters.

'Open.'

Jack hesitated. Oh, Christ, he thought, why can't I just keep them closed? Up to this point in their affair, insatiable fucking had dominated their time together. They had sex literally in every corner of the warehouse. Any flat surface would do. Jack had never experienced such freedom.

When Jack could stall no longer, he opened his eyes and stood bewildered before dozens of male store mannequins – each one with its own layer of exquisite clothing. There were suits by Armani and Calvin Klein; Dunhill sports jackets; shirts by Cardin; flamboyant scarves, silk ties and Italian shoes. To complete each mannequin, Ziggy had painstakingly cut out photos of his face and pasted them to the lifeless figures.

'Have you ever seen so many Jacks in one place?' Ziggy asked with a proud smile. Jack turned back to her, then took another eyeful of his replicas.

'What happens here?' he asked.

'Simple. You make choices.'

'I can't do this, Ziggy.'

Ziggy shook her head. 'Shit, Ella said you might prefer browsing in stores.' She was just about to announce the news of this big American trip for which he'd need the new wardrobe when Jack said, 'How do I do this?'

'Just point.'

Jack turned to Ziggy.

'What? Tell me,' she said, moving up and wrapping her arms around his waist. 'I can have it all sent back.'

Jack hesitated, his face creased with anxiety.

What the hell, thought Ziggy. 'I think I'm in love with all these guys, Jack.'

Jack gave a deep sigh. It was not what she wanted to hear.

'Do you hate the clothes that much?'

'Ziggy . . .' he hesitated again.

'Call me Catherine.'

'Catherine.'

'Yes, Jack,' she smiled cheekily.

'Do you ever get the feelin' that your life's just one big trail of emotional debris?'

Ziggy laughed.

'I'm serious.'

'Debris? Don't be stupid. Look at your life. And you're about to—'

'I gotta problem,' he said cutting across her.

'I'm all ears,' she moved up to him and placed her hands on each side of his face. She looked deep into his eyes and smiled. 'Jack, if we're to build a strong relationship we've got to be honest with each other right from day one.'

'Yep,' answered Jack nervously.

'I'm a big girl – I can help.' She smiled knowingly at him and asked, 'Have you heard of women's intuition?'

'Absolutely.'

'Well then, respect that before you even think of stealing a girl's heart.'

Jack smiled half-heartedly.

'It's all right, I know what's troubling you.' Ziggy said this with such confidence he doubted whether her 'intuition' was up to speed.

Jack just spat it out. 'Ziggy, I'm in love with . . .'

Ziggy placed her hand over his lips cutting off the

remainder of his words. She smiled and savoured the moment. 'I know.'

Oh, Christ, did she know that he was about to say? Why was he stalling? The whole bloody thing should be over and done with by now. Just open your mouth and something will come out.

'Ziggy, I'm in love with Ruby.'

It was difficult to tell Ziggy from the motionless floor dummies that stared at him from every corner of the apartment.

She had gone very white. All sensation had left her eyes. Slowly, ever so slowly – before Jack realised what was happening – Ziggy fell backwards.

'Oh, shit, no!' Jack leant forward and caught her. He carried her limp body through the forest of mannequins and lowered her onto the bed. Jack covered her exquisite body, aware he was seeing it for the last time. He walked across the sink, wet the end of a towel and placed it over her forehead.

She came to slowly. Her eyes darted around as she slowly realised what had happened. Jack smiled down at her. She was beautiful, he thought.

'I was dreaming, wasn't I?' she asked, looking up at him hopefully.

Jack shook his head. A tear slipped from the corner of her eye and rolled down her cheek.

'Shit, shit, shit!' she said, rubbing at her cheek, 'This is just like one of your fucking books.'

Jack shrugged. 'Maybe – without the language.'

His joke was lost on her. Ziggy glanced away, angry. 'What is it? Do I annoy you?'

'No. It's just that I'm in love with someone else.'

Ziggy pondered this and sighed. There was nothing she could do. 'You're meant to be in love with me, you silly bugger.' Ziggy looked back at him. 'So much for women's intuition.'

'It could do with a tweak,' Jack quipped.

They looked at each other, then Ziggy wrapped her arms around him and held him tight for a final moment.

******

The handwritten sign that said *You Touch, You Buy* was still in place in the billiards shop but there didn't seem to be anyone around.

'Hello,' Jack called out. But no one appeared.

Jack continued through the shop towards the counter at the rear. Many times his hand wanted to touch the ornately carved sticks. As he neared the counter, an old man with a felt cap suddenly poked his head up from under a display.

'By Jesus, son, you frightened me,' he barked.

Jack, equally startled, leapt back with such force that he knocked over the nearest row of cue-sticks. They fell like dominos. He reached out but the harder he tried to halt the cascading sticks the more he sent off the stands. They covered the floor – hundreds of them. Jack then stepped on one and slid to the floor pulling down another floor display. The old man watched as the last of the sticks clattered to the floor then without a word, he stepped forward with a pad and pencil and started counting up the fallen cues.

'Hey, what are you doin'?' Jack asked. The old man continued his task without so much as a glance at him. Jack picked up the nearest cue and held it in the air. 'I only touched this one!'

The old man looked at him squinting his eyes to examine the cue in Jack's hand.

'That happens to be a *balabushka*, sir,' said the old man sarcastically. Then he grinned.

'Well then – I'll take it, won't I?' said Jack. 'I'll bloody take it.'

A couple of minutes later he walked out into the street carrying Ruby's *balabushka* pool cue in a black, felt-lined case. Just the ticket. Now he had to hit the road. If Suzie was correct about Hamish and Ruby's departure, he would have to move fast.

Having declared his love for Ruby he was tormented by doubts. What if it was all in vain? What if he'd hurt her so much there was no chance of reconciliation? 'It's going to be one helluva long drive to Lucktown,' he said to himself.

******

It was dark by the time he collected his gear from the hotel and located his rig, still parked in the deserted construction site. Most of the heavy excavating machinery had long gone. The steel personnel and equipment sheds were locked and the security office was empty. Jack pushed in a section of the wire fence and hoped that most of his rig remained intact.

Sure enough, there it stood. A smashed side window surely meant that the tape deck and CB radio had been ripped out. But it took Jack a minute or two to notice that because he was too busy staring. The entire length of the trailer had been sprayed with graffiti. Jack shook his head, but thought, At least it's still here.

He kicked over the engine, crept the vehicle forward and nudged the precarious, wire security gate until it opened.

Then he was on his way.

20

Rain had followed Ruby back to Lucktown. For the weeks she'd been back with Hamish, good steady falls were widespread over most of their stretch of the outback. Many dirt roads became impassable, but that didn't take the cocky smiles off the faces of the local farmers. The rainy season was early this year; reservoirs and dams were slowly filling. Plants that had lain dormant for years burst into life at this gift from the heavens.

Ruby loved the din of croaking frogs and cicadas along the creek banks announcing the change in season with great gusto. And the wildflowers. Even though she'd grown up in the outback it remained a mystery to her how such delicate blooms could spring from such a harsh land. Yet, after one rainstorm, the brown scorched earth could become a miraculous carpet of colour.

Ruby sealed the last moving box with packing tape and stood to stretch her back. Although it had been raining, her white cotton T-shirt was damp with sweat. Ruby surveyed her belongings. Everything she owned, apart from what Hamish had already packed into the Land Rover, sat there in boxes on the verandah.

'What about this, Rube?' Hamish appeared through the flyscreen door wearing nothing but an old pair of football shorts. Ruby told him it was a good look for him.

He held in his hand what remained of Ruby's biplane prop. 'I mean, we can hardly put it above the fireplace.'

'Give it to me.' Ruby held out her hands, feeling too tired for jokes.

'I was just kiddin'.'

'You're lucky that's all I'm takin'.' Ruby placed the broken propeller on top of the boxes and sat down on the edge of the verandah to rest her ankle.

Hamish sat beside her and passed her a stubby of beer. He took a swig and peered out into the night. The rain had stopped and the sweet smell of damp earth filled his nostrils.

'Rube, have you thought again about selling this place?' he asked.

'I sold the Boomerang.'

'No – you gave the Boomerang away.'

Ruby smiled. 'Yeah, I did, didn't I?'

Hamish smiled and shook his head. 'I reckon you could get thirty grand for this.'

'Let's just rent it, Hamish.' Ruby took a swig. 'Haven't asked her yet, but I have the feelin' Suzie's gonna need somewhere . . .'

'Bloody hell, Rube.'

'What?'

Hamish was getting worried by Ruby's generosity. 'What are we now, the Salvation Army?'

'No, she's my friend – and if she takes it she can pay whatever it's worth.'

Hamish gave up; Ruby was not going to change. 'What time's the moving truck coming?'

'Six forty-five.'

'Hell!' he replied, and squashed a huge mosquito that had landed on his neck. Hamish studied his blood-stained hand.

'Look at the size of that bugger.'

'Least you know there's blood pumpin' through there,' she said with a grin.

Hamish wrapped his arm around Ruby and kissed her on the cheek. 'Just think, this time tomorrow we'll almost be there.'

'Yeah.'

A chorus of frogs started up from underneath the tank-stand.

'We should have that plaster looked at when we get to Goondiwindi.'

Ruby wiggled her toes casually.

'Feels all right to me.'

'Well . . .' he said doubtfully, and leaned over the edge of the verandah to inspect her ankle. Hamish's face froze. Fear filled his eyes. 'Rube . . .'

'What?' His tone was frightening her.

'Don't – move – your leg,' he said quietly.

A cold shiver shot through Ruby's body. 'What is it?' she whispered weakly.

'There's a snake . . .'

'Ahhh . . .'

'Shhh. Just don't move till I say.'

Ruby was rigid with fear, paralysed at the thought of even breathing.

Hamish continued carefully, 'Now, when I say, swing your legs slowly up onto the verandah.'

The snake was pitch black in colour with a red belly. Its damp skin glistened from the light off the verandah as it slid past, inches from Ruby's feet. Waiting seemed an eternity. Her body started to shiver.

'Keep still, Rube.'

A smile broke across Hamish's face. 'He's gone!'

Ruby twisted her body around and, in one acrobatic move despite the plaster swung her legs up onto the verandah. 'Oh, shit!' She lay there on her back laughing. The relief was immense.

Hamish, meanwhile, already had a weapon in his hand. He raised the broken aircraft propeller high into the air and brought it down heavily on the snake's back. The snake flicked and twisted in agony.

'Hamish, what are you doin'?' screamed Ruby, sitting up.

Again, the propeller smashed down onto the writhing snake.

'I keep missing the bugger's head,' yelled Hamish.

'Don't, Hamish!'

'It's okay, I'm safe . . .'

'Don't kill it!'

Hamish stepped back a safe distance and looked over to Ruby. 'What?' he asked, bewildered. The snake was already at death's door; the two hits from the propeller had crushed its spine. 'You like snakes?'

'Not particularly – but Jack reckons they do a lotta good.'

'Oh, is that what he thinks?'

She knew she'd said the wrong thing. Hamish delivered one last decisive blow to the snake's head. Satisfied, he then picked up the carcass with the point of the propeller and hurled it out into the darkness.

'Believe me, Rube, when you have kids in the country, the only good snake is a dead one.'

He returned to the verandah, casually returned the blood-stained propeller to its place on the boxes and reached down to help Ruby up. He wrapped an arm around her and rested his cheek against her hair for a moment.

'Let's get a good night's sleep, eh?'

Ruby nodded, and walked with him back into the house.

******

It seemed to take Jack hours to get out of Sydney as he retraced his route back across the Harbour Bridge, out through the northwestern suburbs of Ryde, Castle Hill and Windsor, then finally up the long trail up to the Blue Mountains.

The traffic was thick in these sections of urban sprawl. It took him two long and frustrating hours of changing gears and stopping and starting before he broke loose over the mountains and onto the western plains. Only then did he feel he was really on his way. But the trip was different without Lance on the seat beside him or the comfort of his music.

He stopped periodically – once for diesel fuel, once for food and twice for coffee. By dawn, the familiar outback landscape was a welcome sight. He knew that he was back where he belonged. His soul felt rejuvenated and his tired face showed all of the determination of a man with passion in his heart. In Sydney, nothing seemed possible; out here, the world was truly his. How on earth he was going to deal with the rest of his life, he wasn't sure. But suddenly bright and alive in his mind there was Pilot Officer Boult. 'You're a brave bastard,' said Jack, to his paperback hero. 'What would you do?'

21

Ziggy loved the Sydney Tower Restaurant. Ella, on the other hand, suffered vertigo, so they compromised and choose two stools at the bar facing the elevators. Both women, with their backs to an entirely spectacular view of Sydney, ordered another round of colourful cocktails.

'What more can a woman do,' said Ziggy miserably. 'I did everything. Bought his clothes, arranged his evenings, organised his days . . .' Ziggy was taking her frustration out on a tiny cocktail umbrella, opening and closing it rapidly as she talked.

Ella glanced at her over the rim of her tall glass. 'I reckon none-of-the-above might've been a good start,' she suggested dryly.

'Really?'

'Yeah, and careful with that umbrella – might bring you bad luck.'

'Huh! More?'

Ella sucked again on her elaborate plastic twisted straw, then pulled back and studied the colour of her drink. 'What are we drinking?' she asked.

Ziggy merely shook her head. Ella had never seen her so dejected.

'Oh, Ella – why is love so bloody difficult?'

'Probably because it was lust.'

Ziggy turned and looked at Ella with a sad, pained expression. 'I can't tell the difference.'

'Comes with practice,' said Ella, taking another sip.

Ziggy sighed deeply. Jack was the most intimate relationship she'd had with a man for as long as she could remember. All the other men in her life seemed threatened by her – or she got bored with them.

'So,' Ella continued, 'are you trying to tell me that Errol was so annoyed that Mister Number-one client left town on the eve of his big US trip that, as a result, you and – God forbid – me, need to seek further employment?'

'Not exactly,' said Ziggy.

A businessman with a plain pudgy face and a buzz cut squeezed between Ziggy and Ella to reach for a bowl of beer nuts. 'Hi, girls – I'm from outta town.'

'Fuck off, we're in conference,' snapped Ella.

The man reeled back, withdrawing his hand slowly from the bowl of nuts as he retreated.

'I should inquire more about your personal life,' said Ziggy to Ella, who was still reflecting on love and lust.

'Don't.'

'You know,' Ziggy sighed, 'I've come to the conclusion that I know absolutely nothing about men.'

'Tell you a secret,' replied Ella. 'They know absolutely nothing about you.'

Ziggy was somehow pleased by this statement. 'Yes,' she nodded to herself and took another long sip of her drink.

'You still haven't told me why we're sippin' aircraft fuel on our lunch-hour?' continued Ella.

Ziggy finished her drink and gathered the remaining foam off the bottom of the glass with a loud slurp. She pushed the glass away and indicated to the barman that she would have one more. What the hell, she thought, she had no intention of returning to the office that day.

'I'm quitting the Zane boys' club.'

Ella looked at her in astonishment. Ziggy went on, 'And I want my own company and I want you there with me.'

Ella couldn't believe what she was hearing. 'Are we talking any money here?' she asked with a droll note in her voice.

'A partnership.'

Ella thought about this for a moment. A partnership sounded good. But what did it really mean other than two rather ambitious women sharing a one-room office over a sleazy chemist shop in Victoria Street? Still, that was a start – and where was she ever really heading by staying at Zane? 'What will we do for authors?' she asked.

'Well,' said Ziggy, 'we can start with one hot romance writer.'

Ella smiled. 'I'm in.'

The girls lifted their huge cocktails and clinked glasses.

******

Boult assumed, due to the intensity of the German attack, that the bogus marker-bombing by pathfinder squadrons further west had failed to mislead the enemy defences as to the intended British target. Even worse, many aircraft in the bomber stream had drifted too far north and into the infamous searchlights of the Ruhr defences. Now, with the moon much higher in the sky, everyone knew that it was a splendid evening . . . for German night-fighters.

With bombs fused, Pilot Officer Boult switched off his navigational lights and opened the Lancaster's bomb doors. Sudden flak explosions shook the belly of the plane.

'Don't take any notice, lads,' he barked, 'the bastards are just tryin' to break our morale.'

A few crew members chuckled nervously.

All they had to do now was to continue a straight and narrow run towards the target, deliver their 10 000 pounds of surprise and get the hell out of there.

Boult reached into his uniform and pulled out Susanna's photograph for one more look. He knew he loved this woman with all his heart.

'Oh, God!' The scream from the nose gunner echoed throughout the aircraft as the blinding radar-controlled searchlight cone found them. Seconds later, there was a strafing from above.

'Fighter to port – thousand yards,' screamed the rear gunner.

Susanna's photograph fell from Boult's gloved hand as he grabbed the controls and dived. Without warning, another burst of cannon shells tore violently through the port-side fuselage and into the chest of the navigator. He had no time to scream; he fell, spilling his blood all over the metal deck.

The target aimer struggled aft and tried desperately to secure the navigator's body before it was flung like a rag doll through the aircraft. The mid-upper gunner screamed with fear as he fired tracer blindly into the night. No one could see their attackers. Boult was still trying to avoid the deadly searchlights as he held his dive to seven thousand feet. But the treacherous night-fighters were gathering and moving in like a school of killer sharks . . .

Jack was on a roll, scribbling frantically from Dubbo to Nyngan. He knew his writing skills would return the moment he was back behind the wheel. Yes, Ruby was going to love this one. Especially the chapter when Susanna waits at Waddington for the return of her lover's Lancaster . . .

The night was endless as battle-scarred bombers sporadically limped home in the wee small hours of the morning. Pilot Officer Boult's aircraft never made it. But his silk parachute canopy floated away from danger like a falling angel.

The graffiti artwork that covered Jack's rig looked incongruous against the desert landscape. The rig roared along the highway towards Broken Hill like a huge travelling canvas. A monument to street art, air-brushed and enhanced by a fine coat of brown dust. Jack was nearly home.

22

Highway Thirty-two. A straight run north-east from
Broken Hill via Wilcannia, Cobar and through to
Nyngan. A good six hundred kilometres in a heavily
loaded, aging Land Rover. Hamish expected to arrive
in Nyngan by late afternoon. He and Ruby would
find a cheap motel, get a bite to eat and head off
north first thing the following morning.

Hamish had painstakingly worked on another proposed route to their new home in the border town of
Goondiwindi. He felt, where possible, it was better to
bypass major centres like the wheat towns of Nar-
romine and Dubbo, and cut the distance 'by way of
the crow' even if it meant a few unsealed roads.
Hamish always said that it was far better to travel
eighty kilometres on a gravel road than three hundred on bitumen. All Ruby knew was that if they'd
flown, like she'd proposed, they would be there
already having a cup of tea.

Ruby switched the cassettes in her walkman for the
folk-rock sound of Ani DiFranco. 'Untouchable Face'
was her favourite. She tried to remember what she had

packed. Hamish's things took up most of the room. She had a few items of sentimental value: her dad's flying books and his roll-top desk, a sideboard, her mother's hand-painted plates. Although there seemed to be a lot of 'stuff', nothing much else mattered and she'd left it in the house or at the Boomerang.

North of Gilgandra, on the Great Western Plains, Ruby was looking forward to seeing the famous Warrumbungles – a rugged mountain range that literally thrust skywards through the miles of flat, dry sheep country. She'd camped there once with her school on an excursion. She remembered how mystical the flat-top mountain peaks had seemed – so old that only the very core of the ancient volcanos that had created them remained. They stood erect like huge, ancient corks. She remembered Jack being there, too, with his class.

She removed her headset.

'Do you reckon we've got time to see the Warrumbungles?' she shouted over the roar of the Land Rover.

'You've seen 'em, Rube.'

'Yeah, I know, but you know, if we've got time.'

Hamish glanced down at his map laid out on the seat between them. 'Let's see.' He passed his finger along their proposed route north from Dubbo. 'Nah, sorry, looks like it's gonna be dark by the time we pass through there, Rube.'

Ruby sighed and peered back out the window. 'Doesn't matter.'

An Aboriginal drover waved to her from a distance as they passed a sheep-herding yard by the edge of the road. Ruby waved back.

Some distance ahead of them at a dusty crossroad, a huge road train, four trailers in length, pulled out, blocking the entire highway.

'Bugger me,' yelled Ruby, as she ripped off her headset again.

'What?' asked Hamish.

'We'll never get past him in this.'

'Do we need to?' asked Hamish. He glanced down at the speedometer. They were already doing fifty miles an hour.

Ruby smiled mischievously. 'Give it some stick, Hamish.'

'Rube, this old Rover isn't one of your flyin' machines.'

'Flat to the floor – come on.'

Hamish accelerated. The old diesel engine roared. Slowly they caught up to the rear of the speeding road train.

'There you go,' yelled Ruby excitedly.

Dust and stones kicked up from the roadside as each trailer meandered like a snake and swayed dangerously in front of them. Hamish made his move.

'Go, Hamish . . .' screamed Ruby.

The Land Rover haemorrhaged as it pulled out along-side the road train. The monster was about one hundred and twenty feet long and travelling at sixty-five kilometres per hour.

'Go, go,' screamed Ruby again, as they slowly inched their way along until level with the second trailer.

The driver stuck his arm out and waved them on. Hamish was driving hard.

Ruby had a grin from ear to ear. 'Go, Hamish. Go.'

'I'm flat out, Rube,' he screamed back.

Again, the driver waved them on. There was no more power. The Land Rover was at full speed.

Up ahead, Hamish spotted an on-coming rig. 'There's a truck coming.'

'Oh, shit!' said Ruby, as she flopped back into her seat.

The moment Hamish took his foot off the pedal, the Land Rover started to fall back behind the road train.

The on-coming truck was Jack's rig. He hit the air horns. 'Mad bloody driver,' he cursed. The driver of the road train gave Jack a courtesy wave as the two huge vehicles passed within feet of each other. The Land Rover passed before Jack realised who was inside.

'You know what, Hamish?' Ruby smiled. 'We need a V–8 Range Rover.'

'You just like speed.'

'Yeah, I'll sure miss the old plane.'

'Maybe I could work for the Flyin' Doctor Service,' she added after a moment.

Hamish threw his head back with a chuckle.

'What?' asked Ruby, indignant.

'Yeah, maybe if they hadn't seen you doin' barrel-rolls over the airstrip last Anzac Day.'

'That was a celebration.'

'Of what? Stupidity?'

Ruby didn't reply immediately. She watched as the road train drew farther and farther away, and thought of Jack. She tried to put him out of her mind. She was here; he was still in Sydney.

'My dad used to do barrel-rolls,' she said quietly.

Hamish grunted.

23

Jack pulled up directly in front of the Boomerang Cafe, pulled on the familiar stiff flyscreen door and hurried inside.

Lance was the first to spot him. The old dog ran forward with such glee that his paws couldn't grip the linoleum floor and he half slid his way into Jack's open arms.

As Jack embraced his dog he called out to Suzie. 'Where is she, Suz?'

Suzie looked up to an old electric clock fixed to the wall. It was the shape of an aircraft cowling with propeller arms. It read five after eleven. 'Left hours ago, love. They sped outta here like there was no tomorrow. Can I fix you a coffee?'

Jack's body filled with a sick tiredness. He looked back to Suzie and nodded to the offer of coffee. 'What do you mean, hours ago?' he asked.

'Maybe four,' Suzie said glumly. 'The rain cleared. Their moving truck came real early.'

Jack paced in front of the counter for a moment then sat down wearily on a stool.

'I'm real sorry, love. I didn't think they'd get away until later in the day.'

She placed black coffee down in front of him, noticing as she approached the graffiti all over the side of his rig.

'What happened to your rig?'

'Big city welcome,' muttered Jack.

'It's quite pretty really, isn't it? You had breakfast?'

'No.'

'I'll fix your favourite.'

Jack just nodded. Suzie could see that he was distressed. She walked to the fridge and pulled out eggs, bacon and tomatoes.

'You know, I . . .' Jack stopped, but Suzie understood. There wasn't much she didn't know about heartache.

'What, love?' she said quietly, leaning over the counter towards him. A couple of other truckers had just come in.

'It's all too bloody late, isn't it?'

'For what?' she asked.

'Typical. Everything's staring me straight in the eye an' I'm fuckin' about like a fly on a window.'

Suzie smiled and glanced up again to the clock. 'They headed out on Highway Thirty-two.'

'Yeah,' Jack said with a sigh, 'I reckon I might just catch them by the time they get to Queensland.'

The bacon sizzled the moment Suzie threw it in the cast-iron pan. 'What would you say to Ruby?'

Jack hedged. 'What do you mean?'

'What would you say to Ruby if she was standing right here?'

'Suz . . .'

'Jack,' she cut in, 'be bloody resourceful.' She looked away, then added, 'I think that's the word.'

Jack sipped his coffee while she served the truckers who'd just come in.

Suzie had a point. It didn't matter where he finally caught up to Ruby – what in the hell was he going to say? Christ and then there was Hamish. What about him? Jack glanced around the interior of the cafe. Ruby's presence was everywhere. Suzie had made no effort to change the decor. Everyone liked it the way it was. Jack's eye fell upon a photo of Ruby with her father sitting in the biplane. She was eight when she first wore the goggles, eighteen when she first flew solo. Officially, that is. Rumour had it that her dad had her flying much sooner than that. Jack gripped his head between his hands for a moment and told himself to get going. Christ, he couldn't just sit here gazing at memorabilia. He took one more gulp of coffee and strode out of the Boomerang Cafe. Suzie watched him leave without saying a word.

'What's wrong with him, Suz?' enquired Mad Pete, sucking back hard on another freshly lit cigarette. 'Bugger me, he goes to the city an' comes home a different bloke.'

'I've no idea, Pete.'

******

Hamish and Ruby drove on in silence for a long time. The landscape didn't change much until after Wilcannia. Then they drove across the Paroo River and moved on north-east towards Cobar. Ruby counted the water tanks. It was something to do. All the way along Highway Thirty-two, bores and tanks provided precious subterranean water for cattle and sheep. Many of the tanks had huge, rusted windmills that pumped bore water endlessly to keep up with thirst and evaporation. Ruby liked the elegance of the gently turning blades; they squeaked and groaned like living things. A flock of emus, drinking from a tank, were distracted by the roar of the Land Rover, and scattered through a broken fence like frightened children.

Ruby was able to identify most light aircraft by the engine drone. A biplane was a cinch. A rare Curtis Jenny, a Tiger Moth, a Grumman, Swordfish or a Stearman, like the one she had, were all music to her ears. The drone above them was a Cessna 180.

Ruby leant forward in her seat and squinted out into the sunlight.

'What is it, Rube?' asked Hamish.

'A 180,' she replied casually.

'No, I mean, what's wrong?'

'Nothin'.'

'You're just very quiet.'

Ruby smiled and glanced back out the window. 'You mightn't think so, but all this country is beautiful from the air.'

'I'll believe you,' chuckled Hamish. It struck Ruby

again that a fear of flying was one thing Hamish had in common with Jack.

******

Jack and Mack had flown as fast as the old Cessna could go. Assuming that Hamish and Ruby would still be travelling Highway Thirty-two, they tracked the Land Rover north-east of Broken Hill. Jack knew it was his only chance to intercept Ruby.

He leant forward in his seat beside the pilot and searched frantically for a sickbag. Fortunately, he hadn't yet done the deed but it was only a matter of time.

'There's a Rover, Jack,' yelled Mack, as he dipped the left wing for a clearer view of the highway.

Jack couldn't look; he had his face over the sickbag.

'I'll go down for a geeza, eh?' Mack didn't wait for an answer as he pushed the stick forward and honed in on the Land Rover like a diving Messerschmitt.

'What the hell's he doin'?' asked Ruby, with her face pressed hard against the front window. She was smiling as she watched the plane

The Cessna passed low over the Land Rover. Hamish instinctively ducked, as if the plane were to take off his roof.

'Bugger me,' he yelled.

'They must be having so much fun,' said Ruby, excitedly.

******

Meanwhile Jack was hanging on for dear life. Mack levelled out his Cessna and turned to him with a grin. 'That's them, isn't it?'

Jack nodded.

'Okay then, we gotta get some height.' Mack pulled back on the stick. The little Cessna struggled with the drastic ascent.

'He's bloody mad,' roared Hamish.

'Yeah.' Ruby was busy searching the sky for the fearless flyer and answered without thinking.

'Unless, of course, he's in trouble.' Hamish couldn't imagine anyone flying so recklessly for the fun of it.

'No,' said Ruby confidently, 'he's not in trouble.'

The Cessna reached seven thousand feet before Mack levelled out again. He turned to Jack. 'You buckled in tight?'

Jack nodded. That was all he was capable of. This was his Nuremberg. He hoped Mack had parachutes.

'Okay, here we go.' Mack reached down and pulled a lever beside his seat then, with two hands firmly on the stick, threw the Cessna straight into a dive.

'Ahhhhhhh!' . . . Jack spoke for the first time.

'Hang on,' yelled Mack. He took the Cessna out from the bottom of the loop, hit the rudder, adjusted the throttle and dipped sharply to the left. 'This old girl wasn't really designed for this, ya know,' he yelled cheerfully, as if this information was of no importance.

From the ground, the antics of the little Cessna were now becoming clearer. Ruby watched in amazement as Mack looped, dived and twisted in the air high above them. Out behind the rear of the plane, a vapour trail slowly spelt out her name. The formation of each letter required a punishing loop from the Cessna.

'Oh, Jesus,' Ruby was enthralled. Her face and hands still pressed to the glass.

'Oh, Hamish . . .'

'What?'

More letters strung together spelt, *I love you*.

Ruby turned to Hamish with a look of complete affection. Her eyes filled with tears. 'Is this why you insisted on drivin' . . .?'

Hamish looked puzzled. What was Ruby on about? He slowed the Land Rover and peered high out the driver's window.

'You wonderful, romantic man.' Ruby reached over and threw her arms around him. The Land Rover swerved.

'Careful, Rube.'

Ruby wasn't listening. She looked deep into his eyes as if discovering a side of Hamish she'd never known existed.

'Look what you've done,' she said softly.

'What?'

Ruby gave a coy smile. High above the desert was written: *Ruby I love you*. As she watched there were a few more puffs of white vapour until the word 'Jack' emerged.

Hamish's Land Rover rolled to a stop beside the edge of Highway Thirty-two.

******

'Do you want an exclamation mark?' yelled Mack as he kept the Cessna in a steep dive.

'No!' screamed Jack knowing it was a miracle he hadn't thrown up all over the cabin. Mack levelled out.

'Hell, that was fun.' He peered back over his shoulder to glimpse his artwork in the sky.

'D'you think she's seen it?'

'Hope so.'

Jack was intensely relieved that the plane was flying straight and level. Mack chuckled and slapped him on the shoulder.

'Make a flyer out of you yet.'

Jack was happy to stick to writing books. 'Please, Mack – can we land?'

Mack teased him again by pushing forward on the stick.

'Oh, shit, no!' yelled Jack.

******

Ruby and Hamish shared an uncomfortable silence in the cabin of the Land Rover. The only sound was the spitting and coughing of Mack's Cessna as it glided down to earth.

'What do you want to do?' Hamish's voice was taut.

Another splutter from the Cessna drew Ruby's eyes up ahead as it landed roughly on the bitumen highway.

There had already been tears in Ruby's eyes at the thought of Hamish pulling such a romantic stunt. Now there were more tears, and a deep confusion.

She avoided Hamish's stare for some time by gazing blankly out into the dry desert countryside. By the side of the road a crow was pecking at the carcass of a rabbit hit by a car.

Hamish sighed. 'I had six cups of tea waiting for you in that city cafe.'

Ruby looked back at him. A slight ironic smile came across Hamish's face.

'I hate the bloody stuff,' he said.

'I know.' Ruby grabbed a tissue from the box on the dashboard and blew her nose. Hamish's eyes followed the tissue to the floor as Ruby discarded it.

'I've let you down, Hamish.'

'Nah,' he replied coolly after a moment of thought. 'Nah, I've let myself down. Floggin' a dead horse I think they call it.'

For a moment Ruby rested her hand on Hamish's arm. She could feel the tension in the big man. 'I'm sorry,' whispered Ruby. 'I'm not the one . . .'

Hamish smiled sarcastically. 'Funny, isn't it?'

'What?' asked Ruby.

'How your fuckin' life can turn in an instant?'

There was a long pause before Ruby replied. 'Yeah.'

Hamish chuckled at the irony of his question – never once taking his eyes off the Cessna taxiing some distance away. Mack negotiated his way off the highway and cut the engine.

'I never thought I'd see him in the air.' He turned back to Ruby. The tension in his arm relented.

'Go on, then. I'll send the truck back with your stuff.'

Ruby leant forward and kissed him on the cheek. Hamish responded by starting the Land Rover and waiting for her to climb out. Ruby opened the door, eased her plastered ankle out onto the edge of the road and slipped off the seat. There was nothing more to say. Hamish didn't glance at her as he drove off.

A small dust storm, a whirly-whirly, kicked grit into Ruby's eyes. For a moment Jack's Cessna was obscured. Ruby hobbled away from the wind, which seemed to abate as quickly as it appeared. Again, the desert was filled with a strange silence.

'I reckon I've fallen in love three times in my life,' yelled Jack over the distance between them.

Ruby looked up and shaded her eyes. 'Nice for some,' she remarked.

Jack could see that Ruby was not going to be a pushover. When had she ever been? 'First time . . . Let's see. When you were about thirteen . . .'

'You were too old for me, Jack,' she yelled back.

Jack shrugged. 'Then again, when I saw you in that black dress in Sydney . . .'

'You didn't say much.' Their voices seemed hollow in the sparseness that surrounded them.

'And right now,' yelled Jack.

Ruby took a moment. She was still confused and the hurt on Hamish's face haunted her.

'What, only three times?' Ruby said coolly. She was determined that Jack would make the first move. He hopped out of the Cessna and took his time survey-ing the emptiness. He held a long slender case in one hand.

'I suppose you need a lift?' he asked in a casual way.

Ruby summoned all of her courage and screamed out at the top of her voice. 'You come and bloody-well get me, Jack Willis.'

Jack put the *balabushka* case down carefully and ran to her. The distance seemed huge over the uneven ground. Finally they came together and shared one long passionate kiss. A surge, like nothing before, filled Ruby's heart. She held on tight – tight against the warmth and strength of this man. Ruby wanted to make love right there and then. Right where they stood, entwined in the harsh desert grass.

Eventually, Ruby broke free from their embrace. 'Damn you, Jack Willis.'

'What?' Jack had played his whole hand now. What could be wrong?

'Why'd you take so long?' she gasped.

'Come on,' he protested, 'I was over the limit the whole way from Sydney.'

'I mean . . .' She smiled. 'Doesn't matter now.'

Ruby held his face between her hands. 'I love you, too.'

Jack lifted Ruby up into his arms and carried her back towards the Cessna. 'I gotta wedding present for you,' he whispered.

'How'd you know I was goin' to say "yes"?'

'Just a hunch.'

Ruby couldn't quite determine what the black box was lying on the ground beside the Cessna.

'Microwave oven or a *balabushka*,' said Jack, 'I couldn't decide.'

'You've bought me a *balabushka*?'

'What does it look like?'

Ruby kissed him again, long and deeply. 'And now you're a flyer. What more could a girl want?' she grinned.

Jack struggled and lifted her higher into his arms. 'How come you've got so heavy?'

Ruby thumped him on the arm.

'It's my cast, you idiot!'

'Yeah, sure it is,' smirked Jack.

Ruby took a moment and looked him straight in the eye. 'Jack.'

'What?'

'Make love to me.'

Jack chuckled, then peered mischievously through the low brush and mulga. Mack's Cessna was still some distance away.

'If I get bitten by a bloody green ant, you're in deep trouble.'

Ruby smiled. She couldn't even contemplate the number of kisses she had in store for this man.

The Call of the High Country   Tony Parsons

In the heart of Australia's rugged high country, three generations of the MacLeod family battle to make a living on the land.

As a young married couple, Andrew and Anne work together to make the very best of their property, High Peaks, but at what cost to their happiness?

In time the property will pass to their son David. Handsome and hardworking, he is determined to become the best sheepdog handler in the land. Nothing is going to stand in his way – not even the beautiful Catriona Campbell, daughter of the wealthy graziers next door.

An inspiring and heartwarming saga of a family battling through hard times, of a love that defies all odds, and of dreams that won't be broken.

Bachelor Kisses   Nick Earls

Jon, Rick and Jen share takeaway food rituals, sporadic cocktail nights and the quest for love. Rick seems destined to long, lonely nights beneath his Porky Pig doona. Jen consumes men like chocolate bars. And Jon gets lucky in a way he's never expected – more women than he knows how to handle. A young doctor with grand plans for the hormone of darkness, he finds his life is spiralling way out of control.

Bachelor Kisses is the mess Jon Marshall makes of his life when it stops making sense. It's the story of one man's hilarious search for meaning: a chaotic comedy of misjudgements, misinformation and misguided intimacy.

'Cute, funny, sexy.'
   Cleo

'A fast-paced comedy written with verve and intelligence.'
   The Bulletin

'A chaotic comedy with hidden depths, it's a rollicking read.'
   The Australian

'Buy a Nick Earls novel and you need never be sad again.'
   Who Weekly

PENGUIN – THE BEST AUSTRALIAN READING

Penguin Australian Summer Stories

On the horizon I think I see a light, the fading dark before the dawn. Maybe a boat will come, maybe not, but either way it will be too late. Am I sky? Or am I water? I no longer know.

Water, jealousy, sizzling heat, passion, freedom, death, yearning – all feature in *Penguin Australian Summer Stories*.

From a dark tale of passion to a most unusual ocean voyage, from an exhilarating boyhood joy-ride to a diving tragedy – this collection of stories for summer showcases the talents of well-known and upcoming Australian writers. Their stories, at once hilarious and sad, lively and restrained, make for great summertime reading.

Contributors to Penguin Australian Summer Stories: Glenda Adams • Georgia Blain • James Bradley • Larry Buttrose • Matthew Condon • Raimondo Cortese • Liam Davison • Matt Dray • Nick Earls • Penny Flanagan • Helen Garner • Nikki Gemmell • Peter Goldsworthy • Marion Halligan • Elizabeth Jolley • Nicholas Jose • Gerard Lee • Amanda Lohrey • Phillip Scott • Herb Wharton • Kristin Williamson • Amy Witting